# Destined to Feel

Indigo Bloome is married with two children. She has lived and worked in Sydney and the United Kingdom, with a successful career in the finance industry. Indigo recently traded city life with a move to regional Australia, which provided her with an opportunity to explore her previously undiscovered creative side. Her love of reading, deciphering dreams, stimulating conversation and the intrigue of the human mind led her to writing her first novel, *Destined to Play*.

*Also by Indigo Bloome*

*Destined to Play* (First in the Avalon Series)
*Destined to Fly* (Third in the Avalon Series)

# Destined to
# Feel

Indigo Bloome

HARPER

*Harper*
An imprint of HarperCollins*Publishers*
77–85 Fulham Palace Road,
Hammersmith, London W6 8JB

www.harpercollins.co.uk

A Paperback Original 2012
1

A catalogue record for this book
is available from the British Library

ISBN: 978 0 00 750375 9

Printed and bound in Great Britain by
Clays Ltd, St Ives plc

*For my husband,*
*whose support since this wild ride began*
*has been nothing less than sensational*

*'Do you ever **feel** like you were destined to play?'*
*'Only in my dreams ...'*

**Play:** engage in an activity for enjoyment or recreation rather than a serious or practical purpose, by humans or animals

**Feel:** to perceive or examine by touch, be conscious of experience, to have a sensation of something other than by sight, hearing, taste or smell

# Preface

If I had known then what I know now, would it be any different?

I'm not sure why or how my life changed so dramatically so fast, yet it continues as if nothing has changed at all. It began with one weekend that perhaps, in hindsight, should never have happened, but deep in my soul I have a vague nagging that it was always meant to be ...

This leaves me embroiled within a psychological and sexual tornado that landed without any advance warning or forecast — or maybe I just missed the signs? Either way, what has happened, has happened, what will be, will be. I just don't know how it will end, or whether I will survive the journey.

# Part One

Care about what other people think and you will always be their prisoner.

— Lao Tzu

# Alexa

ere I am, sitting in the first-class lounge, which is another thrilling first for me, with my complimentary glass of Taittinger and snacking on lime-infused salt and pepper calamari. I lean back on the plush sofa and gaze around at the clean, modern lines of the room, with its subdued lighting and every convenience imaginable. Life is good. No, life is great, incredibly great. I can't help but feel a little bit mystified as to how well everything has worked out. Robert and I are getting along famously now that we have finally been honest with each other about our feelings. We've been really focused on the kids together and I've no doubt it has been beneficial for them. They are the quintessential happy little vegemites and it just makes me smile. I wish I could say the same for some of my girlfriends, who are in a state of frenzied anxiety at the sudden change in my lifestyle. Admittedly, it is definitely a weird turn of events to return from a work trip with a new (old) lover, separate from your husband yet still live happily under one roof and suddenly have an international career to meld into your everyday life in Tasmania. Even thinking about it like that seems unrealistic and too bizarre for words. So I understand why a small, close-knit community would want to discuss such a scandalous state of affairs. However, I can't say the harsh, sarcastic edge of some of their statements about my 'illicit' weekend away doesn't hurt. Worse still is the snickering and whispering in huddled groups and the raising of eyebrows when I walk past to drop Elizabeth and Jordan off at school. The unspoken word is what kills me the most. Why can't people just be upfront and stand by their convictions; or alternatively keep their opinions to themselves and say nothing instead of attempting to garner an undercurrent of bitchy gossip at the school gate?

I suppose I brought most of this on myself; I could have said absolutely nothing — so do I regret telling anyone? I don't think so … There is nothing quite like having a few close girlfriends to share the excitement, wonder and emotion of the wild rollercoaster of a ride I have been on in the past couple of months, even though I have to be deliberately evasive of the details, for obvious reasons. To be honest, they have helped keep me sane and I love them for that. I doubt they would believe my version of reality in any case, I find it difficult myself. One thing about becoming a mum is that you are forced to deal with the most judgemental species on the planet — other mothers. From breastfeeding and food to toilet training and discipline, no one is ever short of an opinion. Once you become a mother it is as if you have a god-given right to share your experience and knowledge with newer, less practised mothers who you feel are in desperate and urgent need of your extensive fountain of knowledge — I don't deny I have been known to venture into this category myself on occasion. So we share our all-encompassing sage advice to both enhance our own egos (and reinforce to ourselves that we are on the correct parenting path) and of course, to help each other feel better about our own struggles and pitfalls. That said, I don't believe there is a group in society who will provide you with more support when you need it but it comes, at times, with the cost of some hefty judgement calls.

I keep getting flashes of the many mothers who come to my office emotionally distraught and in need of coping mechanisms to deal with the interpersonal shenanigans of motherhood that no one prepares them for. And now I find myself on the receiving end of their hidden voices questioning whether or not I'm a still a good mother. Apparently I was before my week away, but now? Who knows … and I'm making things worse by leaving again, this time going to London for a fortnight — with *that* man! How do I live with myself? Obviously this must constitute being a very bad mother, mustn't it, even if it is for work? I wonder whether the judgements would be any less severe if I was going on a 10-day yoga retreat with some girlfriends for a bit of well earned rest and relaxation from the daily grind of parenthood. Would that make my choice any easier for others to swallow? I know deep in my heart that I'm a great mum and that I love my children unconditionally, as they do me. They tell me daily I'm 'awesome', which must count for something.

The fathers, on the other hand, have been supportive of Robert although I'm not sure whether they know about his desire to explore his homosexual tendencies. Would that perhaps change things? I'm pleased he will be taking some time for himself when I return home from this trip, I think it will be just what he needs before embarking on the next phase of his life. Imagine the gossip if another man moved in ... Scandalous! I chuckle at the thought. Either way, that is his business and I will respect his privacy as to 'if' and 'when' he decides to discuss his change in lifestyle with others.

I shake my head to clear it from all this circular thinking — it's entirely a waste of time to dwell on other people's attitudes. Everyone is entitled to his or her opinion; it's just the way in which it is shared that has me miffed.

I have a few spare minutes before my flight will be called for boarding and I become more or less incommunicado for the long flight to London, with only a short stopover in Singapore. I decide to make the most of it and take a photo of the decadence before me and send it to Jeremy as a sort of 'thanks for my new life' message with lots of hugs and kisses. A few sips later, my phone rings and it's him.

'Hi, this is a surprise.'

'Hi, sweetheart. God, I can't wait to see you.' His voice is deep and sends a delightful shiver through me.

'Hmm, likewise.' It feels like eons since his magic hands have touched my skin.

'I'm pleased you're enjoying the first-class lounge.'

'I am, but it would be far more pleasant sharing it with you.'

'Not too long to wait now, I should be arriving in London about twelve hours after you; I'm travelling with Sam.'

'Oh, he's with you? That's great.' I can't help but think it might be a little strange meeting Professor Samuel Webster for the first time since the experiment. He had been my PhD examiner and over time had become more like an academic father than a mentor. Over the past year or so, his research team has been focused on female sexology in the field of neuroscience, which is how he ended up connecting with Jeremy and the Global Research Forum. I shift uncomfortably at the thought of him knowing what I have done ... and what I had done to me. But there's not much I can do about it now except try to remain as professional as possible in these unusual circumstances and deep down, I know he will do the same in return. It wouldn't bother me if I were analysing someone else's results, so I resolve to take that approach in my mind.

'There's so much to catch up on, Alexa. We've made some astonishing advances in the last month, it's getting really exciting.'

'You *sound* excited,' I smile. 'I can't wait either and I have a few questions for you too.'

'No doubt you do, Alexa.' His voice reverberates in my ear as my butt tingles in recognition of the meaning behind his words. Oh no, not when I'm on the phone, how would I explain that? I need to focus on something else to distract the flow of memories and their physical effects once again disabling me in public.

'I haven't received any documents yet, Jeremy. Should I have? I want to be as prepared as possible when I arrive.'

'No, nothing yet, I'd rather go through everything with you in person. Just relax and enjoy your time. You'll be busy enough when you get here, I promise you.'

I hear my flight being called for boarding.

'Have to go, they're calling my flight so I'd better get moving.'

'No worries, AB. It's great to hear your voice.'

'I can't wait to see you again, Jeremy, it feels like forever.' Warmth floods my groin.

'I know, sweetheart … well, not long now. You're still wearing the bracelet?'

'Of course.' It's not like I can take it off. I glance down at the silver bracelet embedded with pink diamonds and fitted with a GPS chip encircling my wrist.

'Good, I love knowing where you are.' I roll my eyes but he can't see me.

'Maybe you should get one made for yourself so I can keep track of you and your jetsetting lifestyle.'

'I hadn't thought of that, we'll see.' He chuckles, then adds seriously, 'Far more important that I know you're safe and secure.' Back in protective mode, which I have to admit makes me feel rather cherished.

'Love you, gotta go, final call.'

'Okay.' He sounds reluctant to finish the call, as am I. 'See you tomorrow night and promise me you'll keep out of trouble.'

'When do I ever get into any trouble, unless I'm with you?'

'Alex!' he admonishes me and then quickly adds, 'Love you, too.' I sense his smile all those miles away. 'Later, sweetheart. Stay safe.' And he's gone. I stare at the phone as if in a daze before the final, final boarding call distracts me from my reverie. Unfortunately, with changes in time zones and my increasingly urgent carnal desires for the man I love, tomorrow night is a very long way away.

\* \* \*

I am waiting on the tarmac for takeoff. I would never have thought in a million years this could be happening to me. I feel like I am steadily becoming the person I was always meant to be. I am so excited about seeing Jeremy again that I can barely contain myself as I shuffle around in my seat absorbing all the additional features of first-class. I almost feel like I did when I went on my first 747 when I was seven years old and flying to Disneyland to meet Donald and Daisy

Duck — for completely different reasons, of course. Naturally, this is the adults-only version of such unfettered anticipation. The butterflies in my stomach are still there, just like before I met Jeremy in Sydney, but this time they are big and colourful and I welcome their presence as they let me know I'm vital and alive, more than I have felt for years. I finally settle in as we take off for the long journey ahead.

When I arrive in Singapore I switch on my phone to send a quick text message to the kids. I can't help but smile when I see that I've already received one from them with a photo, all ready for bed in their pyjamas and blowing me a kiss goodnight. My heart swells with love for them, I want to kiss the screen. I take the opportunity to stretch my legs and take a nice long walk around the ever-clean and organised Changi Airport before having a quick freshen up in the first-class lounge. I look longingly at the smooth, curved showers with their giant, rainwater showerheads, but unfortunately I don't have enough time to linger. As I'm facing the mirror to ensure I look respectable enough for the next leg of my journey, I notice the woman at the next mirror staring at me intently. I wonder if I'm imagining this and being a bit paranoid, when she suddenly speaks to me in a rather formal polished, French-accented voice.

'Please excuse my staring, but are you not Dr Alexandra Blake?'

Although slightly taken aback by her intensity, I answer, 'Yes, I am.'

'Oh, this is wonderful.' She visibly softens. 'Please, allow me to introduce myself. I am Lauren Bertrand.'

She is immaculately coiffed, as only the French can be, dressed in a smart suit, matching pumps and handbag. She is an impressive-looking woman, a small powerhouse.

'Oh, hello.' We shake hands and it takes me a moment to search my memory for where I have heard her name before until it dawns on me that she is a member of Jeremy's research forum. Ah yes, Doctor Lauren Bertrand. If I remember correctly I think her speciality is chemistry.

'I work with Dr Quinn. It is so nice to meet you, welcome to the team.' Her smile appears friendly but remains professional.

'Of course, lovely to meet you too. Thank you.'

'Are you on your way to London?'

'Yes, my flight leaves shortly. Are you?'

'I'm heading to Brussels for a meeting and then home to Paris for a few days before meeting up with the team in London. The research Jeremy sent through recently is intriguing on so many fronts. I am very much looking forward to our forum and working with you more directly. Such surprising, fascinating results ...' Her eyes drift over my body and she seems lost in thought for a brief moment. I redden at her appraisal and wonder exactly which results are surprising her so much. How come she has received them as part of the forum, and why haven't I received anything? I can't help but flush with embarrassment and disappointment

11

at the thought of being on the other side of the experiment without any of the analysis to critique and review. I wonder if any of my clients ever felt like this during our sessions. Quite possibly.

I'm thankful to hear my flight being called as the intensity of her gaze is making me feel ill at ease.

'Well, that's my flight. Safe travels and I assume I'll see you in a few days.'

'Absolutely, I look forward to it. Do take care, Dr Blake. I'm so pleased to have had this opportunity to meet you first-hand.'

'Please, call me Alexa.'

'Thank you, Alexa, until we meet again.' She shakes my hand, this time with both of her hands cupping mine. I can't decipher whether it's from affection or possession. Weird feeling. I turn to leave as her cell phone rings and she answers quickly. Her voice is excited and clipped. 'You'll never guess who I've just bumped into ... yes ... she is on the next flight to London from Singapore ...' As I walk out the door as she gives me a quick wave and turns around to continue her phone call.

Back on the plane and flying high, I happily drink a couple of glasses of Cape Mentelle Sauvignon Blanc Semillon. I do so love Western Australia's Margaret River. The wine goes perfectly with my herb-encrusted fish and salad. And I can't resist the delectable passionfruit cheesecake for dessert. As this is the longest part of my flight and I didn't sleep on the first leg, I take great joy in donning my new, not very sexy, first-class pyjamas and socks, and flatten my seat into a bed to snuggle up against the fluffy pillow and warm blankets. I spare a thought for all those people travelling in economy, as I have so many times, and I hope they manage some upright sleep in the hours ahead. My palms moisten as I put the earplugs into my ears and I hesitate before deciding whether to use the blindfold provided. Just the thought of being blind again sends lascivious shivers down my spine and hardens my nipples against the soft cotton I'm wearing. I take a few deep breaths to temper the flow of heat rising within me and squeeze my legs together tightly to prevent the potential ambush. I quickly throw the blindfold towards the end of the bed, away from me; I'm obviously far from ready for anything to be covering my eyes after such an extreme experience last time. Although the thought of *that* blindfold, its silkiness, its lace … it sends me straight back to Jeremy and his tickling feathers, all over my body, his patience, my impatience … Oh dear lord. I must stop these thoughts. Thank goodness I'm in first-class so no one can see where my hands were accidentally wandering. Heaven forbid — on a plane, with people surrounding me! I fleetingly wonder whatever happened to that blindfold. Maybe Jeremy still has it?

But at this moment I need sleep more than anything, not these intense, erotic feelings that need to wait another 24 hours until I am with him so they can finally explode to their passionate content. It's as if the feelings understand that being put on hold will be worth the wait, and they subside enough to allow me to fall into a satisfying sleep.

*I am standing at my bedroom window in my negligee and glance over my shoulder to see Jeremy's tanned, muscled body sound asleep in my bed. The strength of his back and his tousled, sleepy hair remind me of our recent intimate connection. I hug myself in happiness before stepping onto the balcony to see Elizabeth and Jordan playing in the garden. I smile as I wave at them, running and shouting around the willow tree. I step back inside and notice Jeremy is no longer in the bed, which is strange as he was sleeping so soundly just a moment ago. I walk out the door and downstairs calling his name, wondering where he could be. I enter the kitchen, which suddenly feels cold and empty and leaves me with a chill. I follow the draught down another set of stairs and trip over, tumbling further down, deeper and deeper. My negligee is filthy and torn and at the end of my fall I can barely move my legs, it feels like I could be wading in molasses. The stairwell above me goes on forever, too high for me to climb with my leaden legs. I scrape and crawl along the floor, commando-style, unable to see clearly where I am going. I instantly still in absolute terror when I feel something slither alongside my body. As my eyes adjust to the darkness I see the body of a thick, long snake. It pauses as if sensing my presence and my heart pounds hard and fast in my chest. Its forked tongue darts back and forth in its mouth, before it raises its head and moves seamlessly and silently onto the small of my back. I dare not breathe. Its weight is hefty as it follows down the lines of my body. I am frozen with fear as the length of its dark, thick body continues sliding leisurely between my buttocks over what's left of my silky white negligee. Such a strange sensation, it's as if its movement paralyses me. The last of its weight leaves my body and its tail finally smooths past my toes. It climbs up a phallus-like staff. Light is shining from above and I can see that it is bright green and gold in colour as it wraps itself around the Rod of Asclepius, the symbol for medicine and healing. I sense there is something mystical about the vision before me and I can't help but be in awe of the snake's presence — my previous fear is immediately replaced by a sense of peace and calm. At the same time I'm about to turn away, I feel painless drops of blood pool in my belly button before sliding directly downwards. Strangely, it gives me strength and I know I must continue on my own journey to the light. I head towards an archway, momentarily glancing over my shoulder to reflect on the path of my shedding skin. As I round the corner into the*

*glimmer of light, my arms have become wings
and my nose a beak. I carefully poke out into
the air, spread my magnificent wings and fly,
feeling my body strengthen with each passing
second. I fly higher and higher into a majestic
tree. My bird's-eye vision fastens on an owl
resting on another branch. It's as if he nods to
me and I acknowledge him by lowering my head
in return. I see the world like I've never seen it
before, so high, such perspective. As I tuck my
wings back around my body, they brush against
a nest full of eggs nestled discreetly into the
hefty branch. One egg wobbles dangerously over
the edge, as if in slow motion. I attempt to save
it as my body leaves the safety of the branch and
my wings lengthen to protect its fall.*

I wake up suddenly with the feeling I'm falling and gasp
out loud, completely disoriented. What a weird dream.
I don't ever remember dreaming of animals. It leaves
me feeling a little anxious and with a sudden sense of
foreboding — as if there is a path I'm destined to take
that could result in short-term pain for long-term gain.
I shake my head to dislodge the mental images from my
mind. I wish I had my dream book with me. Maybe I
can find an app when I land that will help me interpret
such vivid, colourful imagery. The lights shine in my
eyes and breakfast is being served. I must have been
asleep for a while. I change from my pyjamas back into
my travel clothes and look forward to my imminent

arrival, a step closer to Jeremy and whatever he has planned for me this week. I'm so excited to finally be here and soon to be in the arms of the man I love — have always loved. I can't keep the smile from my face.

* * *

Finally, we touch down in London as scheduled.

I walk through the swinging doors at Heathrow and notice a chauffeur standing with my name on a placard. What a pleasure it is to travel like this, with every detail smoothly organised. We share greetings as he takes my luggage.

When we arrive at a luxury black sedan with the door open, there is another man standing beside it dressed in similar attire to the chauffeur.

'Good morning, Dr Blake. Welcome to London.'

'Good morning. Thank you, it's great to be here.'

I smile as he opens the door for me and the first man takes care of my luggage. As I settle myself in the back seat, ensuring I have everything, I hear my name being called from somewhere in the distance behind me. As I look over my shoulder I am stunned to see Jeremy and Samuel running towards the car I am in. How amazing. What on earth are they doing here? I didn't think they were due in until later tonight? I wave my hand in surprised recognition as the driver's assistant suddenly shoves the door closed and bolts into the front seat. I see the panic in Jeremy's and Sam's eyes and on their faces as they run towards me. Just as I am about to ask the driver to wait for them, the car surges forward and I am flung across the back seat. I ask them to stop, telling the driver that I know those men. Jeremy is now running after the car and banging on the back window and there's fear in his eyes. Something is terribly wrong. I try to open the side window to speak to him, but there is no button. The window tint turns black and I can't see his face any more. The door is locked and as I turn around to look at the driver, a blackened barrier rises between the back and front seats. I scream and bash on the door and the glass. We are moving fast. I start to tremble as the memory of Jeremy's agonised face is etched firmly on my brain. I fumble for my phone in my handbag, only to find there is no service indicated. I don't understand any of this. I am in a blackened car with no phone reception. Who are these drivers? I bang on the windows and barrier, screaming at these men, trying to make sense of what is happening. I attempt to open the doors, urgently checking both of them and bang my palms until they hurt with pain against the black tinted windows. What is this about? Suddenly I feel woozy, faint. Then I don't feel anything at all …

# Jeremy

**M**y world closes in on me in slow motion as I witness the scene in front of me in astonished disbelief. My chest is collapsing within my ribcage. I can't breathe. Alexa has literally disappeared from within an inch of my grasp, before my very eyes.

'Sam, grab that taxi, we need to follow them. Quick, jump in.' We leap into the back of the first black London cab idling in the rank.

'Follow that black sedan in front,' I shout at the driver. 'We can't afford to lose them.'

He drives off much too slowly. 'This isn't Hollywood, mate. Let me tell you right now, I'm not losin' my fuckin' licence for a bit of your James Bond nonsense.'

I slam the seat hard with my fist. What a fucking nightmare!

The driver immediately pulls over to the kerb. 'Get out, get out of my cab, I don't need you bastards smashing things up. Piss off. Go on, get out.'

Shit. I've never been this out of control.

When it becomes clear that the driver is going nowhere with us inside his cab, we scramble out again. Sam stands speechless and shocked as we are left on the side of the road wondering what the hell we are going to do now.

\* \* \*

We arrived at Heathrow late last night as I had a meeting cancelled and could get to London earlier than planned. I couldn't wait to surprise Alexa by greeting her personally, to wrap my arms around her and tell her how much I've missed her, how much she means to me. I had the whole day planned. I took the liberty of taking a larger hotel suite than usual so we could share, but booked a small room in her name too, just in case she had an issue with it — I know Alex has quite fixed ideas when it comes to presenting a professional persona to the outside world. Given this is her first involvement with the Global Research Forum she may have wanted to keep up certain appearances and I didn't want to kick-start our time together making incorrect assumptions. I know it wouldn't take much convincing for her to stay with me, but if it would make her happy to have a room booked in her own name as well, then I'm all for it, particularly after everything she went through last time we met up. God, I just shake my head at the thought. Having her consent freely to what she went through, what she agreed to, for me. What a woman, she just never ceases to amaze me. It literally makes my cock tingle thinking about her — how damn gorgeous she looks when she desperately tries to deny what her body is feeling, sounding all prim and proper. I always try to remain as aloof as possible until it gets so ridiculous I have to hit her with her own redundant attitudes head on — or simply touch her. Both strategies have yielded me endless success in the past. I hadn't decided whether we should consummate our reunion on arrival or later in the day. Even though the delay would be gratifying, I didn't think I'd have the restraint to wait given it's been over a month since I've seen her.

And now I catch a glimpse of her for two seconds and then she vanishes and it's my fucking fault. Shit! I've been briefed on her every movement since she returned to Hobart, every single move. We even had cameras installed to monitor her front gate so we could identify every person who entered her house. I didn't mention it to Alexa, as I didn't want to freak her out, particularly over the phone, and then she'd have to explain to Robert why we needed to take extra precautions so I decided it wasn't worth all the hassle. Better I just make the decisions and deal with any consequences later, it's more my style.

I also haven't told her that my computer suffered an attempted hacking. They accessed some files and, although thankfully they didn't access those I had embedded with additional security, they still have more than enough information about Alexa's involvement in the experiment than I would like. I get the sense that they have an idea of where we are going with the formula. I have no doubts now that they want what we have got. Thank god I didn't send her the detailed documents. If she knew everything it would make things so much worse for her. I just didn't realise they would take things to this extreme and abduct her. Christ! Who would do this, who would take this risk? What a fucking mess. If they lay a finger on her, I swear … Stop! Stop these morbid thoughts, Quinn, and do something rather than standing here swearing and getting lost in your worst-case scenarios. Actions are more important than words. Just fix it!

All these thoughts shoot through my head in the space of a second. I notice Sam beside me staring, mouth open, towards where the car disappeared with Alexa — the one woman in the world I have finally admitted I love more than life itself — leaving us standing in its wake. Fuck, this is so bad! I grab my phone from inside my jacket and dial our driver to let him know where we are. He finally pulls in, after circling the perimeter of Heathrow while we waited for Alexa. As we quickly settle into the car my brain finally kicks into action mode rather than shock.

'Sarah, get me Leo on the phone, now. It's an emergency.' I wait impatiently as my assistant connects me. I end up reaching Moira in New York, his 'be all and end all' personal assistant who knows almost every facet of Leo's life. We have liaised often during the past decade since Leo is never in one spot for too long.

'Moira, it's Jeremy. Is Leo there? Where is he? Jesus fucking Christ. The Amazon?' She tells me that he is deep within the northern region of the Amazon basin living with the Wai Wai people, studying soul flight with the village shaman, and he can't be contacted for at least three weeks. Bloody hell. That's Leo for you. 'We have a massive problem. Alexa has been abducted. Yes, now … right now … right in front of my eyes. Yes, I'm with Sam, he saw it too. Two men, obviously posing as chauffeurs. They just shoved her in when they saw us running towards her … No, I didn't recognise them.' I raise my eyebrows towards Sam. He shakes his head. 'No, he doesn't either. Yeah, we lost them. Shit. They could be anywhere now.'

Moira shifts immediately into gear, just as Leo would. She's already been intimately involved in trying to find out who hacked into our computers and the attempted blackmail, so she's across all the details. Leo also organised for her to secretly compile personal dossiers on each of the Global Research Forum members, just in case the leaks and threats were coming from one of our own people; anger pumped through my veins at the thought, but I couldn't deny he had a point. I haven't mentioned it to Sam or any of the others. Moira has the ability to access resources to handle emergencies on behalf of Leo, though we never imagined anything like this. She's calm and efficient, but my panic makes me feel like shouting given the seriousness of this situation. I take a deep breath before responding in an attempt to control my rising fear.

'Okay ... and Martin's available?' Martin Smythe looks after Leo's security issues. He's ex-CIA, quick-thinking and highly capable and it's a huge relief he'll be involved. Leo had organised for him to be at Avalon just in case anything unforeseen occurred. 'That's great, he can organise the team and can you make sure they have a contact in Scotland Yard? We'll need to monitor London's security system.' God, in this city, we'll never find her with so many millions of people swarming around. No, can't think like that. My hands begin to shake. Control it, Quinn, I admonish myself as Moira asks what else I need.

'Can you send through the latest information you have on the hackers and we'll also need anything you have on what drugs the top five pharmaceuticals are taking to market in the next five years, as soon as you get it together. And get some people working on the next five companies, just in case. We need to work out who is this fucking desperate — there must be a link somewhere that we've been missing! Okay, yeah, will do ... and thanks Moira, I really appreciate it. I'm desperate to get her back.'

I press 'end' and realise my hands are now trembling. I shove the phone back in my pocket and rub both hands through my hair in sheer exasperation at this diabolical situation. I turn to Sam who is still speechless which, given my internal fury and dread, is probably a good thing.

As we silently make our way to Covent Garden, I absently stare out the window and thank god for Leo and I connecting when he had his accident all those years ago — my life changed for the better as soon as I met him and, ultimately, he was able to orchestrate my scholarship at Harvard and essentially my future career path from that point forward.

Leroy Edward Orwell — the philanthropist who has sponsored my work at every level for more than a decade. He has been the financial backbone of every breakthrough and discovery I've been involved in. He comes from a family with a long history of inconceivable wealth, providing him with incredible access to global contacts and resources. We first met when I was in the Royal Flying Doctor Service and was on call. He was abseiling near Kings Canyon in the Northern Territory and had a bad fall when he was rappelling off the rock face and one of his anchors didn't hold. He ended up breaking his leg and had to be airlifted out. We bonded during his recovery time and learnt much about each other's ambitions and motivations. Even though he is ten years older than me, the nurses used to joke that we could be brothers, although I've always thought he was more of a Rob Lowe type. Either way, aging has been kind to him and he keeps himself incredibly toned and fit. There has always been a healthy competition between us in relation to the state of our bodies, and we keep each other in check. We certainly don't want to risk letting ourselves flab into middle age.

Leo's passion is anthropology, more specifically biomedical anthropology — his nirvana is the holistic integration of Western 'science and medicine' with Eastern 'philosophies and spirituality'. He's a big thinker and has studied extensively. He has an extraordinary mind; I'd be lying if I said I wasn't in awe of his brain. Global phenomena intrigue him and my work is just one piece of the myriad projects he's indirectly involved in. His seemingly extrasensory perception has certainly worked in his favour when it comes to ensuring his continued financial success, having managed to quadruple his already substantial wealth over recent years. His only requirement of me is to maintain his anonymity in public. I don't have the opportunity to see him in person much, but it's great when we do get together. He enjoys his private, more reclusive lifestyle and I respect that in him, but we have a lot in common and his conversation is always enlivening.

Leo was intrigued with my theories and suppositions regarding blood types and depression and even flew out to Sydney and attended Alexa's lecture with me, highly irregular behaviour for him. To this day I'm not sure whether it was for the project or whether he sensed that my meeting up with Alex was potentially something far more significant. He really is one of those people who seem to have a sixth sense about things, and I suppose he was spot on. Alexa always called him Charlie — as in *Charlie's Angels* — as she has never met him, only heard about him.

Actually, he was posing as the maître d' and served martinis to me and Alex at the InterContinental during our weekend together. Obviously she didn't see him as she was wearing the blindfold and he didn't want to be introduced. He was a little shocked when he had to cuff her at my request. Afterwards I had to explain to him that she did her first thesis on the instinct and suppression of sexual behaviour, and why I believed this was an important part of our journey together should she resist and not acknowledge her true feelings.

This was also coincidently just after I received an anonymous letter at the hotel threatening me in relation to her pulling out of the experiment. I couldn't tell if it was a hoax or not and had no time to explore it further during the scope of the weekend, which admittedly put me a little on edge myself. I knew I couldn't risk her walking away from me for many reasons, let alone the heightened danger the letter presented.

Either way, it certainly created both playful fear and extreme arousal in Alex (her body has always proved a more accurate radar for reflecting her true disposition), which she admitted afterwards she found truly fascinating. Leo asked if he could have a copy of her thesis and Alex generously sent a copy through for me to forward on to him. I was only ever allowed to read her original hard copy all those years ago but thankfully I have a great memory. No doubt it would have been intriguing for her to read it again after our experience together — or rewrite it perhaps …

Anyway, Leo's funds have enabled him to acquire properties around the world that he believes hold either mystical or spiritual significance to cultures past and present — they are known as Avalon. It's his concept, his baby if you like, and he offered me his executive treehouse on Lord Howe Island to ensure Alexa's safety and wellbeing after our weekend together. His only condition was that she was not to know its location. I remember wanting to ask him why, but the look on his face stopped me, even though his demeanour remained calm and placid. I've learnt over the years when to question and debate with Leo, which most of the time he embraces with gusto, but this was not one of those occasions, so I maintained my silence and kept my promise. He doesn't ask too much from me and he has done so much for me, it's the least I could do. Thinking about it, in hindsight I wonder if he had a sense that she was at greater risk than we originally thought, or whether he felt there was something unique about Alexa, even before we further tested our hypotheses, given his direct involvement and his insistence that I take her to Avalon. I sigh as these thoughts and memories flood my mind while our car smoothly drives past Buckingham Palace and on to Pall Mall. So much for her safety now …

* * *

Sam and I check in at One Aldwych. I stare aimlessly around the suite in which I had invested such high hopes and expectations. I can't deny the emptiness I'm feeling without Alexa here by my side, or the rising turmoil in my gut as to where she could be. I stare blankly at my laptop as if her whereabouts is going to miraculously appear before my eyes. I haven't heard back from Moira yet, which is driving me mad, but I know she's efficient and does her job like no other. I don't want to bother her unnecessarily, but every second counts and I feel like I'm in Alexa limbo. I'm half tempted to call Scotland Yard myself to sort this hideous mess out. I can't get my mind off the letter I had received during our weekend away that indirectly threatened the safety of Alex's children if I didn't go ahead with the experiment. It must be the same people. Shit. If only I could turn back time we would not be in this mess. I should have organised for the whole family to be with me in the safety of Avalon until all this crap passed over and we figured out who was behind it but as we didn't receive anything else, we instead just increased security and surveillance at Alexa and Robert's house as a precautionary measure. Now this, they've abducted her — if they're willing to go to these extremes, will it ever be over? I slam the laptop closed in frustration — it's not as if it's giving me any of the answers I so urgently need. What I need is a strong drink. I'm driving myself crazy. I pass by Sam's room and tap on the door before opening it. He's absorbed in his laptop, maybe hoping for answers just as futilely as I was.

'I'm heading to the bar, can I get you anything?'

'I'll join you in half an hour or so. I want to reorganise the priorities for my team in Sydney so they are on standby to research the information Moira will be sending through and I'll offer any assistance to Martin in setting up a more sophisticated tracker on Alexandra's bracelet. You never know, they might find something. I know it's a long shot but ...' He sounds despondent as he looks up from his work and his eyes register both our misery.

'Thanks Sam, it will all help and they're a bright bunch by the sounds of it. I'll let McKinnon know we'll need to defer the forum indefinitely and he can inform the other members.'

'Of course, I should have thought of that, he is the Chair, after all. I'll see you downstairs. I suppose there's not too much else we can do until we hear back from Moira.'

I close his door and trudge towards the lift. I'm not used to being this useless. I need action, to hunt down her abductors, not just make phone calls, damn it. Being forced to wait is killing me.

In the lobby bar I stare aimlessly into the flames of the candelabra, jiggling the ice around in my double shot of Glenmorangie. Some slick chick asks me if I want company tonight and I motion her away with a wave of my hand. As if I could think of anyone but Alex at the moment, as if I ever will again — even my dick concurs. My mind flits back through the many times we have played together. She never disappointed me, has always been willing to try anything with me, explore and push the boundaries. Of all the women I have been with, and there have been many over the years, she is the one I keep coming back to. The one I couldn't get out of my head even when I was being pleasured by two buxom blondes in California, or getting a blow job from a lusty redhead with a mouth to die for. It was Alex — her body, her mind, her heart — that kept floating erratically through my mind during those moments of random pleasure, preventing me from committing further to any other woman in my life. I never spoke about her of course, they didn't need to know.

Marie was close and wanted our relationship to go further, but I couldn't bring myself to commit, not when I knew Alex was still out there, even if she was unavailable and on the other side of the world. We are still friends but she's as wrapped up in her career as I am in mine and marrying Marie would have been like a business deal, Kardashian-style, all for show but without any grounded substance. Marriage should mean more than that.

Besides, I needed to know once and for all, where I stood with AB. I knew she was married with kids; I'm Jordan's godfather after all, even if I haven't exactly been a major presence in his life. The weekend away I organised with her meant everything to me. I knew from the second she agreed to stay that, finally, this was our time, our destiny and that my philandering ways were over. This was the real deal. There was no way I was ever going to let her go again. And it couldn't have worked more perfectly. My meticulous planning paid off in every way possible. I had to ensure our lives would be entangled together somehow from that point forward — whether it was professionally, sexually or psychologically. I didn't mind which one, actually, if I'm perfectly honest I was obviously hoping to achieve all three and hit the jackpot. Breaking through her boundaries, removing all the layers of defensive constructs she'd built up over the years and finally witnessing her willingness to experiment made me fall even more in love with her all over again. Not to mention her effect on my research. The results are absolutely extraordinary but shit, at what cost? What would have happened if she hadn't agreed to be involved? I would never have forced her into anything she wasn't willing to do herself and ultimately she did it willingly, but with the blackmail letter I received on the Friday night of our weekend hanging over my head, threatening the safety of her children … I just couldn't risk it. Anything could seem like an accident when they were travelling in the wilderness of Tasmania. I certainly didn't want to scare her or put her children in any danger, all because of my work. They mean the world to her; they are her world. In the end, I was pleased that I hadn't caused her any worry by mentioning it to her and I thought it had all worked out, but now the letter, then the computer hacking, and finally the abduction, all tumbles into one sordid picture — but who is behind it? Who would stoop so low? Who would take that risk to put her in so much personal danger? They must have a lot at stake or maybe I have more enemies than I realised ... My head literally aches as my brain runs through numerous scenarios.

I remind myself that Alexa is strong, has always been strong and oftentimes is stronger than she realises. Christ, look what she did for me! At least I know they won't want her dead. She is no use to them dead; these results require that she is very much alive. Thank god! But I also know it is highly unlikely they will achieve the results we did. My stomach churns at the thought of what they may put her through, how they might want to touch her. It sickens me to the core. The only way I want my Alexa to receive pleasure is under my instruction. No one knows her body the way I do, and at least that knowledge calms my churning gut a little. Hang in there, sweetheart, we'll find you. The light from the candles continues to flicker. I swipe my finger through their flames, feeling the heat but not the burn, and it sparks a memory from a happier time.

\* \* \*

We are in the middle of a five day skiing trip to Val d'Isère with a group of friends. It's such an amazing resort, the snow and weather have been exceptional as is the chalet we are staying in. We have a dedicated chef and as much wine and champagne as we can drink. We've been skiing hard each day and chilling out when the sun goes down.

Alex has improved dramatically on the slopes in the past two days. She has only skied once before. I'm really proud of her perseverance, she never gives up and today we managed some red runs together, so it's a massive improvement. She has one spill when some dickhead trying to show off loses control and bowls her over. She hurtles over the side of the run and I only know where she is when I see her poke her stick up from the body-deep snow. Once I can see she's not injured, we can't stop laughing, which makes it even more difficult for me to haul her out of her predicament.

'Could you be covered in any more snow if you tried?' It's taking all my strength to keep a grip on her, as I try to control my chuckles. She looks like the sexiest, cutest snow creature I've ever seen, white flakes caked through her hair and sitting on top of her eyelashes. I decide there is no way I'm sharing her with the others tonight. We'll stay in and this has given me the perfect excuse.

'It's not like I planned it this way, Jeremy. Is that guy okay?' Her voice is muffled under the snow. Typically she's more worried about the idiot who did this, than herself. I give one last heave and out she pops, landing on top of me — which I have no issue with whatsoever.

'The maniac who took you out? He's long gone, but are you sure you're okay?'

'Yeah, I'm fine, but I've got snow everywhere, absolutely everywhere, inside and out!'

'Well, maybe we should call it a day. I've got an idea that should warm you up nicely.'

Oh yes, there's the mischievous look in her eyes. I've piqued her interest.

'What did you have in mind, Dr Quinn?'

'Let's just get you inside and de-snowed. We'll be staying in tonight.'

No arguments from the lady.

It's the chef's night off so our friends head out for a big night — more than likely till about 4 a.m. I'm pleased we now have the chalet to ourselves and I have important plans for our evening together. My cock has been twitching for action all day and is very happy to be free of the restraints of my ski clothes.

As I walk past the bathroom, the door is left slightly ajar, which is convenient because I catch Alexa's reflection in the mirror ... hard for me to miss when she's in the shower naked. That's all the encouragement I need. I immediately strip off my boxers and T-shirt and join her, fully erect and raring to go. Her smile confirms I'm a welcome presence as I slide the soap from her fingers and skilfully take over the cleansing process in her place. She doesn't resist me and is used to me taking the lead, she loves it and god knows, so do I. I could devour her breasts, they're more than a handful and I have large hands. I slide my soapy palms all over the curves of her body as my eyes greedily take her in. I love watching the impact my touch has on her body, it's the only thing that tempers my impatient cock. I massage her thighs as I watch her mouth open to let out a sigh, yes, she knows what's coming, I kiss that mouth, those soft, full lips and taste her desire for me, so I slow my strokes, knowing she will soon need the support of the wall or my body.

My cock is furious with this strategy so I'm forced to quicken my play. I turn her around so she's facing the wall, my hands continue to massage her plump, full breasts and play with her taut nipples. Her eyes are closed so she's already to the point of no return, just as I want her. My cock rests between the crack in her arse while my fingers find her opening, teasing it wider. Her head rests back against my chest exposing her delectable neck, but my needs are too raw, too immediate. She's panting rapidly as her body presses tight against the wall. I spread her legs and butt cheeks to clear the passage for my cock to slide through her welcoming flesh so I can push as far as I can into her soft, enveloping centre.

As I take her from behind, my hungry shaft penetrates her layers further and higher, and she groans in ecstatic response. Her sounds encourage me to completely fill her and pump harder and faster. I love the power she surrenders to me, that I have over her responsive body, and my cock is in heaven before it explodes into her sweet tunnel. It's my favourite place in the world, as if our bodies were made for each other and she never disappoints. Ever.

A little calmer now that my pent-up sexual tension has found its release, I put on some music, light the fire and a few candles around the room — quite a few. I have a thing about candles, and tonight the whole concept of warming her up propels me into action. I'm impatient waiting for Alexa, so I entice her out of the bathroom with promises of a Cointreau and ice, some stinky cheese, oozing brie and crunchy bread. Finally, she emerges flushed and glistening from the bathroom.

'Santé.'

'Santé.'

'Dr Quinn, you're not going all romantic on me, are you? You do have certain playboy standards to maintain.'

'That I do, Alexandra. You just bring out the best in my imagination.'

'Imagination? Surely you can do better than candles, Cointreau and cheese?' She does like to tease … I can indeed do better, but I remain silent and just give her a 'watch this space' look. Which she misses because she is settling all cosy-like into the lounge. There'll be none of that!

'Drink up, I want you naked and on the floor by the fire.'

She looks up at me carefully, assessing my seriousness, before slowly taking another sip of her drink. Will she, won't she? I ponder. I give her a moment to do as I ask of her own free will, and take another sip myself, tempering my impatience to have her where I want her, immediately. Our eyes are locked as we play this game of psychic cat and mouse. I let her continue with her little charade. She defiantly takes another sip before placing her drink on the side table. She's very deliberately taking her time; she'll pay for that later. She stands up and slowly undoes the tie of her robe before letting the robe fall off her shoulders. God, she looks hot and she isn't wearing anything underneath. Love your style, Alexa, what a legend. I can't take my eyes off her glistening skin; my arousal is piqued all over again. She casually saunters over to the platter, helps herself to the cheese and bread. She munches away, still not saying a word, jiggles her tits to the music as she returns across the room to her glass, and this time has a giant mouthful of the icy drink, swishing it around her mouth before swallowing the citrus liquid. There is nothing about her I don't want this second. She raises her eyebrows and I place my palm out towards her, which she gracefully accepts, finally. She likes the notion of having some power, even in the process of her submission to me. I congratulate myself for my patience (which always pays off when it comes to Alex) and lead her to where I want her, naked, on the rug and at my mercy.

'So, now that I'm here, what are you going to do with me?'

I have to stop the carnal visions that penetrate my brain as a result of her words. I don't bother responding verbally, I just run my fingers along the outline of her body. I start with her big toe and take my time bumping over her smaller toes, around the side of her foot, her calf, her outer thighs. I follow the curve of her butt and the indent of her waist, allow my little finger to languidly caress her nipple on my way past her breast, but not enough to create any real friction so I know I have the complete attention of both her body and mind. The softness of her skin never ceases to amaze me; my fingers and my eyes absorb its texture and tone.

Of all the women I have been with, none ever feels like Alex beneath my touch. As I move past her arm, I take it with me and raise it above her head so her breast is lifted upward. It takes every bit of willpower to prevent me lowering my lips to her nipple to nibble and suck, knowing it will instantly arch her back and wet her sex. If my cock had a voice it would be groaning, but my brain is still in control, as it should be. I continue my journey around her face, knowing her eyes are locked on mine. I must concentrate on the sensations I am causing on her body, not lose focus. I raise her other arm above her head. This is more like it, unfettered access to my gorgeous plaything. I notice her breaths becoming shallow in her chest and I know this is turning her on, big time, and she knows it's the same for me. I don't lose sight of my mission as my fingers continue to glide along her sexy contours, I can't wait to arrive at her thighs and notice my breathing is also shallow. It will be worth it, I remind myself. Finally, I'm there, sliding along the softness of her inner flesh, wanting to bury my head between her legs and my tongue in her opening, but I deliberately tease before meandering past and back down to the toe where I started. At last!

'Now, are you ready to play?'

'Jeez, Jeremy, you're slowly killing me here.' There is nothing quite like the sound of Alexa's voice when she's almost begging for it. Absolutely worth the tortuous slowness of my journey around her body.

'I don't think you'll have the willpower to stay in this position, Alexandra, so I am going to bind your wrists.' When it comes to women, I have learnt that statements are far more effective than questions; that way, they don't have to give themselves permission (which is always the case with Alex). If they say nothing, you have told them what will happen. They can always say no, but never seem to, in my experience anyhow. I grab the tie from Alexa's robe and securely fasten her wrists together above her head. She knows she can stop me, but given the playful look of feigned horror in her eyes, she won't. Oh no, she definitely wants this as much as me. It intrigues her as to what I'm going to do next, just as it excites me.

'Seems like you are taking a few liberties tonight, Jeremy.' She doesn't resist me whatsoever.

'Only you could inspire me to take such liberties, Alexandra.'

Okay, almost ready.

I move one of the lounge chairs over so I can tie her bound wrists to the leg of the chair. I know she'll be shocked by what I'm going to do, but she'll love it once she gets used to it. One of my friends-with-benefits at Harvard did it to me, and although the feeling was fascinating, I couldn't stand not being in control. All I could think about was how Alexa's body would react instead and I've wanted to try it with her ever since. Now, I have my chance.

'Is this added security necessary? Anchoring me to the base of a chair? What if the others come home early?'

'They won't.' I know this because I have organised for Craig to call me if it looks like anyone is leaving early. As if I'd be that unprepared … she should know me better than that by now. I take a moment to absorb the sight of her exposed and trapped body. My cock springs spontaneously out of the split in my boxer shorts.

Alexa laughs. 'I'm not sure who's more turned on by this scenario, you or me.' I always wonder if she's aware that she sinks her teeth into her bottom lip when she says things like that. I don't want to mention it in case she stops doing it.

I lower my head to her sex and sniff, animal instinct taking me over. She smells sensational and there is no doubt in my mind she's ready. I lick, darting my tongue between her lips and around the edges of her hot, wet layers. She groans in response, arching her back but unable to move her arms from over her head, and I kiss and suck a little more, teasing her swelling clitoris, before raising my head from between her thighs, her sweet juice on my lips, and grin at her shocked face.

'I'd say it's a dead heat at this point, sweetheart. But that's not why we're here.' I reach over her body lowering my groin over her head, my dick dangling deliberately close to her lips, so I tease her knowing she can't lift her head high enough to fully take me. God, this is fun — she is so frustrated by desire but trying to be so contained. I love it! I pick up one of the candles from around the fireplace and bring it back to our position on the rug.

'Jeremy ... what are you doing? You're not really going to use that, are you?' She sounds a little nervous now.

'Have you ever done this before?'

She shakes her head. No words, she's silently debating pros and cons in her mind. It's so obvious I can almost hear it. Best get moving before she talks herself out of it.

'I've done it before, and I know you'll like it, Alexa. Trust me. I'd never hurt you.'

She closes her eyes, a good sign; she's silently giving in to herself, giving in to me.

'I'll start slowly, somewhere less sensitive, you choose. That way you can get used to the sensation.' Always good to let her know she still has a say, some power.

'Where do you recommend?' And the power returns so gallantly back to its rightful place ...

'Feet, and I'll work my way up. Ready?'

I locate the remote control from behind me and turn the volume of the music up; we both like Chicane and it will help Alex relax into the experience.

She nods. She is ready and I can't help but be in awe of her willingness to experiment sexually with me, the absolute trust she places in me. No one on earth compares to Alexa when we are like this together. It's exhilarating. She closes her eyes and holds her breath as I position the candle over her legs and I carefully drop a small amount of wax on the front of her foot, and wait. She sighs and visibly relaxes. Not as bad as she was expecting. Her consent allows me to continue. As I move slowly up her legs, her body shivers and her skin responds with goosebumps.

'Keep your eyes open, sweetheart, I need to see you.' I'm utterly absorbed in her reaction as I eventually move closer to her belly, lust clouding her eyes. I ensure the candle cradle is full of liquid wax as I tip enough on her skin to fill her belly button.

'Oh … my … god …' She gasps, arches her back in response and a light moan escapes her lips as her trapped wrists continue to anchor her body to the floor. I hope I don't come before this is over. She looks even hotter than she does in my dreams; I had no idea that was possible! If her arms were free she'd cover herself, but she can't and I'm pleased I went to the effort of restraints. Even so I'd better check in to make sure; I'd never want to hurt her, even accidentally.

'Are you okay? It's a shock, isn't it?'

'Yes, a complete shock. So hot, but it doesn't burn, then the warmth follows … It feels so weird in my bellybutton, as if you've tapped into my core.' Bless her. Such abandon and analysis at the same time. I watch as the wax hardens on her belly like a plug and place my palm over it, feeling her heat. I can't prevent myself from kissing her sensuous lips and penetrating her mouth with my tongue as she lies beneath me, mesmerised. She responds with such immediate and unexpected passion that after a few moments we are both rendered literally breathless. This wasn't part of my plan but I'm certainly not complaining. I fleetingly wonder if she has any idea just how much sexual energy and raw lust is screaming out of her pores. It shocks even me. Either way, her nipples are exactly how I want them now, hard, pert and ready for action. I straddle her body, ensuring her legs are as anchored as her hands. I need to get a move on now, otherwise it will be my juice over her nipples instead of hot wax.

'Oh god, Jeremy … Are you sure?'

'Very sure, sweetheart, you'll love it. I've been thinking of this since we arrived. I want moulds of your gorgeous tits. Now lie still, I don't want to miss.' She takes deep breaths, no doubt attempting to control any nerves or anxiety. And now she waits. 'Open your eyes for me.'

I love it when she follows my commands. It makes her that much more perfect for me.

My intention was to do one nipple at a time, but I'm so ready to explode I pick up another candle, swivel it around to ensure it has the same level of liquid wax and decide to trust my medical precision to do both nipples at the same time. The look on Alexa's face is priceless — apprehension, curiosity and excitement all at once.

'Trust me, I'm a doctor.' I wink at her as I position each candle high above her breasts. The suspense is killing her, which I love, so I wait a little longer to coincide with the chorus in the music. I ask her to calm her breathing because it's moving her breasts too much, knowing full well she has a snowball's chance in hell of doing anything about it. She groans loudly in frustrated excitement. I know she'd slap me at this point if she could. The time is right and I pour the silky hot wax on both nipples and she writhes and screams at the shock of it; I can only imagine the sensation, knowing how much more sensitive her nipples are than mine. But I also know the initial shock is worth the feeling and the pleasure that follows. I'm thrilled that she is experiencing this, knowing she'll love it.

'Ahhhh, god, Jeremy. That's hot, so fucking hot. Fuck, fuck, fuck!'

Swearing, that's unusual for her. She strains against her bound arms and her hips are bucking against mine as my weight pins her to the floor.

And then the wax starts to cool against her delicate pink buds. I need to distract the tsunami building within my balls, so I carefully place the candles down, keeping one close by and I wait till her need for me inside her replaces the sensation of heat penetrating her nipples.

'Fuck me, please, for god's sake, Jeremy, fuck me, *now*!'

It would be rude to deny such a delicate, polite request.

I quickly raise my body and gently flip her over, lifting her gorgeous arse into me so she is positioned on her knees and elbows. I make sure I position my penis slowly and carefully into her moist vagina, allowing her surrounding cushioned flesh to feel full and tight around me. There is nowhere else on earth my cock would rather be.

'*Jeremy*!' Her patience is non-existent and she pants her frustration into the carpet, her swollen wax-capped nipples dangling in the air towards the rug below. Her body looks fucking sensational from this perspective. I pick up the candle by my side and pour a steady stream of the melted wax on to the top of her crack ensuring its predetermined path flows directly downwards. Her behind bucks and jolts with the shocking intensity of the sensation, and she releases an almighty scream as her vagina tenses around my cock causing tight, twisting exquisite pleasure as I explode into her. We lose ourselves in the magical connection of each other's bodies and simultaneous orgasms rip through our muscles before she ultimately surrenders beneath me.

From the moment I laid eyes on her, I sensed she was the one for me, the connection to my heart and my soul. But we were too young, had so much of life to explore. I had to test the boundaries outside my feelings for Alexa, push her away before I understood how much she meant to me. The years flew by and my feelings grew deeper, more intense, my connection to her like the root structure of a majestic rainforest tree in fertile soil.

# Part Two

Emotions occur precisely when adaptation is
hindered for whatever reason.

— E. Claparède

# Alexa

As I come to, my head hurts and my body feels heavy. I'm sitting up but my limbs are securely bound, restricting all movement. I am travelling smoothly through a crowd, people rushing in every direction. I can only see fast-moving legs and bodies and I have to look up to see into their faces which makes me dizzy.

I realise I'm strapped to a wheelchair. My heart pumps fast with adrenaline fuelling my fear as the clarity of this nightmare crystallises in my mind. I attempt to scream, only to discover it's stifled, my mouth taped shut. I look down to see full-length black robes covering my clothes. I shake my head but my hair, nose and mouth are covered by the same material. Only my eyes are open to the outside world, one pair of petrified green eyes that can't talk or scream; they can only gaze out towards the normality that surrounds them. Someone has dressed me in a burqa. I am horrified. It isn't right to use religion in this way. No one can see that I am held captive under these garments. Amidst the bustling activity, I am completely incognito. I'm too low for people to discover the terror in my eyes and, anyway, they're too focused on their own business to notice.

We glide through a security gate with barely a glance from the bored-looking female guard. I silently cry out to her as we pass, pleading with her to look directly into my eyes so she can detect something is fundamentally wrong. Efficiency and effectiveness triumphs over potential security delays as I am guided to the disabled access with a curt nod from a face lacking a smile. I try to struggle but can barely move as we continue our uninterrupted journey towards the platform and the awaiting train. I hear broadcasts in English and French announcing imminent departures. Oh god, they're taking me out of the country. Jeremy's tortured face flashes through my mind and a wave of nausea threatens to overcome me. I tell myself sternly that I will *not* be vomiting and, after a moment of psychological determination, I win the battle over my tumultuous stomach.

Reality slices through me like a machete. This is no game. This is exactly what Jeremy was afraid of during our last discussion on the beach at Avalon — his greatest fear realised. I have been abducted amidst of millions of people in London and it has been as easy as picking me up from the airport and wheeling me onto the Eurostar. No eyebrows raised, no questions asked. Simple and effective.

I am manoeuvred on the train and into a cabin. The person wheeling the chair leans over me, opens the front of my robes via a Velcro seam, unfastens the seat belt around my waist and frees my legs and wrists from their binds. Arms heave me up from my seated position and deposit me into a lounge-style chair. Before I can get a proper look at my captor, the person leaves the cabin, taking the wheelchair and closing the door behind them. I am left sitting alone in the small, neat cabin, although, thankfully, in my own clothes. My chair is next to a foldout table near the window with a tray of food and some bottled water. In the corner is a small cubicle with a toilet and basin. I immediately check the window but already know in my mind that the blind will be locked closed. I can't see out and certainly no one can see in. I automatically check the door, which of course is locked. I feel more alert now and I bang against it in raging frustration. I sense we are pulling out of the station as I lurch a little on my already unstable legs. I can't prevent the icy fear within my core. An uncontrollable trembling starts in the tips of my fingers before the feeling overcomes my entire shaking body and I collapse haphazardly back into the chair wondering what the hell is going to happen next.

My hand subconsciously grasps my bracelet, my fingers seeking the reassurance of the pink diamond chips and the Gaelic inscription against its otherwise smooth surface. Anam Cara — soul companion. I offer a silent prayer to Jeremy, to the universe.

*Please, please let this bracelet work the way you said it would. Please be able to find me. I don't know where I'm being taken or what they want with me, you never explained that in detail. Please let me be strong enough to survive whatever happens until we are together again. I need you so much.*

I can only hope that he is true to his word and that he can track my whereabouts 24/7 anywhere in the world via this encoded piece of jewellery. If he can't, how on earth will I be found? As my grip tightens around my only link to him, I try to subdue my rising panic by breathing deeply and reflecting back on our last night together at Avalon, where our lovemaking took on a whole new dimension that had never existed before, as if our paths were now spiritually connected somehow and the universe was conspiring for our togetherness. Well, it felt like it was for me at least ... My fingertips fondle the bracelet as the tender memory attempts to calms my nerves.

\* \* \*

After everything I have been through since meeting Jeremy at the Intercontinental Hotel, I know I have never felt more alive or sexually charged in my life. I can sense an iridescent spark within my soul that he has ignited and now will never be extinguished. It's as if my life's purpose is to ensure its continuous, growing flame. I feel like I need to become one with Jeremy like never before, take him to a place with me that's beyond sex and almost beyond our love for each other, after everything he has initiated within me. No more experiments, swabs, blood tests, toys or restraints. No more recording of my hormone levels. I need to bond with him naturally, passionately — as two sexual beings connecting as one. There is now an intense force driving my sexuality as if it is has taken on another persona within my body. It's impossible for me to deny and it propels me to take the lead with a man who doesn't like to be led.

I silently take Jeremy's hand, intuitively knowing words will diffuse the energy of the moment, and guide him purposefully over to the bed. There is something about the circular nature of this treehouse that gives me the courage to embrace the deep passion dwelling inside me and continue on my quest. He allows me to remove his robe with a raised eyebrow, no doubt wondering where I'm going with this and his fingers twitch by his side as he makes a deliberate attempt to remain still. The powerful force within propels me to take control here, so I deliberately remove my robe as well, leaving them pooled together on the polished floor. He visibly relaxes and his eyes glaze over as he soaks in the sight of my body. I can feel the heat rising between us. He awaits my next move and I know exactly where I want him. He allows me to position him spread-eagled in the centre of the giant round bed and he looks magnificent. I greedily absorb the vision, his presence and majesty almost disabling me. I take a few breaths to compose myself. I lightly kiss the softness of his lips as I carefully straddle his naked body, wanting my touch to be deliberate, not accidental. I gently raise my index finger to his mouth, cautioning him to silence. The look in his eyes acknowledges that he will concede his power, enabling me to take control when I know this is so difficult for him. He allows me to play with and stroke his firm, glorious body as he lays still, my perfect Vitruvian Man, surrounded by the white and gold sheets, surrendering his body beneath me. My heart swells with love for him; he is doing this for me, without moving, without touching me. Allowing me to twist and turn over his body, kissing, touching, sucking, at my own pace, in my own time, backwards and forwards, above and below. I love that he is the one and only person I have ever connected with in this way and I am finally able to experience what he has been able to elicit from me for so many years, time and time again.

I'm in awe of the sexual power emanating from our bodies and minds, and his willingness to give himself over to me. He tries to stifle his strengthening groans as my sensuous playing and exploring continues unabated and takes on new dimensions. My mounting lust fires my groin. The only movement in his body besides involuntary shivers is the growing magnificence of his phallus — eagerly awaiting the eventual attention of my hands, lips and mouth. His strength, patience and resolve is otherworldly as I lower my mouth over what's mine and his groan can no longer be withheld.

I take my time, wanting him to build slowly, and allow my tongue to lick and play only gradually strengthening momentum. His body tremors beneath mine and I know he is close — as am I. My belly aches for the completeness only he can provide. I manoeuvre my body until he is perfectly positioned beneath me so I can sheath his beautiful cock. I open my legs over his hips to accommodate the fullness of his girth within me.

I notice beads of sweat on his forehead, perhaps from his determined stillness, or his burning sexual desire … but his hands refrain from touching my body as if he completely understands why I need this, why we need this. He doesn't prevent me from establishing my own harmonious rhythm. I'm rapturous with the feeling of him surrendering himself to me, his strength penetrates my entire being. I love this feeling, the control he is conceding to me. It's as if he is sharing his power, his manhood, his fountain of life deep within my very core and I can feel every thick inch of him deep within me. Our eyes meet as I continue my grinding rhythm against him. We are both so very close as he raises his head slightly, questions me silently, beseechingly. I can't deny him a second longer, this man I love, asking for permission. I throw my head back as I anchor myself around his girth and grip tight around him. He immediately explodes with a fullness that is intoxicating. I collapse on top of him in a magical, spiralling state of complete euphoria. The slow burn, now liquid lava, intensifying our love and connection to each other as we hungrily find each other's mouths and tongues, speaking in a passionate, silent, universal language of unadulterated sexuality, until eventually we lay still together, completely sated both physically and emotionally.

'Thank you for doing that for me, I know it's not easy for you.' I smile lazily at him.

'Thank you for the opportunity. I've never allowed myself to experience anything like that before.'

'Relinquishing control?'

'Mmm, letting you dominate. You know it's not my preference but it was undeniably amazing.'

'So why did you?'

A pause. 'I did it because it was important for you and I will never deny you any sexual experience that you want or need. You know I'm all for you exploring and discovering every aspect of your sexual nature, even more so when it's between us. And this seems to be a pretty important milestone for you, particularly after everything you've been through in the last few days.' He looks at me quizzically. 'Am I right?'

'Yeah, you are,' I admit. 'It was as if there was a force inside me compelling me to take control. I've never had such a strong sexual urge before, so I just went with it.'

'I can't tell you how much it pleases me to finally hear you acknowledge that sexuality is a major part of who you are, Alexa. It just seems to have been buried and forgotten in recent years,' he adds with a chuckle.

'Thanks to you, Dr Quinn, I'm beginning to doubt whether I knew myself at all before this weekend.'

Jeremy snuggles me to him. 'How are you feeling?'

'A little light-headed but I feel so full, so content, safe and complete ...'

'My life is only just beginning to feel complete now that I know we are together,' he murmurs.

Oh, and how wonderful does that make me feel ... Our limbs are entwined as he spoons me closer to his chest.

'I love you, Jeremy.'

'And I you, Alexandra, more than I think you'll ever understand.'

They are the last words spoken as I drift off into a beautiful sleep in Jeremy's warm embrace.

I find myself in tears at the memory and in fear of the situation I'm in right now. My distress reaches hysterical proportions at the thought of what could happen to me, at my disconnectedness from Jeremy and my children. I'm a scared, emotional mess and I lash out at the tray of food that my stomach can't remotely contemplate, sending it flying into the wall. This is truly a nightmare! What do they want from me? I rise unsteadily from my chair and get a sense of the speed of the train as I step into the tiny bathroom and splash my face with cold water. I would give anything to collapse into a bed and wake up in Jeremy's arms knowing this was all a bad dream. After attempting to freshen up I make another futile attempt to force the door open, and then the window, but eventually I am left with no alternative but to sit in the secluded silence of this cabin cell with my own frightening thoughts of what might happen next.

The train eventually slows and I wonder if I will have to endure the humiliation of being tethered to the wheelchair again. I vaguely remember hearing about the burqa being banned in public spaces in France; I wasn't sure whether this was the case in surrounding European countries. The door opens, startling me, as terror returns to shake my body to the core. God help me. Two large men enter the cabin, seeming to fill the space, not making any eye contact with me. A quivering mess, I can only remain seated in my chair, as one of them walks towards me. I can't utter a word — I can barely look at him. He motions for me to stand. He doesn't realise I'm frozen with fear and can't follow his command. I'm hoisted roughly into a standing position and he hastily cuffs my wrists together. Oh, dear god. Some kind of gas mask is securely placed over my nose and mouth and I attempt to hold my breath, not wanting to lose consciousness again. Realising this logic is futile, I am left with no choice but to inhale, allowing myself short, shallow breaths, not sure what substance is infiltrating my lungs. The first man holds me still as the other attaches a container to my back, which looks like a bit like a fire extinguisher or small oxygen tank. It is carefully secured with straps around my waist and under my arms — my own self-sufficient breathing apparatus. My legs are efficiently taped together at both my ankles and knees and I feel myself becoming a little groggy. A warm softness enters my limbs and I go slightly limp against the man holding me upright. This warmth is actually pretty good and I feel myself relaxing. I remember this feeling from the dentist. Happy gas, nitrous oxide — it dulls sensations such as pain and makes you feel euphoric.

One of the men leaves the cabin briefly and returns wheeling a larger-than-average suitcase. As if on cue I get the giggles as my mind wanders and I randomly wonder whether it would be used to cart around outfits for Paris fashion week — that is, until he opens it and I am scooped off my feet and literally folded into the awaiting piece of luggage. It's lined with some kind of foam padding. I am aware, in a detached way, that this is not good, but as I don't actually feel too bad, it's difficult to decipher any of my emotions about the whole situation. I attempt to dislodge the gas mask attached to my face, pushing against the foam material, so I can think more clearly but to no avail. I am tucked into a foetal position. I attempt to scream and struggle, sensing that I should, but don't have a strong desire to muster the energy required. My body feels warm and rather heavy, but surprisingly comfortable given the position I'm in. Either way, I can't move and the mask stifles any sound before it can escape. I can't believe I'm small enough to fit in a suitcase; they'd never be able to do this to Jeremy, it would have to be tailor-made! The lid is closed, making my world once again black and if I weren't so relaxed, I'm sure I'd be shaking violently with fear. I hear the sound of a zip closing and the suitcase is positioned upright. I'm silently thankful for the generous padding that softens my impending ride; I shudder at the thought of the bruises otherwise. The wheels are in motion and I have no idea where I'll end up. I can't see, I can't hear, I can't talk or taste or smell. What I can feel is an immobile body that is awash with relaxant. All I can do is just keep breathing.

# Jeremy

I linger at the bar, aimlessly shuffling food around on my plate, ignoring everything else going on around me; my thoughts about Alex are all-consuming and endlessly disturbing. Apart from the terrifying thought that she might be hurt, I can't stop thinking about missed opportunities, my inability to come to terms with my own feelings for her — and now, shit, I may never have the opportunity to make amends. I can't even say whether Alexandra was ever aware of the complexity of emotion I feel for her, have always felt for her. It took me a while to admit it to myself and, once I had, I didn't want to scare her away so I deliberately kept things light and playful between us. Ultimately, I wanted to give her the world and be the focal point of hers. But I was too driven back then, knew the path of my future differed from hers.

My younger brother suffered from serious depression, and just before my twenty-fifth birthday I found him dead in our garage. He'd gassed himself in our father's car, which he'd locked from the inside. My world perspective changed from that moment on, my ambition fuelled by pain and the inability to provide him with the help he had so desperately needed. My parents, bless them, handled the devastating loss of their second son more graciously than me ... at least, I thought so. My grief was so raw, so incredibly confronting and completely overwhelming. I blamed myself. If only I knew more, had studied more, had understood him, spent more time with him ... if only the medication he was taking had helped him deal with life more effectively, rather than take it from him. I found it impossible to reconcile the loss of Michael's life in my mind. There was so much I needed to sort out in my head, to understand. Why my brother, why not me? Why did this happen to our family? Was it part of our gene pool or something unique to him? God knows, my family and friends tried to support me but I wasn't ready for their help. I didn't want their pity or anyone else's, so I pushed them away, including Alexa, to work it out for myself.

I had to get away from the pulse and stress of the city and find some perspective. I had an overwhelming urge to bury my pain, needed to be hands-on rather than lumbered with textbooks, theories and lectures. I needed to prove I was alive, unlike Michael, whose life was lost at the vital age of twenty. The flying doctor organisation and the outback provided me with space, sanctuary and distance from everyone and everything I had known. Thankfully, they were in desperate need of medical staff and accepted my application as soon as I secured my pilot's licence, as I could provide both medical and flying roles for them. An extra set of strong male hands never went astray when working in the harshness of our great southern land either. Everything seemed to fall into place when I met Leo. He too, had lost a cousin to suicide and we spent many hours discussing our theories as to why and how such acute depression happens to some and not others, never being able to decide on whether the contributing factors were psychological, chemical or environmental or how they connected. He provided me the mentorship I needed to get my life back on track.

I needed that then, just as desperately as I need Alex now. Back then I had to let her go so we could pursue our futures independently. I wasn't ready to give her the family she longed for and I couldn't be diverted from my mission to find a cure for depression. I had to prevent other families going through the pain and anguish we had to deal with when we lost Michael. But now I know she is my connection to the earth; my love for her is so great I will not allow her to slip through my fingers again. She is the oxygen that fuels my life.

I remember the conversation we had in Santorini that secured our separation for the next decade. It began as an inspired discussion on our paths in life and ended at a fork in the road, like the tongue of a serpent and stung just as badly. For me, anyhow ...

'I'm ready for something more meaningful, Jeremy. I'm just not getting the buzz out of work that I used to. It's becoming routine, monotonous. The business world is all about the money and I need to know I'm helping people, not just making money for money's sake. Besides, I'm not as driven as you and I know I need more than work in my life to satisfy me …'

'So what are you going to do about it?'

We are basking in the sun on a warm rock by the warm waters of the Aegean Sea and I'm doing my duty, rubbing sunscreen on Alexa's back. It's a tough life!

'I'm thinking of going back to psychology full-time.'

'Wow. That's a big move. Are you ready for it?'

'Yeah, I am. But it's more than that. I think I'm ready to settle down.' I keep up the sensuous strokes along her smooth back.

'Settle down. What do you mean?' A small wave of apprehension shudders through me. Settle down, shit … not my Alexa!

'You know, start a family, maybe return to Australia. I don't want to raise a family in central London.'

'You're serious?' I inadvertently splat more sunscreen than necessary on her shoulders and quickly start rubbing it in to distract from my shock at her words.

'Of course I'm serious, Jeremy. Why wouldn't I be? My maternal clock's ticking, and I'm over the club scene and the frantic pace of London.'

'But you're not even close to thirty, you have heaps of time.' God, I need to come up with something, she's slipping away from me, from beneath my very fingers. I know I'm not ready for a family or to 'settle down'. I've just started to make headway in my career. My research at Harvard is only serving to make me more certain I am on the right path. I've never been closer to a significant breakthrough in managing chemical imbalances in the brain. After all these years, I know I'm finally on the right path, on the cusp of finally doing something real and tangible to help prevent families going through the pain and hell we went through with Michael. I can't stop now and I can't split my focus between work and a family. My hours of study, my research, it would be a disaster. And there is no way Alexa would tolerate a partner who isn't around for their kids, there's just no way.

'I know,' she replies calmly, while my mind reels, 'but it's only just around the corner and you never know how long these things can take. One of my friends who just turned thirty has been trying for two years without success. I don't know how I'd survive if that happened to me. I can't ignore it much longer, Jeremy. Every baby I pass in the street is … well, it's as if my heart spasms and contracts. The yearning to nurture my own biological child is like nothing I've felt. Each time I see a pregnant belly I smile at the mother and then tears well up in my eyes. And I can't deny it, the feeling gets stronger each day. It's as if everything else has faded into insignificance for me.'

I drag my brain back from morbid thoughts on how depression can devastate the happiest of families to concentrate fully on Alexa's words. My lover … my best friend … clock ticking … Jeez, does she expect me to be the father? What if she's already pregnant? Bloody hell. I'm so not ready for this. She sits up from her lying position and looks directly into my eyes, as if sensing my fear, my rising anxiety as to where this discussion is leading.

'It's okay, Jeremy.' She laughs her delightful laugh. 'You don't need to look so scared! I know your career is everything to you, it always has been — and it's not like we have ever had a monogamous relationship. We just have incredibly great sex when we're together. You've made your views on marriage very clear over the years.'

'Oh, yeah, sure, I suppose I have.' She looks at me with a gorgeous twinkle in her eye and her dimple appears next to her smile. I breathe a sigh of relief and relax but surely she must know she means more to me than incredibly great sex … doesn't she? And as for my anti-marriage views … well, we've been on opposite sides of the world for the past few years and I haven't had the chance to explain to her that such views only ever pertained to every other woman in the world until I was ready for her.

'I've met someone.' Fuck. That's a bombshell. My thoughts come to an abrupt halt. My heart pounds deeply within my chest at her words. 'And it's getting serious, I think.'

My breathing temporarily stops before I realise she is waiting for me to respond.

'Really, what's his name?' I have to pretend I'm coughing as I choke out the words.

'Robert. He's English but seems quite keen on moving to Australia with me and he just loves kids. I met him a few months ago at a friend's christening and ….' I see her lips forming words but I don't hear her voice thanks to the loud thrumming in my ears and the pumping pain in my chest. This is it. I'm losing my Alexa. Doesn't she realise she is mine, has been since we first met? Now she wants to settle down, have babies, move back to Australia. All three things are impossible for me at this juncture of my life. I love her, surely she must know that. If she doesn't, how can I possibly tell her now? She looks so happy and animated talking about 'Robert' and their potential new life together. Fuck! How did this conversation end up like this? I shake my head as her voice cuts through my daze.

'Anyway, I just wanted to let you know, because if Robert and I move in together, like we're planning, you know, as a couple, well, I won't be able to have any more weekends away with you, like this. It just … wouldn't be right, would it?'

She looks up at me, both resignation and longing in her puppy dog eyes. This is it. My playful, experimental Alexa is closing herself off from me because I can't give her what she wants at this point in time. And she's right. I can't — or won't. I don't know which it is, but it's too soon, we're still too young. And besides, it really sounds like she loves him so how can I, in all fairness, deny her this happiness just because I'm not ready to commit? Shit, I feel sick to the pit of my gut. Too much for me to dwell on right now. I force my voice to sound calm.

'No, sweetheart, it wouldn't. I'm pleased you're happy and thanks for letting me know. But know this, if he hurts you, upsets you, lays a finger on you that you're not happy with, or doesn't treat you like the goddess you are, he'll have me to contend with and you know what I'm like.'

She smiles her gorgeous smile and I can't help but try to grin back. 'Very theatrical Jeremy but

70

yeah, I do know what you're like.' She gives me a fun, playful, loving thump on my upper arm. 'Always my protector.'

'I will always be there for you, Alexandra. It's very important to me that you know that.' I seem to be drowning in solemnity which I'm sure must be freaking her out, particularly if she loves him and not me. I must try to get my head around supporting the choice she's making and I need to lighten things up — urgently. 'In the meantime, he doesn't have you this weekend, I do, so if this is our last weekend together before you "settle down"' — I can't keep the bitter undertone from catching in my voice — 'then rest assured, we will be making the most of it.'

I can't bear to look at her face as I experience the unusual sensation of hot tears pooling in the corners my eyes so I pick her up instead and she squeals as I carry her to the edge of the rock shelf and leisurely throw her into the warm, aquamarine water. I wait till she rises to the surface, then promptly jump in to retrieve what's mine, at least for now. I desperately need the diversion of the water against my skin, which helps to wash away my turbulent emotions and lighten my heavy heart.

I will *not* let her slip through my fingers again! I slam my fist hard on the wooden bench of the bar, my skin burning with determination.

'Jeremy, are you okay?'

'Oh, Sam, hi, I didn't see you come in.'

His usually jovial face is lined with worry and concern. I quickly wipe any sign of moisture away from the corner of my eye; he shouldn't have to see me like this. Fuck it, we shouldn't be in this situation at all.

'Yeah, I've been a million miles away. Any update?' I raise my hand to the barman to indicate we need service and order more whisky which momentarily takes the edge off my pain but it will be the last one. I can't afford to be playing anything but my A game when it comes to Alexa.

'Actually, I do have some news. The signal from Alexandra's bracelet has been traced to St Pancras station, they believe she boarded a train to Paris. The tracking device on the bracelet is not as effective on high-speed trains but we have been able to correlate the timing of the train departures and the bracelet and we are ninety per cent sure. Unless —'

'What?' I say harshly, frustrated by his seemingly longwinded explanation. 'Unless what, Samuel?' Shit, I really do need to control my temper.

'Well, they could have tampered with the bracelet to throw us off the trail. Do you think they could know about it?' Samuel asked.

'There was nothing about the security of the bracelet on my system at work, that was kept in another department. What about yours?'

'Same. So we should be all right for a while, or at least until they try to remove it — and realise they can't.'

'Well, we need to get going. If they think she's in Paris then that's where I'm heading.' Finally, something to focus on rather than drowning in sorrow. I start to rise but Sam puts his hand on my arm to stop me.

'That was a few hours ago, Jeremy. She could be anywhere in continental Europe by now. I hope you don't mind, but I took the liberty of speaking to Martin directly, knowing how upset you —'

The look on my face stops him in his tracks and I take a deep breath to calm my anger. Control it, Quinn. 'Sorry, Sam, of course, yes, please continue.'

He visibly relaxes, I must look scary. Sam is not easily unnerved.

'Anyway, we detected the signal at Gare du Nord for a short time and lost it again. The security guys are assuming she must be on another train travelling southeast from Paris towards the Swiss border but we won't be 100% sure until she is stationary. We should have an exact location in the morning. Martin is hoping to finalise the team in the next twenty-four hours.'

'What?' I am shouting. 'We can't wait that long, Sam, they've fucking abducted Alex!'

'These things take a while, Jeremy, and they don't want to get the authorities involved just yet ...' Sam's tone is placatory but I don't want to hear it. Why the hell haven't Martin and Moira been calling me and instead talking to Sam? I grab my phone out of my jacket pocket and see that I've had five missed calls and that it's been on silent. Shit! How the hell did that happen? I slam it down on the bench top in complete frustration; absolutely nothing is going my way.

I shake his hand off and stand up.

'You have to be kidding me?' Blood pounds through my head. Samuel's calmness inflames my anger and I'm teetering on the edge of civility. I pick up the phone again, my fingers fumbling in my attempt to make the call to sort this mess out. Sam interjects quickly.

'Apparently, they're trying to avoid any red tape if we are forced to act quickly, if you know what I mean.' He looks flustered at these words and adds hastily: 'Anyway, we'll take the first flight to Paris in the morning, and hopefully have a more comprehensive picture of where she has been taken.'

I reluctantly consider his words and try to temper my fury. 'Oh, right, I see where you're coming from. Yes, if we need to act quickly, we don't want to be asking permission from anyone, for anything.' I take the last swig of my whisky in an attempt to take the edge off my nerves and my fear for AB's wellbeing. If only she were in the safety of my arms right now. A burst of rage fires in my belly that is so strong, I feel like I could kill the bastards who have taken her captive. Not an appropriate emotion for a medical professional but I don't give a fuck at this point.

'I need to be on the first flight out, Sam, as soon as we have a location. Let Martin know.' I need some fresh air quickly, I'm feeling so claustrophobic.

'Will do.'

I'm becoming a rude arrogant bastard and it's not fair to take it out on Sam when he's doing everything to help. I take a deep breath and make a determined effort to control my threatening emotions. I soften my voice and place my hand on his shoulder. 'Thanks, Sam. I appreciate it. It's just killing me, not knowing if she's okay. I need to get her back.'

'I know, Jeremy, and we will.'

# Part Three

While the doctor is reflecting,
the patient dies.

— Italian proverb

# Alexa

After scrubbing my skin to remove the filth, jetlag and tears, I allow the steaming water to cascade over my tired and exhausted muscles, my emotions numb. My heart feels frozen. I don't know how long I have been under this scorching rain of water and I don't care. My brain seems incapable of making even the simplest of decisions. It isn't until I realise I am in a crumpled heap on the floor of the shower and the water temperature is cooling over my limbs that I shudder and consider getting out. To what? I wonder. Where am I? Who has done this to me? Who could do this to me? There are no tears left to shed. I have more than used my quota.

Even the plush towel I absentmindedly wrap around my shoulders feels raw and harsh against my skin. I glance in the direction of the mirror and am grateful it is steamed over. If I saw my face it might make this nightmare more real, more tangible and I don't have the nerves to deal with that. I hesitate as I open the bathroom door, not completely sure what I have seen on the other side. I briefly remember glimpsing classical, almost antique-style furniture, a cupboard, bedside tables, a higher than normal double bed and a floral chaise longue as I emerged like an unidentified creature hatching from the case that held me prisoner for so long. I think I was in shock when light finally infiltrated my eyes and I realised I was breathing free of the mask. My binds had been discarded just as efficiently as they had been applied. No one was in the empty room when I cautiously peered about, stretching each of my agonised limbs slowly and carefully to allow the blood to flow back into my extremities after being confined for so long. The light of the bathroom had attracted my immediate attention as I crawled over to haul myself up onto the toilet. The shower quickly became my next point of call as I hastily removed the clothes I had been in for however many days or hours since I departed Melbourne. It seems like a lifetime ago.

The curtains are open, nothing is shrouded in darkness and I marvel at being able to see out into the world. My eyes take a few minutes to adjust to the view before me. The countryside is beautiful: rolling hills and pastures with the sun sinking rapidly behind them, the sky being teased with the colours of dusk. Majestic mountains provide a picture-perfect backdrop — only if you were on holidays, I reprimand myself, which I most certainly am not! I place both hands on the window ledge to steady my balance as I continue to gaze, taking long deep breaths to fill my lungs and attempt to calm my returning panic. I notice how high above everything I am situated, the view all-encompassing. *Too high to escape* ... the thought flitters through my head, although I do try the window but it cannot be opened.

I am captured, imprisoned behind this small window in what appears to be some sort of castle. A distant memory reminds me that I have only ever stayed in one chateau before, just outside Reims when visiting Champagne in France, but the vision of the mountains before me must mean I am further east towards Austria, or Italy maybe, or perhaps on the outskirts of Eastern Europe. It's impossible to be sure. I shudder at the unfathomable reality I face, compared to the delightful European adventures of my younger years. How did I end up in this mess? I know how it started and I just don't want to go there. I notice the towel is pooled around my feet and I am naked as I continue to peer out the small window frame. I feel like Rapunzel without the luscious long locks to provide a means of escape, nor the handsome saviour — at least not yet. I desperately hope that Jeremy can trace my whereabouts, as I hold on tight to the only item on my body, my cherished bracelet. I raise it to my lips, willing Jeremy to sense where I am, willing him to save me from whoever has abducted me.

No, I tell myself, no more tears, no more emotion. I am alive, albeit a little battered and bruised, but essentially unharmed. I need to focus on the positive aspects of this dismal situation. If they wanted to harm me, or worse — I shudder — kill me, they have had every opportunity since I stepped into that toxic car at Heathrow. As stoically as possible, I pick up the towel from the floor, wrap it around my body under my arms and search the room for any of my belongings.

I notice the revolting piece of luggage I arrived in is no longer in this room, they must have removed it while I was having a shower. Relief washes over me — that claustrophobic journey is certainly not something I ever wish to experience again. I open the antique mahogany cupboard and notice a dress hanging in there, covered in plastic with an elegant handwritten note neatly attached.

*Please be dressed and ready for dinner by
7.00 p.m. sharp.*

I glance over to my clothes lying on the bathroom floor. Clothes that by my calculations I must have been in for at least thirty hours or so. I pick up my shirt, take a quick sniff and immediately discard it, physically and symbolically kicking the pile aside, never wanting to wear or touch them again after what they have been through, after what I have been through. But do I want to take what is being offered in the cupboard? My emotions threaten to unravel yet again as I take a deep breath and unpeel the plastic. One elegant, classic cream dress. Not quite the virgin bride, but even so ...

What the hell is going on here? How can I be deposited in a room, presumably somewhere in Europe, in a frigging suitcase and now this? *Please be dressed and ready for dinner* — what the hell? My head starts to spin as I think, for the first time, to check the door of the suite. Locked, as anticipated. I don't want to dress up. I can't play dress-ups under these circumstances. I was never good at it, until ... my mind floods with images of the stunning red designer dress Jeremy had made for me and I almost crumble under the stress of the anguish it causes. Why aren't I with him right now? Because I am imprisoned in here. I bash my fist against the door in exasperation, my legs give way and I'm a crumpled heap on the floor. I glance towards the window and opportunistically wonder if someone will come shattering through it and rescue me from their hovering helicopter, à la James Bond or *Mission Impossible*. I race over to the window desperately searching for any sign of movement, rescue attempt, anything. Nothing. Absolutely nothing. Why do such rescues only ever occur in movies? Darkness descends on the rapidly diminishing pink and purple hues of twilight. I run my fingers through my hair in both fear and frustration as I contemplate the dress beckoning me from the other side of the room.

My stomach rumbles on cue, reminding me that it has been some time since my last meal. Nothing like basic physical needs to assist with the decision-making process. Damn it! I walk tentatively over to the dress — it's not like I have other options available at the moment and I am stark naked. God, what if they arrive and I'm like this? This thought provides me with enough momentum to pull the dress off the hanger even though I'm filled with disgust as I touch it. They've even supplied cream underwear to match — how considerate. At least I won't be knickerless again. I hastily get dressed in this flowing, sophisticated ball gown without wanting to dwell on it any more than I have to. I notice a box at the bottom of the cupboard, knowing that it will contain high heels and take them out, desperately hoping they won't be too high. Reasonable, I sigh, in the scheme of this insanity. I quickly comb my wet hair and leave it sleek down my back. I don't want any more fanfare than is necessary and I don't have anything to put it up with. Either way, I don't care how I look and have no interest in checking in the mirror. After cleaning my teeth — grateful a toothbrush and paste have been supplied — and splashing my face with cold water, I go and sit on the edge of the chaise longue, the bed being a bit too high to be comfortable. The longer I attempt to sit, the more anxious I become. I start to notice the suppleness of the dress's silky material against my skin and I don't want a bar of it. I decide to lie on the carpeted floor, even though I'm in heels and a full-length dress, and attempt to meditate. Savasana, there's nothing like a good corpse pose!

Breathe in, breathe out, breathe in, breathe out, close your mind, relax your body … Doing this, I realise how tense my body actually is and I make an effort to relax my shoulders, which are high and bunched towards my neck. I deliberately tighten each muscle group so I can release it while I continue my breathing. All this concentration is helping to distract me from my reality for a few seconds at least. It feels good to be lying flat on the floor, stretching out what has been cramped for so long. I allow my breath to flow in and out of my body carefully, ensuring each one is relevant and worthwhile until I eventually calm into a deeper state of being.

\* \* \*

The shout at the door disrupts my mental solitude.

'She's down, we need attention immediately!' the urgent, accented voice calls.

Someone is suddenly by my side checking my pulse. My mouth is open with no words coming out. I stare upwards focusing on the scene before me. An intense-looking man wearing a white coat comes racing towards me as I am raised into an upright position. He waves something under my noise that makes me shudder away from it. God, smelling salts! Do they think I've fainted? They're talking amongst themselves in a foreign accent I don't immediately recognise. I shake my head in dismay. My chin is held firm as a bright light shines in my eyes. What is it with doctors and their damn probing and blinding flashlights? I blink and try to squirm away. My pulse is checked again before I am escorted to my feet, though a combination of my attempted meditation and high heels makes me a little wobbly to say the least. Who are these people? A young woman in a maid's outfit, the doctor type and another male who looks like a butler. I stand in shock before them.

'Dr Blake, what happened? How do you feel?' They speak to me in English.

'Can you talk, Dr Blake? Please answer us, are you okay?'

Well, they certainly *appear* to be concerned about my wellbeing, which has to be a positive sign. I can only hope. I stare at each of them intently, one by one, wanting to soak into my memory the faces involved in my captivity. Under different circumstances I may have noticed that the doctor, hiding beneath his white coat and furrowed brow, is actually a very attractive man, a pair of funky glasses covering his chocolate-brown eyes, dark blondish hair and a smile that could light up a room. The butler is an average-sized man but looks more brawn than brain, a bit of a miniature Muscle Mary, and the maid looks like a sweet innocent girl in a ridiculous uniform with a long dark plait down her back and wide hazel eyes. How dare they ask how I am when they have done this to me, put me in this situation? I could scream as anger and panic simultaneously well up from deep within me. Just as suddenly, I realise they are eagerly anticipating my answer, awaiting my response. Well, they can shove it! I vow then and there to remain mute, silent, until I know exactly what is going on. They may have shipped me from London to wherever we are, against my will, but these people are not, will not be hearing my voice or response, to anything!

The doctor removes the stethoscope from around his neck and places the cold metal on my chest; its temperature alone makes me automatically inhale. He moves silently around my shoulders and above my breasts, his fingers alternating between barely touching the fabric of my dress and my sensitive skin as he makes his way around my body. I'm not sure whether to hold my breath so he can't hear what he is hoping for or attempt to maintain a regular breathing pattern for him to report on. He stops before my decision is made.

'She is fine, stable.' He nods to the others. 'Fetch a glass of mineral water, immediately.'

The maid flies into action at his command. His hand remains firmly on my elbow as he guides me to a seated position on the chaise longue. It is only at this point that it dawns on me how weak I actually feel. It takes me by surprise.

'Please, drink this.' He hands me the water the maid has fetched.

I accept it from him and drink. The cool liquid bubbles refresh my dry mouth. I raise my eyes again, staring at the doctor's face, seeking any information or understanding as to my situation. I can see concern and professionalism, nothing more. I don't think he'll hurt me. I hand the glass back after finishing the last mouthful, which he passes quickly to the maid, all the while never taking his eyes off me.

'Well, Dr Blake, I see no reason for you being unable to attend dinner this evening with Madame.'

What? Who is Madame?

Oh, so close … I almost uttered the words out loud.

I notice a small smirk curl the edge of his lips, which quickly vanishes with his next words. 'Please, allow me to introduce myself.'

I nod to acknowledge his request. Somehow his manner puts me more at ease. 'My name is Dr Josef Votrubec. I will attend to you during your stay with us.' He takes my hand in his own and gives it a firm but steady shake before assisting me to my feet. 'Louis, Frederic, I am comfortable that Dr Blake is ready to be escorted to dinner. She is in good health and will benefit from some fine food and wine.'

Louis, the butler-looking one, appears instantly by my side while Frederic, a much larger man, miraculously appears from outside the room and maintains a massive presence in the doorway. Well, it's not as if I would have been successful should I have decided to run, they have all exits well attended. I glance anxiously between Doctor Josef and the foreign bouncers allocated to 'escort me to dinner' and I'm not sure whether to roll my eyes at this ridiculous scenario or not. The apprehension still coursing through me prevents such frivolity. The doctor's smirk reappears on his face as if he can sense exactly what's going on in my brain. I'm furious that he finds my situation so amusing. Louis has his elbow crooked towards me expectantly, his face a mask. This is absolutely farcical.

Does he honestly think I am going to loop my arm through his and waltz elegantly off to dinner? Moments pass as if we are all frozen in position and time, only their eyes moving silently back and forth between each other before settling on me, awaiting my next move. I exhale both from nerves and the realisation that I have no choice but to play along.

Through all those hours when I was crunched up in that suitcase, I had honestly imagined that my destination would see me thrown into a skanky cell, locked behind bars, lying on damp, concrete floors with only a bucket for company. This just doesn't make sense, dressed up in a cream ball gown and high heels, and two butler-cum-bouncers waiting to escort me to dinner with Madame, whoever the hell she is. Even though this situation proves to be more comfortable physically than I had imagined, it is the emotional consequences that seem to be creating my extreme discomfort. Stockholm syndrome penetrates my scattered thoughts and I give myself a harsh reminder of my commitment not to speak. It is with that conclusion that I am able to take my first step towards the door, bypassing the butler-bouncers, ignoring an outstretched elbow — I don't want to touch them and certainly don't want them touching any part of me.

As I stride towards the door, I sure hope I'm looking more confident than I feel, and I wonder what on earth could be waiting for me on the other side. Frederic stands back to let me pass which surprises me as I have no idea where to go. Louis whisks past me so fast my dress swishes around my legs as if I'm standing in a gentle breeze.

'Please follow me, Dr Blake.' He starts off at a rapid pace down a long, carpeted corridor. I turn to look at Frederic, who extends his arm to invite me to continue, confirming my options are limited to one way — forward. I glance back into the room to see the doctor repacking his equipment in his small black case. As he completes his task, he looks up towards me.

'*Bonsoir*, Dr Blake.'

Once again, I have to catch myself from answering '*Bonsoir*' back to this perplexing man.

'Enjoy your dinner, I have no doubt you will feel better after some food.'

I quickly turn my head away, resigned to the fact the bouncer behind me is less than patiently waiting for me to be on my way. The vision before me mentally transforms into a horizontal version of Alice and the rabbit hole. As nerves get the better of me, all I can think is, 'Oh fuck, here we go again!' And I really don't like to swear very often unless it's absolutely necessary.

* * *

After walking along what feels like the longest corridor that I have ever experienced, we eventually turn into what seems like a great hall. I take a tentative step onto a parquet wooden floor that enables me to hear as well as feel my legs as my steps clatter nervously forward.

Louis is setting quite a pace, so I focus on the task of following close behind him as we pass beneath an enormous chandelier and subtle stained glass windows. Towards the end of the great hall are two enormous wooden doors, which when closed make an elaborate arch. I lift the front of my dress slightly so I don't trip over it. As we stride across the superbly polished floor, the dress wafts behind me. There are two guards standing on either side of the massive doors and I am intrigued as to the history of their ornate uniforms.

As I continue to stare and stride, I almost smash straight into Louis and step back in the nick of time to avoid a collision. It takes a very concentrated effort on my part to not let out an 'Oh, sorry'. I gather myself quickly. They both stand either side of me, Louis only slightly taller than me, in my heels, and Fred (I decide the more Australian version of his name makes this whole situation less ominous in my mind) towering over me, the top of my head barely reaching his shoulder. We are standing rigid in front of the great doors before us. What am I walking into here? I wonder fleetingly if it would be easier to faint, but I look toward the guards and feel the presence of the butler-bouncers either side of me and decide that wouldn't be such a good idea.

Louis nods toward one of the costumed guards, who then turns to a piece of technology I hadn't noticed. He mumbles something I can't hear into it and enters a code, which seems to take some time. My heart pounds frantically in my chest and my hands are twisting anxiously in front of me, as we stand waiting. I tentatively glance behind me, more to absorb my surrounds than anything else. Louis and Fred immediately close in on me and take a slight step backwards to block my view. Tension builds within my belly. Now the only thing I can see behind me is the black and white of their butler uniforms.

As I turn back towards the doors, they slowly swing inwards, allowing me to feast on the vision before my eyes. I'm overwhelmed by gold and crystal and paintings, enormous paintings that belong in museums and churches. Good god, what is this all about? The sheer opulence is astounding. I'm nudged along by the butler-bouncers until I eventually step unassisted into another great room — I have no idea what its proper name would be. There is too much to take in, I just stand in awe of this place. Why am I here? Who owns this? I fleetingly think of Jeremy and the consequences of me asking questions. I still remember the tantalising sting across my arse and the overwhelming pleasure that came after, over and over again. My head starts to spin with the memory. Oh no, I scold myself, please no, not again, not here. I feel warmth swell in my groin, steadily and determinedly heating my sexual parts. After all I have been through, how can I still have these sensations cascading through my body? Oh please, no.

Too late, the ambushing rhythm sets itself in motion as if it has finally been granted permission to release itself after being on hold for so long and I find myself leaning against an antique chair, holding myself up, desperately trying to maintain physical balance and mental perspective. Oh god! The rhythm continues to course through me as my body remembers the exquisite pain of the lashes and the delicious aftermath that followed. The feelings linked to the memory threaten to overwhelm me as I try to catch my breath and my knees begin to buckle. Heat and desire pool between my thighs and I feel as if my temperature is rising as it spreads to my nipples and my behind, perspiration beading on my forehead as I bow my head to accommodate the shallow breaths that escape me. How can this still happen so quickly, so automatically?

My mind commences its descent into oblivion as my sensate body overrides everything else. I start to tremor as my body writhes in pleasure. The problem is I love this feeling, but it just can't happen now — not here. Control yourself, you weak woman. Get your act together — *immediately*.

I inhale deeply, knowing that my brain needs oxygen to focus, and that finally helps to bring me some relief. I inhale again as I realise my head is bent between my arms and I'm clinging to the chair in front of me. I feel a light sheen on my face that I know from experience will be accompanied by a deep blush. Oh dear me! How could I? It takes a minute or two before I am composed enough to maintain a standing position, albeit with my hand still gripping the chair for balance. Deeply embarrassed, I quickly glance towards Tweedle-dee and Tweedle-dum who are staring at me unabashed, disbelieving of what they just saw. Oh shit!

'Well, well, well, Dr Blake. Welcome! I must say, that was quite an entrance!'

I hear the female voice from the other side of the room. It's unnerving to say the least. I focus my eyes towards the voice and the attached body comes into my line of sight.

'Please, perhaps you should take a seat in order to fully recover from your, what shall we say, episode?'

I don't know what to make of this woman nor her words as she gestures toward a set of ornate lounges to my left. She, too, is dressed in a full-length gown, of pale gold chiffon — no wonder I hadn't noticed her in the room when I entered, as she blends in perfectly with the gold and crystal, enhancing the majesty of this room. She elegantly adjusts her gown to accommodate her now seated position. My breath is still weak from my 'episode' and I wish I had a tissue to wipe my forehead. At that precise moment, Louis offers me a handkerchief from his pocket. I take it ungraciously from his hands, pat my face quickly and hand it straight back to him. He accepts it with a bemused look on his face, placing it back in his coat pocket. He then places his hand on the small of my back and motions me forward towards Madame Goldy. I stare at both bouncers, before whisking up my dress and less than elegantly taking a seat on the lounge opposite her.

'Dr Blake, shall we start over?' She doesn't wait for a response before continuing. 'Once again, welcome to Chateau Vilamonte,' she states proudly and warmly. Is she serious?

'It is our sincere pleasure to have you here with us.' Her voice is low and has a slight accent. It is as if she is welcoming an invited guest. I stare at her aghast. 'I trust the rather unfortunate circumstances of your arrival are now behind you and you are feeling refreshed and revived?' She raises an eyebrow. I notice the slightest glint of amusement in her eye as I realise she is enjoying this charade. It takes all my energy to recommit to my vow of being mute. Am I making the right decision? I'm not sure but resolve that it can't hurt in the short-term. At least until I understand what is going on and why I'm here.

'My name is Madame Madeleine de Jurilique.' She pauses as if this announcement should be of significance to me. I would dearly love to assure her it isn't. 'I am the European Managing Director of Xsade Pharmaceuticals.'

More like the Managing Director of Kidnap and Abduction, I think to myself viciously. I can only hope that she can't read my thoughts on my face as I continue to maintain 'nonchalant' eye contact with Madame Goldy.

'I am assuming you understand why you are here?' She tilts her head to one side in anticipation of my answer.

No, actually I don't and I'm really, really trying not to let my mind explore this question further as I'm sure it would elicit questions from the mouth which I want to keep firmly shut. I continue my silence and attempt to assume a vague, blank mask on my face.

'So this is how you want to play? Silence, *oui*?' Ah, finally she understands. '*D'accord*. So be it. You can listen to my proposition over dinner and consider your options overnight.'

Her last comment sparks my interest — options, I have options? She catches my slight head movement in recognition of her words and I mentally kick myself that I'm not better at ensuring my feelings aren't reflected in my facial movements. Damn.

She carefully rises from her seated position and slowly glides across to the head of the dining table, which could seat perhaps thirty people but has only been set for two. Excellent, I think sarcastically to myself. Two large hands grasp both my elbows as I am firmly guided to the dining table. The additional place setting is in the middle of the table where my two bodyguards stand either side of the chair, waiting patiently for me to be seated. This whole situation is becoming more insane by the minute.

Goldy looks more than comfortable in the silence of our elegant surrounds. There is a calm gracefulness about her demeanour that I find quite disconcerting. Our entrées arrive simultaneously and my stomach growls in anticipation of being fed. I thought I'd be feeling too emotionally overwrought to eat, but I surprise myself by polishing off every morsel of the smoked salmon salad in record time. Madame seems pleased with my appetite. I grimace at her smile and distract myself by dabbing the sides of my mouth lightly with my serviette. I haven't touched the glass of champagne sitting before me as drinking it would just conjure too many of the memories that threaten to overwhelm me. I wait until I see the wine being poured from the same bottle Madame is drinking from and decide at least that it would be a safer, non-spiked option. It is fresh, dry and has a delicious bouquet, just as you would expect from good French wine. Its taste momentarily distracts me from my circumstance.

Main course is delivered — succulent duck à l'orange with assorted veggies — and still we continue to sit, chewing in silence. This is just too weird, but I'm thankful I can focus on eating dinner without interruption and it helps keep my anxiety in check.

We finish our last bites at the same time. After swallowing another mouthful of wine, I look in Goldy's direction to assess her body language in an attempt to ascertain what on earth she wants with me. She looks just as deliberately at me for a long moment before nodding briefly. This results in one of the guards disappearing momentarily and returning to the table with a document of some sort. With a quick flick of her finger she signals for the document to be placed just out of arm's reach from where I am sitting.

'I hope you enjoyed your meal, Dr Blake, it seems you haven't lost your appetite, which is very encouraging.'

I stare toward my glass of wine as I absentmindedly fondle the smooth stem of the crystal glass, observing the changes in colour as it refracts the light.

'The document beside you is a contract my company would like you to consider very carefully. We don't mean you any harm, Dr Blake, and we hope we can anticipate your cooperation.'

Well, well, here we go ...

'I would like to present you with an extraordinary opportunity, related to your recent studies with Dr Quinn. You must have been exceptionally impressed with the results he presented, based on your case study, last week in Zurich.'

What the —? He presented findings in Zurich that I don't even know about? How could he? He wouldn't. He wouldn't do that to me without my knowledge. Would he? As I sit silently, attempting to quell the emotional ambush of his words, Madame Goldy doesn't miss a trick.

'It seems as though this is perhaps a shock to you, Dr Blake. You're not telling me that the great Quinn neglected to copy you in on his results, *non*?'

Beads of sweat form on my forehead and my palms moisten at the insinuation. He would never do that to me, she's goading me to speak. I straighten my shoulders, fasten my eyes on the almost naked Renaissance woman featured on the artwork on the opposite side of the room and inhale deeply in an attempt to lock her out and maintain some form of composure. I'm not sure that it works but it's worth a try.

'Surely he would inform you of such a significant document?'

Control and composure, Alexa. I do remember he sent me an email about doing some presentations in Europe but not specifically about *what* he was presenting. Keep silent. She's obviously desperate for a reaction and I desperately don't want to give her one — which is becoming an increasingly impossible task.

She continues her charade with all the finesse of a quintessentially aristocratic French madame. 'The accuracy with which he has been able to detail the transudate excretion fluid in combination with natural serotonin and testosterone is positively miraculous. We are in awe of his research and it's all because of you and recognising the distinct characteristics of the AB blood group. It has been staring at us for years but we never considered isolating and recombining the factors as Dr Quinn did with you, Dr Blake. Just *magnifique*.'

Has he used my name in the report? He promised me that I would remain incognito, that no one in the public domain would ever know that I was the case study in this scenario. What is happening here?

'I see this one-sided discussion is disturbing you somewhat, Dr Blake. Surely Dr Quinn enlightened you this past week on his breakthrough? Why else do you think you are here?'

I remain rigid, mortified that I have been caught so off-guard. Doesn't Jeremy trust me enough to share his findings about me, with me? Or is it more important for him to be centre stage making his global breakthrough discoveries … I wish he were here to explain himself, to explain what is going on. But he isn't, so I must continue not believing a word she is saying; that's what he would do for me and that's what I must do for him. At least I think he would. I continue to stare directly at Renaissance Woman's breast, refusing to give Goldy an inch. Out of the corner of my eye I see her shake her head.

'Oh, such silly games we must play, Alexandra. I thought your approach would have been a little more mature. So disappointing.' Oh, it appears we are on a first name basis now, and after having me abducted she has the audacity to treat me like a child. I open my mouth and utter the slightest of sounds. Thankfully I stop myself in my tracks. So close. I sigh in relief.

I can't help but notice the satisfied smirk on her face at her success in goading me into making a sound.

'This is becoming a bore for me. It appears my word is not good enough for you so perhaps concrete documentation is more your style.' With another flick of her finger, another document and fetched by Fred and yet again, placed next to the other one, just out of my reach.

'I would ask that you take some time to carefully review the documents before you when you return to your room, which will be locked, as much for your own safety as anything else. You have suddenly become hot property in the pharmaceutical world. Frederic and Louis will be placed outside your room should you have any needs. Please note any queries you may have as we shall discuss them in the morning.' She raises one eyebrow and gives me a knowing wink with these words, as if daring me to continue my silence. I suspect it won't be in my best interests to continue my mute position tomorrow as I get the feeling she's not an overly patient woman.

'Our aim is not to harm you, Dr Blake, we simply need to borrow your body and mind for a few days. Then you shall be free to leave, intact. Some of your options are, of course, more open to negotiation than others. This will become obvious to you as you digest the offer on hand. *Bonne nuit*.'

With that, she politely and elegantly extricates herself from the table with a level of sophistication that certainly doesn't come naturally to my casual Australian nature, and disappears through a discreet door at the opposite end of the room from the one through which I arrived. I am left sitting in silence with Lou and Fred waiting in the background. It is difficult for me to absorb everything that has happened to me in the last 24 hours and I figure the best place to do that is to be alone in my own room minus the presence of these beefy butlers.

I push away from the table and stand up. Fred darts forward and hastily gathers up the documents from their position on the dining room table and places them into a file with my name on it. I am escorted back through the arched doorway of the entrance and, eventually, via the extraordinarily long corridor, back to my room.

The file is placed on the antique desk in the corner of the room and the desk lamp is switched on ... presumably for my reading pleasure, I think sarcastically. They both nod curtly as they leave and I hear my bedroom door being locked. And here I am, left alone again, wondering what Jeremy has managed to place me in the middle of this time.

I notice that my suitcase has appeared at the foot of the bed and relief washes over my entire body. This one act of seeing my own belongings in this austere environment is enough to ensure I am once again overcome with emotion. But I gather myself together and try to convince my heart and mind to remain aloof and professional. I desperately miss Elizabeth and Jordan, more than I ever have in my life. I wish I had my phone and the most recent photo they sent through. They say you don't appreciate something until it's gone. I feel as if they have been torn away from their mother's embrace and I have stupidly and naively allowed this to happen. Would other mothers have made the decisions I have made the past couple of months? Quite possibly not, I have to concede.

It is hard enough to come to terms with myself, let alone worry about others' opinions of my actions, but what if something had happened to me and they became motherless? I can't bear to linger on this thought as it threatens to break my heart violently in two. A more rational part of my brain wonders whether Robert and I have updated our wills. I must make this a priority when I return ... if I return in one piece. Oh god, how the hell did I end up here? This feels so very different from my week away with Jeremy. Then, the excitement and the continual adrenaline rush of not knowing what was coming next seemed to keep my mind from the emotional turmoil I was in and, of course, it was Jeremy who was in the driver's seat, making all the decisions, taking control. I knew deep down I could trust him with my life, knowing he would ensure I was reunited with my children, my world. But now, who do I trust in this environment? What hasn't Jeremy told me? I don't even know exactly who knows I am missing — maybe Jeremy is keeping that information to himself as well ...

I abruptly halt that train of thought, knowing it is getting me nowhere and has the potential to unravel me entirely. Professional and businesslike is my new mantra. No time for threatening emotions. You have survived exceptionally well in the business world before, Alexa, I say firmly to myself, and that is all this needs to be. If you play your cards right, you'll be out of here in a few days time, just as Madame said. Hopefully ... if you can trust her ...

I scrunch my fists into a tight ball in an attempt to marshal my strength of mind before stripping myself out of this ludicrous dress. I open my suitcase and staring up at me is my newly acquired very slinky negligee, which was reserved especially for meeting Jeremy. Now I wish I still had my other bag with my British Airways pyjamas! I decide to opt for the only truly casual clothes I have packed and slop on my gym pants, comfy bra and a T-shirt. If Madame Goldy wants to negotiate, then that is exactly what we will do. I determinedly settle myself at the small desk, not knowing what I will find inside the dossier labelled: 'Dr Alexandra Blake — Private & Confidential'.

* * *

To say that I'm shocked is an understatement. It appears that Jeremy has indeed presented to the International Scientific Advisory Board on depression, bipolar disorder and related conditions. In doing so, he has *referenced results on a live pre-menopausal, Anglo-Saxon female with type AB blood grouping* ... yes, that would be me, how convenient. *The results identified the missing element in the hormonal comparisons of realising natural serotonin without the harsh side effects of existing drugs and returning all chemical balance to the brain to normal ranges within three to five days.*

I'm pleased he thinks I have 'returned to normal' because I certainly feel anything but normal given I've been experiencing 'episodes' ever since then, which he knows nothing about because he has been too busy spouting forth about his results instead of tapping back into his clinical research. Shit, what has he done? Why, Jeremy? Why didn't you tell me you were going to do this ... you didn't mention a word about it during our recent chats. Why are you still keeping me in the dark? There is so much more I need to talk to you about.

*Today we aim to submit a comprehensive
funding proposal to approve the testing of up*

*to 100 females of AB blood type. Anglo-Saxon
and pre-menopausal are prerequisites for testing
of these subjects in clinical environments; half
will have been previously diagnosed medically
with some form of relational depression and
the other half will never have experienced
diagnosed depression. They will undergo a series
of tests and be administered drugs in relation to
placebo ...*

Why the hell hasn't he mentioned this to me? Where is he conducting these tests? How will he secure these women? Is he going to subject these women to the same experience as he did me? Did it all mean nothing to him? I feel blood pounding through my veins in fury as I continue to read through these documents. Please don't let Madame Goldy be correct. How the hell could he have neglected to tell me anything about this? Did he give me other drugs during our time together, drugs I didn't know about? Heaven knows he could have, and it may more appropriately explain these damn 'episodes'. He said he gave me a sedative after my experience and I woke up somewhere he called Avalon, dazed and confused for what felt like days. Anything could have happened and I wouldn't be any the wiser. Then there was the drip, the need for a catheter, and blacking out again. Oh, dear god, could I have been that naive? Did I trust him so implicitly that I didn't even think to ask these sorts of questions? With this realisation, my stomach feels like it is doing a complete three-sixty degrees in my belly and I lurch up from the desk and stumble into the bathroom, instantly heaving up the contents of my dinner. Did I concede that much of myself to him? I know the answer to the question. Of course I did. I handed everything over to him that weekend.

My sight. My body. My mind.

I was totally at his mercy, before allowing myself to be ensconced in the supposed warmth of his care — now more obviously his absolute dominance over me. A shiver thunders down my spine as an entirely new version of our time together flashes before my eyes and an ice-cold feeling settles in my bones.

I tightly grip the basin as I consider a completely different perspective on what was not so obvious to me before. His absolute control over every detail, every interaction. The ever-present ominous undercurrent of his tone. His absolute refusal to negotiate any of the predetermined conditions of our weekend together. No sight. No questions. Holy fuck! How could I have been so blind? What a stupid statement. Of course I was blind. He ensured I was blind — and bound when necessary — for the entire 48 hours, which was all centred on the experiment, and it enabled him to do whatever he chose to do.

And now, for the first time, in this chateau, I am questioning exactly what that was. Was I so caught up in the sheer sexuality of the experience that I intellectually overlooked everything else? What an easy target I would have been for the oh-so-suave and sophisticated Dr Quinn. My passionless marriage; our shared sexual past; his connection to my body being like nothing I've ever experienced with anyone else; his remote control button facilitating my orgasms. What hope did I have? How could he lose?

I have a sudden flashback to just before we jumped out of the plane when he told me I was in perfect health. I questioned how he would know such information as we went hurtling out the plane. He'd said he needed to make sure there was enough adrenaline pumping through my veins to get through the evening — this all occurred before we had even discussed my involvement, let alone me agreeing. Damn him. Had he been researching me long before our weekend away?

Obviously he had, because he knew everything about my medical history. Would it have honestly made any difference whether I had agreed to the experiment or not? Maybe not, maybe my whole decision-making process was inconsequential and I played right into his hands regardless!

Flashes of the hot chocolates flitter through my mind; anything could have been in them. His casual conversation regarding his knowledge of my rare AB blood, as he was so confidently extracting his fourth instalment from my veins. As if he owned me! He never told me he was going to do that and I didn't even know about the first three times. Would he have told me? And why subject me to that dreadful catheter and drip when he has always known how much I hate that stuff? Was that really necessary or was there so much more at play?

The memory of his words and my version of events somersaults in my mind as my heart feels battered and bruised by these entirely new insights. It is as if I have been shining the narrow beam of the flashlight only on the components of our time together that I wanted to see, rather than turning the room light on to see the entire scene. Am I that gullible, that naive? I have always been an easy target for the great Dr Quinn and it appears nothing has changed. I am still a medical experiment to him, a means to an end in his all-encompassing search for a cure. He has chosen to present his results professionally before I am privy to them myself — and they are about me! Once again, I'm a mere pawn in the masterful game of his life and he has deliberately chosen to keep me in the dark.

My body trembles with betrayal and rage. How could he have put me in this situation if he honestly loved me? Did he ever love me? His desperation and drive for a cure has catapulted me into danger and into taking more personal risks than in my worst nightmares. He doesn't care about me, about my children. I could never contemplate doing what he has done to a person that I love. And he has carefully and callously manoeuvred me into this point of no return. On the flight over I was like an excitable young puppy looking forward to the next instalment of Jeremy-esque experimentation on my body and my mind. Which is actually really bizarre when I think about it in this context. He was my world and I would have done anything for him, including leaving my kids for almost two weeks to eagerly take part in whatever was on offer.

What a bloody idiot I am. No sex is worth this risk, damn it, and now I've been abducted in a bloody suitcase because of him and his silence. Well, fuck him! I'm so angry at him and so very disappointed with myself. I swipe at the stinging hot tears sliding down my face; I can't deal with any more emotion.

I quickly brush my teeth to remove the awful taste in my mouth and collapse on the bed, overwhelmed by fatigue and complete exhaustion. I'm unconscious in seconds, my sleep too heavy and absolute to allow any dreams to seep through.

# Jeremy

I toss and turn during the night, completely disturbed by the dreams and imagery I have in my head about Alexa's plight. At some stage, I decide it's useless attempting any more sleep given the tense state I'm in, and spend a few hours poring over the information Moira has collated in the personal dossiers on each of the forum members. I obviously can't do this when Sam's around, as he would be shocked to think I might even consider he would ever intentionally harm Alexa. I know he loves her like a daughter.

I sense that I'm missing something but I just can't put my finger on it. I send a quick message back to Moira asking if she can access the mobile phone records of each forum member from the time of my trip to Sydney to see if that provides any leads before jumping into the shower to freshen up. It's a long shot and possibly illegal, depending on who is paying the bills, but I can't afford to leave any stone unturned. I quickly get dressed and pack up my belongings, desperate to be on the move. Just as I'm about to call Moira for a more thorough update, Sam knocks on the door.

'Morning Jeremy, did you sleep —' He doesn't bother continuing with pleasantries, he can sense my anxiety.

'What's the update, Sam? I was just calling Moira.'

'They've tracked Alexandra to Slovenia.'

'Slovenia? What the hell would they take her there for? I only know of two pharmaceutical companies based there. Zealex, which is only small and I doubt would be involved but you never know, I suppose, and I think Xsade has only a small office, not a large factory or other concern there, but I could be wrong. This is good, Sam. At least now we have something more concrete to work on.'

'Maybe it's best if you read this for yourself, it just came through.' Sam hands me a file and my eyes scan its contents rapidly.

'So, they believe she is being kept somewhere near Kranj and has been stationary for the past few hours. Right, we need to get going, Sam, we can't waste another second. When's our flight?'

'Martin's organised the team to assemble in Munich as it's more accessible for everyone to fly to, particularly from the States. We'll have a room set up at the airport Hilton and will coordinate our plan from there.' I grab the map that has been included in the file.

'It's too far away, Sam. We can't afford the time

or the distance.' I study the map in more detail and decide Ljubljana is a better option. I pick up my phone and speak to Sarah, my assistant, before covering the phone and turning back to face Sam.

'I'm organising my own flight, I'll let Martin know when it's done. What do you want to do? Are you coming with me or going to Munich to coordinate with the others?' I can't keep bitter sarcasm out of the word 'coordinate'. Its passive undertones are making me even more determined for direct action. I wait for his decision.

'I'll come with you.' I nod and return to the phone

'Right, yes, Sally, that's one for me and one for Sam. As soon as we can … Stansted? Sure, and we'll need a car when we arrive. Make it safe and fast. Yes, we're ready, have the car meet us outside One Aldwych. Thanks. Keep me posted as any news arrives. Yes, we will. Bye.'

I then call Martin who isn't too impressed that we aren't following his master plan, but he'll survive. He hopes to have a trained bodyguard meet us at the airport, but it may take too long to organise, given our direct flight.

Finally, I feel like we are moving a step closer to saving Alexa.

* * *

Our bodyguard is a few hours behind us when we arrive in Slovenia and I decide we can't afford to wait.

He can catch up with us as best he can. Sarah organises a BMW M5, which is the only bit of good news we've had. I jump in the driver's seat and we make our way into Ljubljana to pick up some supplies before heading north towards Kranj. While I drive, Sam's on the phone to Martin for an update.

'Yes, we're here, on the road now. Sure we have a GPS, give me the coordinates. Has she been moved? Still there, good, that's one thing at least. Okay, can you organise accommodation as close as you can without it being too obvious? No, we don't have guns.' I turn to glance at Sam and he looks considerably paler. 'Jeremy, can you use a gun?' I confirm that I have in the past. 'He has but ... okay ... right, we'll see. Hopefully he won't be too far behind us. No, we aren't stopping.' Sam glances towards me and I deliberately accelerate to reiterate his point. 'Okay, good, send it through when you have the details.'

We sit in anxious silence as I concentrate on driving towards the place where we believe Alex is being held captive.

\* \* \*

Our accommodation is nothing like One Aldwych but I don't give a shit. It's the Eastern European version of a basic outback hotel — that is, nothing flash. The village is small and old, with cobblestone bridges crisscrossing a small river that meanders between the houses and shops. It would look quite picturesque under any other circumstances. The main thing is we are closer to Alex and that's where I need to be. According to the GPS signal from her bracelet, it appears that she is being held in a castle high on a hillside behind the town and there is nothing else close to it. We settle in as much as we can. I turn to look at Sam and he looks absolutely exhausted, poor bloke, all this has to be tough on him. His face looks like all this drama has certainly taken its toll, particularly as he has almost twenty years on me.

'Why don't you rest for a bit while I go for a walk, Sam? There isn't too much we can do now except wait for the bodyguard to arrive and the team to assemble in Munich.' He doesn't disagree, at least, and I have so much adrenaline pumping through me I need to do something physical and outdoors.

'I might do that, and I'll give Martin a call again to see how everything is going.'

I start throwing a few things in the backpack I bought in Ljubljana as I want to hike up the hill to check out the castle — anything to feel closer to Alex and the activity helps temper my nerves. As I turn to walk out the door, I look back towards a stressed and tired Samuel.

'Thanks for everything, Sam, I really appreciate you coming with me today. I know this isn't easy on you either.'

'We just need to find our girl. Be careful on your hike, Jeremy. Please don't take any unnecessary risks. We can't afford two of you missing.' It's as if he understands my intentions exactly without me having to disclose them.

'I will, just doing some reconnaissance while we await the arrival of our highly-trained compatriots.' I can't help but give him a wink and I see a tiny smile appear on his face before it vanishes just as quickly.

'We will get through this, Sam.' He nods in silence and I depart.

The fresh air is chilly and crisp as I locate a path that winds from the small village up towards the hillside castle. On any other day, I'd take my time to look around. Alexa would love the cutesiness of this village. My thoughts wonder what Alexa is going through at this moment. Does she know where she is? Are they treating her well? Is she in pain? God, I realise I'm beginning to sound like her as questions continue to flood through my mind.

The exercise is doing me good and I'm pleased to be out in the fresh air. I continue along the path which climbs steeply up the mountainside. Eventually I turn a corner and can see the castle clearly in the distance. It is literally built into the mountainside and looks both majestic and defiant. Its whitewashed walls and turrets appear to be Renaissance style and centuries old, but I'm no expert on architectural history. I climb higher until I am almost at eye level with the front of the chateau, with only a small valley between us. I settle in behind a rock to protect myself from being seen and locate the binoculars in my backpack.

I scan the entire chateau and notice figures moving around the entrances. I zoom in as much as I can and it looks like they are armed. Of course they would be if they are willing to abduct someone. I don't know why I would have been expecting otherwise. I move my vision slowly up towards each of the windows and scan for any movement.

As I reach the highest turret, I see a figure moving in a window. As I refocus the binoculars I notice I'm holding my breath in anticipation. I see a woman staring out of the window into the countryside. I gasp in shock and can't believe what I'm seeing as I focus in on Alexa. Her wrist is across her chest and she looks like she is rubbing the bracelet. My god! My heart almost lurches out of my chest and into her hands as she continues to caress the bracelet. The vision of her is utterly mesmerising and it's almost if time stands still as I reflect on her beauty. How can she be so close yet so impossibly far from me? I pick up my phone to call Sam but there's no reception from here.

I continue to gaze through the binoculars, mesmerised by the sight of her. As far as I can tell, she looks well enough. Scared and unsure but still herself. Thank god. I feel the first pang of relief in my heart since she was taken. I try to will a message to her that I'll come for her soon, it won't be long. Just hang in there, sweetheart. Hot tears well in my eyes and spill down my face but I don't care. The emotion is too raw to contain. I need her back in my arms. My vision blurs and I have to look away to wipe my eyes.

When I focus in again, I can see the shapes of more people in the room, but they are difficult to see clearly.

Alex steps back from the window and then they all disappear from my view.

At least I know that's she's alive and exactly where she is, the bracelet firmly intact. This is great news. Now, with the help of Martin's men, we just need to get her out of there. I slump against the rock, suddenly fatigued by the nervous energy that has been coursing through my body. I grab some water and a piece of fruit, aware that it has been a while since I've addressed the needs of my body. Anxious to update the others, I prepare for the long journey back down the hill.

As I descend I notice an ambulance driving through the chateau's gates. Once it is parked, the driver and passenger quickly emerge, run around to the back and slide out a stretcher before being ushered into the huge front doors. There are a few other people in strange uniforms milling around as well. The stretcher returns, moments later, with a body strapped on it. I grapple with my bag and retrieve my binoculars, focussing them quickly, and am horrified to see it is Alexa strapped to the stretcher, lying so still with only her face uncovered, her dark hair cascading over the whiteness of the pillow and sheets. Shit, what is happening now? They carefully manoeuvre the stretcher into the back of the ambulance, and a man, presumably a doctor given the stethoscope around his neck and black medical bag he's carrying, accompanies her in. A silver Audi Q5 pulls up behind the ambulance and a well-dressed female is escorted into the back seat. The colourful guard signals both drivers and they slowly pull away from the chateau towards the village.

I realise I have barely been breathing as I watch this scene unfold before my eyes. As if I've been suddenly released from a spell I start running and screaming after Alexa. I lose my footing and tumble down the hillside towards the cars, my cries completely silenced by the sound of the siren that pierces the still afternoon air.

# Part Four

To judge well
To comprehend well
To reason well
These are the essential activities of intelligence

— A. Binet & T. Simon

# Alexa

I wake up in the morning with a pounding headache. I search through my bath bag until I find some Advil. Thank heavens I packed it; I'd hate to break my silence and have to ask Tweedle-dum and Tweedle-dee for pain relief. I think how normal it is for people to swallow pills for so many of our ailments — most of the time treating the symptoms and not the cause, yet we expect them to work effectively and fast and complain bitterly if they don't. I've never stopped to think about how such pills come to the market — how they were tested and on whom before they reach the shelves in our homes to be ultimately popped into our mouths. Distracted by this, I know I really need to focus, as I'll probably be having one of the most significant discussions I've had in my life very soon. I can sense the contract silently taunting me from the corner of the room. I tell it I'm not ready yet. A knock on the door signals that it will be opening and I'm grateful to see the chambermaid carrying in a breakfast tray. Eggs Florentine. As if I would be able to say no to that. My stomach growls on cue and the maid vanishes quickly from the room.

My appetite doesn't seem to have wavered one bit in these shocking circumstances, although last night I did lose a fair amount of what I'd eaten thanks to my reaction to Jeremy's treachery. Should I have ever let him back into my life? I think of Robert and can't deny Jeremy's reappearance triggered the discussion we should have had years ago. No, I don't have any regrets and I refuse to live my life that way. My relationship with my estranged — albeit still under the same roof — husband is now probably better and more honest than it has ever been.

Why couldn't Jeremy just talk to me, tell me about his results, his plans? Does he not think I'm strong enough to handle it? Well, watch this space, Dr Quinn.

After fully devouring every skerrick of food on the plate, I wash it all down with some fresh orange juice and settle myself in front of the contract.

So absorbed am I in my reading I barely notice mademoiselle chambermaid enter my room again to remove the tray and deliver a perfectly timed café latte. I have a strange sense that they have a dossier prepared on my likes and dislikes and are now trying to make up for my horrifying abduction. Either way, my headache has cleared thanks to the food and painkillers and I am grateful the coffee has arrived. I nod in silent thanks and watch her as she and her black-and-white frilled uniform depart my room — they can't be serious dressing her in that, can they?

Onward! It's as if I'm gearing myself up for all-out war, though against whom is still be to determined. For the first time in days, a chuckle escapes me. I'm not sure whether it is from constant nervous anxiety or perhaps sheer relief that Xsade Pharmaceuticals don't appear to want to hurt me. It seems they just want to verify Jeremy's discoveries. I still don't comprehend why they specifically need *me* to do this — I must be missing something. Deep down, I know there is a certain way to find out and I need to muster the personal strength to go through the required motions.

Using the elegant pen and engraved stationary provided in the drawers of the antique mahogany desk, I summarise the contents of the contract to the best of my understanding to help solidify the key elements of the agreement in my mind. I can't help but think that this is a far more professional way of engaging my services than a damn blindfold and handcuffs! I sense my anger building again at the thought of what Jeremy put me through, but at the same time I can't deny the tingle below when I think of the memories. Why do they excite me so much? Why is nothing simple with him?

Enough of this torture to my heart. Back to business.

**Duration**

A total of 72 hours within the clinical experiment facility — excluding travelling time to this location (undisclosed within this document)

Maximum of four days in total in the absolute care of Xsade

**Conditional agreements — to be negotiated**

1. *Human penetration* — With strangers? Good grief, no!
2. *Non-human penetration* — Possibly …
3. *Testing of the purple pill: female Viagra* — I can't help but admit this intrigues me, I wonder what it would be like? Definitely a maybe.
4. *Sampling and testing of orgasmic excretion fluid* — Oh, here we go again. <u>No catheters.</u> I need to underline this to remind myself this is non-negotiable.
5. *Sampling and testing of blood type* — Hmm, more blood tests. Something about this doesn't sit well with me. My gut says no.
6. *Monitoring of neural activity and pathways* — The psychologist in me can't deny that I'm intrigued to see these results and at least this way I'll be given access to them, unlike Jeremy and his hidden documents. So that's a yes.

7. *Monitoring of blood flow to erogenous zones* — I suppose so, whatever.

8. *Enema* — What the? I will certainly be discussing this in more detail.

9. *Establishing emotional and physical baseline* — Well, at least this confirms that they are taking a scientific approach.

10. *Non-Disclosure Agreement — Access to all data research, findings and conclusions will be provided to the Experimentee at the conclusion of day four.* The NDA looks pretty basic, yet doesn't prevent me from showing the results to Jeremy, for example. That's if I care to share them with him at all after his secrecy. I get a strange inkling that they almost want me to share them — weird!

11. *Xsade undertakes to be wholly responsible for the safety and care of the Experimentee and to return the subject unharmed to a destination of her choice at the conclusion of the experiment —* Well that's comforting.

Suddenly, for the first time since arriving here, my children don't feel so far away from me. I relish the warmth in my heart and decide I just need to make it through the next 72 hours. That's what I must focus on, for them.

12. *At any time during the process of clinical experimentation, the Experimentee may halt proceedings due to emotional or physical discomfort.* I can't help but think how I would have 'halted' proceedings mid-parachute jump! Imagine if that had been one of the conditions of my weekend with Jeremy? It would certainly have guaranteed a different outcome, I'm sure. However, in the scheme of things I certainly don't have problems with this term.

13. *A sum of GBP one million shall be deposited into the bank account of the Experimentee on completion of the clinical experimentation process.* Holy shit! One million pounds — are they serious? How on earth could I be worth that much to them? Jeremy offers me a position on the Global Research Forum and then refuses to keep me in the loop — on anything! And they offer me this? Now I'm *really* intrigued, what are they so desperate for? Why not choose any other 'Anglo-Saxon, pre-menopausal' woman? This is just too weird for words. What if they don't find what they're looking for? Do I still receive the money? Based on the terms of this contract it appears that I do. What *are* they looking for?

The familiar tingling sensation ripples across my buttocks as I ask these questions but instead of leading to feelings of orgasmic sensation, it is quickly negated by my anger at the lies and deception that have now become so obvious to me. These tingles — are they sensory memories of my previous experience? They can't possibly just be based on emotions can they? Damn it, I'm going to find out what all this is about myself since Jeremy doesn't think I warrant receiving the research findings. How dare he treat me like this? Well, Madame Jurilique, it seems we have a contract to negotiate.

While one part of me feels slightly nauseated at this thought, another part is ready to embrace the experience with a 'bring it on, don't mess with me' attitude of high resolve. I must admit, my own determination scares even me a little.

A tap on the door indicates my reading time is over. I quickly glance over the rest of my notes and the contract, confirming that it is fairly standard. I slip the papers back in the folder.

'Dr Blake, Madame Jurilique is ready for you in her office.' I look at Fred and can't help but glance down at my attire. I raise my eyebrows in his direction.

'The discussion is far more critical than your state of dress of this stage, Dr Blake.' I have to agree; maybe he is more perceptive than I've given him credit for. I mentally withdraw my 'brawn' judgements. I scoop up the dossier from the desk and follow him out the door.

Madame Jurilique is seated behind a large desk in a pale blue Chanel suit, looking all class. I look like a casual Aussie ready to go for a power walk along Bondi Beach. Oh well, I didn't ask for this. She can take me as she finds me! I sit down opposite her.

'*Bonjour*, doctor, I trust you slept well.'

'Yes, as a matter of fact I did.' It feels weird to hear my voice out loud. It seems like forever since I last spoke. Her smile is cold and professional.

'Excellent, well let's get down to business. I assume you have read the documents and have some questions, *oui*?'

Here goes nothing. I decide to launch straight into the details and cut to the chase. Best get this over and done with.

'Enema?' I have never had one before and always wondered what it would be like, but in this scenario?

'Liken it to colonic irrigation, which many people experience on a regular basis as part of their overall health regime.' She pauses to assess my response. I remember one of my friends has a monthly appointment for exactly this process and raves about how fantastic she feels every time. 'It's important to us that you begin the experimentation process "clean", allowing us to control and monitor your body more effectively for the next seventy-two hours.' She looks directly into my eyes before continuing. 'Alternatively, we can monitor your motions back in your room until such time —'

I quickly interrupt. 'That won't be necessary. I'll do it.' I don't want to spend any more time here than required.

'Good. I'm sure you'll have no regrets, it's a very safe procedure.' It's not so much the safety that concerns me, but I don't really want to dwell on the messy details, so I move on.

'I am not comfortable with any form of penis penetration as part of the experimentation process.'

'No problem, I shall note it down. No human penetration?' Oh jeez, this really is the weirdest discussion I've ever had in my life. That was a little easier than I was expecting. Madame looks at me expectantly. Next. 'Excretion samples?'

'Yes, from your orgasms. This is non-negotiable.' She seems incredibly confident that I'll be having orgasms ... we'll see about that. I feel like I'm signing up to a Kinsey experiment.

'This is what you need to test to confirm Jeremy's results?'

'We believe so, yes.'

'Will it hurt?' My voice falters a little.

'It is not our intention to do you any harm, Dr Blake. If it did not hurt with Dr Quinn, it will certainly not hurt in our environment.' Well, it could be described as sheer unadulterated pleasure with Jeremy, but that's what got me into this trouble in the first place. Concentrate, you are negotiating your life, your freedom, Alexa. Focus! I glance quickly at my notes.

'I don't want a catheter.'

'You will not be required to have one. You will see that the equipment in our laboratory is state of the art and designed to make our clinical patients as comfortable as possible.' That's a pleasant change from what I had conjured up in my mind.

'Okay. Good.' I continue. 'No blood tests. This is non-negotiable for me.' For some reason, the memory of Jeremy's discussion with me about my blood makes me not want them to have access to mine.

She frowns. 'That provides us with some difficulty, Dr Blake.'

'I'm sure you are able to access blood samples from other people with AB blood.' I say far more confidently than I feel.

'True, however ...' She seems lost in thought, her finger rhythmically tapping the top of her clipboard, as if her brain is trying to find a way around this impediment. 'How many vials did Dr Quinn take when you were under his care?'

Under his care ... what an interesting way of describing it. She seems almost desperate for this information? I notice the skin above her lip is beading in perspiration. This is obviously extremely important to her.

'I'm not sure.'

'Not sure, or unwilling to disclose, Dr Blake?' The undertone in her voice is cutting. She stands up from behind the desk and stares out the window before returning her steely gaze to meet my eyes.

'I honestly don't know,' I state more firmly. 'Jeremy is aware of my dislike of needles and hospital equipment.' Although it still didn't stop him from using it, the thought shudders through me.

'Hmm. This could be problematic.' She looks thoughtful. 'Definitely non-negotiable, *oui*?'

'Definitely.'

'Why so, Dr Blake? It's only a bit of blood.' Her eyes penetrate my brain as if she is trying to decipher just how much I know and might be hiding from her. God, I wish I knew more, rather than simply running on gut instinct as I'm doing right now. The obstinate look on her face leaves me with no doubt they could take my blood by force right now and I couldn't do a single thing about it. Why am I so adamant? I harden my resolve in an attempt to play her game and even out my odds in this bizarre negotiation.

'I am willing to undergo your experiment, Madame Jurilique, for seventy-two hours as requested. I have agreed to allow you to penetrate my anus for an enema which, for your information, I have never had before. I am willing for you to stimulate me enough to capture the fluid secreted from my orgasms, which is what I believe you need for your research. I am not willing for you to extract vials of my blood.' I hope I am sounding more convincing than I feel.

She looks lost in thought before continuing: 'As this is a negotiation process,' she states rather reluctantly, 'would you be willing to consider a pinprick of your blood every twenty-four hours, so we can at least link it directly to our laboratory results?'

I return her stare as she stabilises her hands against the desk awaiting my answer.

'I suppose that would be fine.' For some reason, I just don't want them to have enough of my blood to run a whole series of tests with it and I just hate needles. A pinprick I can live with.

'Good. Any other questions?'

I quickly refer to my notes. 'I will then have access to the results and be released?'

'Yes, of course.'

'I will be going to one of your clinical facilities, but I won't be told where, is that correct?'

'That is correct.'

'How will I get there?' I live in dread of being stuffed into a suitcase with happy gas again.

'You will be escorted there in an ambulance. This is the safest way.'

'By ambulance. Is that necessary?' I query.

'Be under no illusions, Dr Blake. We are not the only pharmaceutical company interested in securing your unique results. There are other, shall we say, less scrupulous companies who, should they lay hands on you, would not be so accommodating of your requirements.' She raises a perfectly sculpted eyebrow in my direction. Jeez, I hadn't even thought of that!

'Your safety is our utmost priority, Dr Blake, so I would ask that you go along quietly with our requests. That way we can minimise any danger we may find ourselves in.' This would be a great time for my James Bond version of Jeremy to come crashing through the door or window with his special agent troops and rescue me from this scene. Where are you, damn it?

Where are these special teams you told me about? Do you really not care any more?

'Are you waiting for something, Dr Blake?' Yes, waiting for something that is just not going to happen. My bravado seeps away as I resign myself to my fate.

'No. When will I be going?' I can't help dejection colouring my voice.

'At the conclusion of this discussion, and once you have signed the required documents. I am sure you don't want to prolong this process more than necessary. I, like you, want to be reunited with loved ones as soon as practicable.' At this point, I'm glad to be sitting, as my body feels leaden at her words. Will I be returning to Jeremy's love or his betrayal? My children feel every bit as far away as they physically are. For some reason, it is slightly reassuring for me to know she has loved ones as well. It gives her a more sympathetic side and I get the sense that she also wants this over and done with as soon as possible.

'And the money?' I have no idea what I will do with this 'blood' money but have no doubt it could be put to good use in a number of charities I'm involved in.

'Will be deposited in a bank account in your name at the conclusion of your time with us. The details will be included in your exit package.'

'And if I said no to being involved at all, in any of this?'

'Let's not taint such a fruitful discussion with such suggestions, Dr Blake. I believe we have both come to a very satisfying conclusion under unusual circumstances.'

How can she sound simultaneously so polite and so threatening? Any sympathy I detected has vanished in her last statement. It's as if her 'loved ones' could be a pit full of venomous snakes. In a businesslike manner she crosses out some parts of the contract and adds some handwritten notes presumably based on our discussion before placing the revised document and gold pen before me on the desk.

'I can assure you, your involvement in this research will be of benefit to women around the world, most significantly the more than 40% who report lack of sexual interest or desire as a key factor impacting their lives. Now we have a very real opportunity to develop a solution that can benefit women and significantly enhance their sex lives which has to be a good thing, don't you think?' This is obviously a rhetorical question, she continues without a pause as if she's delivering their marketing plan to an audience. 'If all goes according to plan, we should be in a position to release this drug early next year. It is near perfect, Dr Blake, as you will experience in our laboratory.'

I can't imagine a sex life better than the one I have with Jeremy but being at the edge of a scientific breakthrough suddenly excites me, particularly one that may affect the lives of women so dramatically — if it does, in fact. Her words still linger as I pick up the gold pen and quickly scan her amendments. If Xsade's purple pill targets female arousal, not just the physical aspects such as increased blood flow, just imagine the potential impact for both women and men alike? Good grief, this could change our lives as we know it. No wonder some companies are willing to take frightening risks.

I can't deny that there is definitely a part of me that is really intrigued to find out if it works, first hand. I think about my friend Mandy in the States, who recently paid thousands of dollars to have her sexual arousal tested at a specifically designed clinic. Although I suppose if women can have reconstructive surgery on their labias, it shouldn't really be such a shock that there seems to be no expense spared either by corporations or individuals in some cases.

Is this really what has become so important to us? I reflect on the impact that Viagra has had on our society. Men unable to achieve an erection due to drugs for HIV, anti-depressants or age, or even men just wanting to stay harder for longer, are suddenly able to engage in sex again, all due to the little blue pill. I have only had one experience of Viagra and it was when Jeremy and I were in Santorini and although it started very playfully, it didn't end well, from my perspective at least. The memory pervades my mind.

\* \* \*

We've just arrived back at our hotel, all whitewashed walls and blue painted round rooftops, which is embedded into the side of a hill. The Greek islands are such a great place to relax and chill out away from the stresses of life. It is a big hike up the hill and we are both hot from the climb, even though we had been in the clear waters of the sea only ten minutes ago. I decide to jump in the small hotel pool, and Jeremy continues on to the coolness of our cave-like room. He's been in a funny mood since our chat on the rocks. Maybe he is just preoccupied with his latest research project.

I wasn't sure how he'd react to me telling him about Robert and wanting to settle down. It's obviously the furthest thing from his mind and I can't say it didn't sting a little that he doesn't ever see us being together like that at all. I had always suspected we weren't that way inclined, but I can't deny I always had this nagging hope that one day … maybe, it might work out for us … when we were so good together in other ways. But we experienced such extreme highs, perhaps we wouldn't be so good together in a more mundane day to day scenario.

Anyway, at least now I know once and for all. He had his chance to say something and he didn't, so I suppose our lives must continue on their separate tangents. He certainly seemed more intent on making the most of this holiday and having frivolous fun together, than seeming to want anything else longer term, and I felt he reinforced this by throwing me in the water. Always playing and mucking around. Oh well. I dry myself off and return to our room, knowing

I have a little surprise for him that will hopefully cheer his mood and distract him from whatever is on his mind — maybe.

'Hi, I'm back. What are you up to?'

'Just packing some work papers away so I can focus fully on you for the rest of the weekend.' Work, just as I thought.

'Excellent. I have something for you but I want you to promise to use it this weekend.'

'Sounds intriguing, particularly when you are looking so cheeky over there. But you'll need to give it to me before I promise, sweetheart.'

'Oh Jeremy, go on … why can't you promise me without knowing, just this once … please?' My voice is pleading and to my great surprise, he seems to have a change of heart.

'Okay. I promise. As long as you're not trying to kill me.'

'As if I would ever do that.' I act like I'm mortally offended. 'Thanks, J. I can't wait to see the impact it will have.'

'Okay, now you've got me worried. What impact?' I hesitate for a moment as I try to second-guess how he'll take this.

'Come on, Alexa, don't go all shy on me now. What is it?'

'Remember you promised?'

'Yes, I promised.' Excitement washes through me that he has promised me something but he doesn't know what, very unusual for him.

'Okay, just give me a sec.' I race into the bathroom, rummage through my toiletries bag and locate a plastic bag with two little blue diamond-shaped pills in it. Hiding it behind my back I saunter out to the lounge room, a wide smile spilling over my face. I wonder what he'll say when he finds out.

'Are you going to give it to me, Alexa, or do I need to wrestle it out of your hands?'

'Hmm, as tempting as that sounds ... here.' I hand over the bag and wait patiently while he inspects its tiny contents.

'What the? Where did you get these?'

'They're authentic, I promise, nothing dodgy. I just thought you might, well, we could experiment, see what they are like, what impact they have while we are here.'

'Sweetheart, you want me to take Viagra? Since when am I not hard enough for you?'

'Since never, Jeremy, it's not that. I just thought it would be interesting for us to experience together... You promised remember.'

'Yeah, I know. I just wasn't expecting this.' He holds the plastic bag toward me as if it is an unidentified specimen. 'Where did you get them? Oh never mind, it doesn't matter, anyway.'

'So you'll have one?'

'I promised, didn't I? I have to admit, I've always been interested in what impact they'd have on some one not suffering from erectile dysfunction. Which I'm sure you know that I don't!' he states emphatically. I link my arms around his taut, tanned waist and reassure him of his virility with a kiss.

'I would never, ever say that about you, J. I just thought it would be fun while we are away and they're obviously no use to me.'

'Okay, I'll take *one* tonight and see what happens. I hope you are prepared for the repercussions.'

'I'll do the best I can to accommodate your needs, Dr Quinn.' A rush of lascivious anticipation settles in my bones.

'Will you promise me something in return?'

Oh, I knew it was too good to be true. 'What did you have in mind?'

'I think it's only fair that if I am taking something to, um, how should I state it in medical terms ... give me a full on stiffy for hours, then the least I can do is put you in the mood so you are more able to accommodate me.'

'What do you have in your bag of tricks this time?' I look at him dubiously.

'How did you know? You must promise to choose at least one of the items ... actually no, I think I know which one will go best with the Viagra.' He returns from his suitcase with a small, stylish bag. Before he hands it over to me he says with a cheeky grin, 'Promise?' Thank goodness happy Jeremy is back and the moody one has gone.

I can't help but feel a little sentimental that this may be the last time I am in a position to promise Jeremy anything, after all these years. 'Yes, I promise.'

He reaches into the bag and hands me a very cute decorated box with a funky purple egg in it that looks like it has been ever so slightly squashed in the middle and a narrow rectangular box with press pads.

'No wonder you were so happy to promise me,' I say sarcastically. His face explodes into a mischievous grin. I take a closer look. Luxury vibrating wireless egg, effective within a ten metre radius.

'Oh no, not you with a remote control again? Honestly? You know what it did to me last time. I spilt drinks everywhere.' I raise my eyebrows toward him knowing full well he can hardly contain his enthusiasm.

'At least this time it is for use in your desired orifice, sweetheart. This way you will be able to directly track the impact the Viagra is having on me.'

'And how is that exactly?'

'I will let you know via remote control. As my erection strengthens, I will increase your vibrations so we are evenly matched.' He looks thoroughly pleased with himself. 'Oh come on, you were the one who was excited that I had to take the blue pill not five minutes ago. Now who is becoming the prude?'

'Oh, all right, I suppose it could be worse. But what's with your obsession with remote controls, Jeremy?'

He turns towards me and cups my cheeks in his palms and says seriously, 'Nothing pleases me more than being able to control your pleasure, Alexandra.'

He kisses my lips so softly and gently, it makes me weak at the knees until I crumple back onto the bed beneath him. His tongue steadily pries open my mouth and the depth of his kiss is so impassioned I wonder if I am in some hot love scene at the movies. His hand slips through my bikini top and fondles my breast, his fingers flicking my nipples to attention. My butt crushes the new toy beneath us as we roll around, hungry for each other.

'Be careful, Alex, I want to make sure this is in perfect working condition for tonight.' He picks up the box as if it is injured and I'm not treating it with the reverence he believes it deserves. I'm left panting on my side as he decides to open it up. 'Actually, I might just make sure it's in full working order. And besides, you should probably be saving your energy, I have the feeling you'll need every bit you can muster for tonight.' He slaps my behind playfully. 'Why don't you have the first shower while I get this organised and I'll choose what you'll be wearing for dinner.'

I open my mouth to respond and promptly close it again. So what if he wants to decide what I'm wearing for dinner? I packed my outfits to bring on holiday, so he can't go far wrong.

'Sure, why not? Then you can have your shower and I'll choose yours.' I swat his behind in return and head into the shower as per the instructions of my bossy best friend. I can't help but eagerly anticipate the night ahead.

In keeping with our Grecian surroundings, we are both wearing white linen, which looks good given we've been touched by the Mediterranean sun. My dress is reasonably skimpy but not too short, thank goodness, and Jeremy has chosen a tan belt to bring it in around my waist. He doesn't like shapeless clothes on me whatsoever. He looks hot with his shirt unbuttoned just past his pecs. You can get away with that on Greek islands without looking sleazy and he looks anything but. His hair has grown since I last saw him and it's hanging tousled and wavy around his face, its darkness framing the intensity of his smoky, green eyes. He looks like an Aegean sex god and I could honestly take him right now, but he reminds me that we have a dinner reservation.

'So when are you going to take it?'

'After the entrée at dinner, just in case the impact is too fast.'

'Do you think we should try and last as long as we can out and about? I wouldn't mind going for a boogie.'

'You think you'll last that long with this inside you?'

'Oh, that's right.'

'We should try it now.'

'I thought you already tested it?'

'I mean inside you. I'd hate for it to malfunction.'

'I suppose it's better to sort out any issues in the privacy of our own room. How far is the restaurant?'

'Just up the road.'

'Okay then, hand it over.' I wait for him to give it to me and he looks at me with a twinkle in his eye.

'Allow me.'

'Really?'

'Please?'

'Oh, alright then.'

'Great, place one leg up on the lounge. Do you need lubrication?' No, not after my thoughts about how hot Jeremy looks just moments ago, I'm raring to go.

'I should be fine.' I lower my knickers to provide him with direct access.

'Okay, ready?'

'As ready as I'll ever be. Jeez, the things I do for you.' He slides it carefully between my thighs into my vulva and I feel the pressure as he moves it higher, into position.

'Hmmm, ready as always, Alexa.'

'If I wasn't starving, we wouldn't be leaving this room, Jeremy.'

'Such little patience, sweetheart. I'm sure you're a stronger woman than that.'

He places my leg back on the floor. 'How does it feel?'

'Fine, at the moment.'

He takes the control out of his trouser pocket and I eye it dubiously.

'Just testing and I promise I won't start it again until I take the "innocuous" blue pill.' He presses the button and a low vibration stirs within my core and it feels good. Slowly the intensity increases and Jeremy's eyes are absorbing every reaction of my face. It feels really good. 'Okay?'

'Hmmm, indeed, good choice.' The vibrations continue to grow in intensity until I quickly grab the control out of his hand. 'Yes, all working. No problem, no malfunction. Just go easy on those high levels, or I won't be able to speak, let alone walk.' He turns it off.

'Great, perfect. We're ready to go then.' I place the pill in my handbag for safekeeping along with the remote control. He stares at me in disbelief.

'It's only fair, J. I will give them both to you after entrée, like you said.'

'Well, let's get a move on.' He sounds as anxious as I am for our night to begin and his arm sweeps around my waist as I'm escorted out the door. I can't help but do pelvic floor exercises with each passing step, ensuring my purple friend is snug and tight within me.

We quickly devour vine leaves and stuffed eggplant for entrée, both excited to explore the next phase of our evening. Jeremy orders a shot of ouzo to mark the occasion with an elaborate 'Cheers', which our waiters applaud, and I discreetly hand him the pill. 'Is it okay to drink with Viagra?'

'We'll find out, I suppose.' He downs it in one gulp with his water.

'And the remote?' He places his hand on my leg under the table so I can give him the control and I fumble and miss. The waiter comes scurrying by and quickly retrieves the control, handing it into Jeremy's outstretched palm. 'Thanks very much.' He smiles without any embarrassment whatsoever and places it smoothly in his pocket. I close my purse and take a quick gulp of my wine to distract me from our table antics. I decide it might be sensible to go to the bathroom now, before the sensations begin. I excuse myself from the table.

'You will be leaving everything intact, Alexa.' It's a statement not a question.

'Of course.'

'You know I will be able to tell immediately?'

'Yes, Jeremy, you have gone through with your end of the deal so I will follow through on mine.'

'Thank you, don't be long. I think I'm starting to feel something.' Oh dear, I move quickly to the ladies.

I am settling down to a delicious seafood platter when the first buzzing sensation begins. I cross my legs just to ensure I'm as contained as possible. Jeremy's cheeks are looking nicely flushed and the next increase in my inner sensations confirms the Viagra is definitely having an effect on him. His hand caresses my thigh under the table and he shifts closer so my hand can feel the bulge develop in his trousers.

'Wow, impressive, it hasn't even been half an hour.'

Another increase in buzzing intensity confirms his status.

'You might need to eat a bit faster. The way I'm feeling it will be impossible to keep my hands off your body for much longer. This pill is making me impatient for action.'

'What, no dessert?' Another increase. I start to squirm in my seat in an attempt to adjust to the stronger vibrations. It's becoming increasingly difficult for me to sit respectably still. 'Okay, okay. No dessert. But no more increases until we finish this. I'm starting to break into a sweat.'

'I'll do my best, but we did agree to keep pace with each other. You can't begin to imagine how hard I'm feeling.'

'Believe me, I'm getting the gist. Do you like it?'

'It's quite intense and I feel like my dick is trying to rid itself of my undies, as if it's becoming more of an independent beast, if that were possible.'

'Is everything okay for you here, sir?' The waiter pours more wine in our glasses. We both shuffle in our seats with sexual impatience.

'Yes, it has been great. Just the bill when you have a moment, please.' It is the first time I've heard Jeremy a little out of control and I like it. Even his voice is wavering.

'No dessert tonight?'

'Not tonight. We'll be having dessert elsewhere and we're late. Thanks.' The waiter registers our urgency with a full grin. With these words we look across at each other's flushed faces and dissolve into a fit of giggles at the situation we have created for ourselves.

As I sip the last of my wine, the intensity inside me almost doubles its strength.

'Jeremy,' I gasp, 'god no, please.' Tingling sensations literally emanate through my entire body toward every extremity. God, it feels so good and so bad all at the same time. He raises his eyebrows and his grin widens in delight, fully understanding the meaning behind my heavy eyelids.

'Oh, Alexa, just you wait. I'll be able to tame that urge and then some with the state I'm in. Let's get out of here before it is indecent for me to be in public.' Jeremy slams some euro notes on the table and helps me from my chair. My legs quiver beneath me as I attempt to walk in a straight line under the influence of my hidden purple egg. He anchors his arm firmly around my waist to provide me with additional support, for which I'm grateful.

'I may need to borrow your jacket.'

I look down at his trousers and quickly hand it over. 'Holy hell, look at you. Can you even walk?'

'Barely, let's just stay close and move as fast as we can.'

'It would be much easier if you turned this thing down.'

'Oh, I hear you, Alexa, but if I can't turn this pill off, it's hardly fair, is it? I know how you feel about equality of the sexes so it would be wrong on so many levels for you if I turned it down.'

I groan at the reasoning of his argument and jab my elbow into his ribs in reproach. We continue shuffling awkwardly along the cobbled laneway towards the water. The half moon looks absolutely stunning shimmering in its path before us. I try to focus on its beauty to distract me from my need for urgent release; the intensity of the build-up is almost crippling me.

'Oh, stuff it, I can't wait another second.' He leaps off the ledge without letting go of my hand and I follow, tumbling into his arms. He charges off dramatically and we end up behind a large rock.

'Sorry, sweetheart, but your purple friend needs to make way for a far more important priority. I can't wait another second.' He pins my back against the sheer rock that is still warm from the afternoon sun. Jeremy holds my face as he kisses me deeply before devouring my décolletage. With this intensity, he'll be taking no prisoners. His other hand impatiently dives into my knickers to urgently rid me of the vibrating device.

'Gently, careful,' I pant as he pulls it out of me and shoves it into my handbag before allowing his trousers to fall to the ground. I'm gobsmacked at the size of him when he loosens his undies and unleashes the beast.

'Oh my god! Does that hurt?'

'It won't in a few seconds when it's buried inside you.' He dons the obligatory condom in haste and tears at my flimsy panties, which immediately break under his hands. I can't take my eyes off his throbbing member and wonder whether I will be able to fully accommodate the length and girth of him. I mean, he's always been bigger than average but this … it's monstrous. I'm suddenly very grateful I've been fully prepped by the intensity of my purple friend. Seconds later, he hauls up my leg with determined urgency and immediately penetrates my core, stuffing me with a fullness so complete and so gratifying, I'm given no choice but to shatter around him while he pumps into me with the pure force of his masculinity. I'm left breathless.

'Oh god, Alexa. Hold on tight, sweetheart, I'm not done yet.' His cock pinions my body against the rock as I grip my arms tight around his neck and he wraps both my legs around his waist. In this position he attempts to control his raspy breathing as his hands grab the flesh of my buttocks and he pulls out of me and pushes in to me more slowly, enabling me to feel every decadent inch of him. In and out, slowly and completely re-establishing his control over my body until I am weak with desire.

'You know I love you, don't you?'

'Of course, Jeremy, we've loved each other for ages.'

He looks beseechingly into my eyes, as if he is trying to tap into my soul. It's a weird sensation, as if he is trying to inject some romantic element into this highly-charged sexual encounter.

'But I really love you, Alexa, like no other.' I can only assume the Viagra is affecting his emotions as much as his blood flow, but at this minute, my needs are extreme.

'Please, Jeremy, faster,' I plead into his ear, while my fingernails scrape into the flesh of his chest. The excruciating slowness of this rhythm is frustrating the hell out of me, particularly after the torment of the vibrating egg and I don't want to have to beg for release. My teeth bite into his hardened nipples in an attempt to make him understand my desperation and spur him into action. Oh, and finally …

'Thank you,' I groan out as he rides me as hard and fast as he ever has. My brain collides with images of the stars in the sky as his precision fingers detonate my swollen clit and I instantly dissolve into the bliss of the universe as he continues to pump into my core. We stumble to the ground, entwined together, the shattered shells and sand beneath us cushioning our fall. He remains within me, rock hard and ready for more action.

'Are you serious? I need a breather.'

'Sweetheart, you did this to me. It was your idea.'

In a tricky wrestling manoeuvre I find myself on top, my legs straddling his thighs and his cock still firmly planted within me. Oh, the pressure in this position is divine and I take a moment to adjust to the depth of this sensation.

'You feel amazing inside me.' I rock gently around and around, my juices smoothing my motion. God, this feels good.

'You're killing me, Alexa, I need to explode but I can't.' He grasps my hips to still my movement.

'Really? I'm loving you like this.'

'Alexa … I'm warning you …' I continue with my grinding movements over, around his enormous, throbbing shaft. I'm lost in a delightful haze above his body.

'You won't be loving it when you're raw inside and out.'

Suddenly, I'm flipped over so fast that Jeremy's instantly on top. How does he do that? He pinions my arms and bites and sucks my nipples hard as he again pumps into me. I cry out at the piercing pain and my back arches dramatically in response. My nipples are definitely hardwired to my clitoris and the sweet agony is intense. Oh, good lord. It's hard and it's fast and it's hot, carnal sex. This time I can't temper my voice as my continuing whimpers turn into full-blown cries of ecstasy, completely ignoring the fact that we are far from the privacy of our hotel cave. His mouth and tongue instantly close in on mine, equally as hungry and dominating as his member inside me, he ravishes my throat and stifles my orgasmic screams. I reunite with the stars again as his fingers continue to silence my lips and his mouth massages my breasts. I am utterly lost beneath the presence of this masculine hunk of physicality, my body a mere plaything to use as he desires — and I love that he can do this to me, and does, as often as he pleases. I eventually notice that his giant penis is not in the least deflated after our recent activity. In fact, it's quite the opposite, still rigid as hell and raring to go — inside me. Oh, dear god, what have I done? I let out a groan in recognition of this fact, as I flop my head back, feeling rather fatigued by the force of our sexual rampage.

'Oh, sweetheart. Will I have to carry you back to our cave?' Moments pass in my delirious state until I feel the hollow inside me as he attempts to pack himself ineffectively back into his trousers. I can't help but stifle a giggle.

'You think it's funny, do you?'

'Well, it is a bit. I can't believe you are still that engorged after all our activity.'

'I can assure you, our activity has only just begun, Alexa.' He straightens my dress over my now panty-less arse, hands me my handbag and jacket and scoops me up in his arms, wasting no time getting back to our room. Such energy, it really is astonishing, even for Jeremy! He quickly undresses himself and I swear his erection must be getting painful. Even I'm feeling a little bit sorry for him; at least my sexual desire has now been sated considerably. His eyes are still carnal as I register he is honestly ready to go again, frustration and lack of release definitely taking their toll on his patience.

'Maybe a cup of tea, a glass of wine?' I try to delay the inevitable.

'Maybe me, inside you, now!'

I'm on the other side of the table as he lurches around to grab me. I dodge in the nick of time and run towards the bathroom. Unfortunately, his steps are bigger than mine and he catches me, scooping my legs from beneath me and catapulting me onto the bed. I scream in shock and anticipation. My dress is discarded in seconds, the virility of his naked body hovering above me.

'You look like Eros.'

'Eros in desperate need of Psyche.'

'Okay then, take me however you want me.' What can a girl do?

He needs no more encouragement and the potent force of Jeremy and the impact of the little blue pill dominate my entire being, and most surfaces of the cave, for the next hour or so.

'Hydration, required urgently.' I can barely breathe the words out I'm so shattered by his dedicated attention to every part of my body. I feel like I've been pulped. Jeremy jumps up and returns with a bottle of water and a carafe of wine, happily spilling both over our bodies as we settle together naked and sodden on the lounge. He fills his mouth with wine and empties it into mine via a strategic kiss before settling, with some difficulty I might add, my head and shoulders on his lap. I can feel his erection against the side of my head but, thankfully, not like it was before. I open my mouth for more and he tries to aim the stream of water from the bottle into my mouth, but is lacking his usual precision. Whatever, it's not like I have clothes on. Some water makes it between my lips eventually. I can't move, I don't try. I'm utterly spent after such a heroic session. I'll certainly be aching and sore tomorrow, but I'll be far from complaining. His hand is gently caressing my hair and face and I snuggle into the softness of his touch, it feels serene.

'So you really are going to settle down and move back to Oz?'

I wasn't expecting this conversation to reoccur.

'Hmmm, well, yes. I think so. It had to happen at some stage. Life can't be one big party all the time.' I look up into his eyes; they look far away.

'I won't get to see you nearly as often.'

'I know, which won't be great.'

'Things will be quite different between us, not like this.'

'Yeah, more than likely. I'll miss this.'

'Hmmm, me too.'

I must have dozed off to sleep because when I wake up, I'm in bed and alone. I find a note on the table.

*'Can't sleep, gone for a drink. Back later. J xo'*

For some reason I'm worried about him. He seemed really forlorn during our last conversation before I dozed off. I whip a brush through my hair, dab on some lip gloss, throw a light summer dress on and head to the bar to see if he is okay. I'm as tender as all hell as I gingerly take each step knowing his penetration has done this to me, and I mentally note that when it comes to Jeremy, there is absolutely no need for Viagra. I could well be battered and bruised tomorrow even though he didn't hurt me. I liked the feeling and bizarrely enough, the idea that his passion could physically mark me actually turns me on more than I imagined. As I round the corner to the open entrance of the bar, I see him in the company of two overtly friendly females who look very pleased to be sharing themselves with Jeremy and his chemically-enhanced erection. I hesitate for one last look at my non-committal, playboy best friend and decide, at that moment, that I am making the right decision in being with Robert and will at last have some relationship security in my life. After all, I can't be hanging around playing games with Jeremy forever.

* * *

'Dr Blake, excuse me, Dr Blake?'

'Oh, sorry, yes?' I am instantly returned to the here and now.

'Do you have any other queries before we proceed?'

'Ah, no, oh, actually yes. I do. I don't want my eyes covered. I need to be able to see. At all times.'

For some reason I feel like she gives me a knowing smile before responding. 'When you are in our clinical facility there will be nothing that inhibits your vision unless you request it. There will only be one point where you will be required to be in darkness, and that is in transit to our facility. We shall let you know when it will occur so you can be prepared.'

'Right, okay.'

'Anything else?'

'And the purple pill? You will want me to take it?'

'Naturally, but the choice will be yours when the time comes. Rest assured, it is perfectly safe. And of course, your professional opinion on its effectiveness will be greatly appreciated also.'

It's not like I haven't heard that before! I feel light-headed and slightly ill thinking about what I'm signing up to. I can't help but ask one more thing.

'Madame Jurilique, may I ask, have you tried it?'

'Oh, indeed I have, Dr Blake. For drugs such as this, I believe it is imperative for our executives to be able to experience what we are developing first-hand, from a marketing perspective at the very least. Therefore, I can unequivocally state that I believe women the world over will be more than satisfied with the results — at least they have been to date.' Her face looks as if she is lost in a very pleasant memory as her eyes glaze over. I can't help but stare at her in shock as she slides her fingers languidly down her neck and chest towards her breast. Good grief, this just gets more bizarre by the second. She returns from her reverie and states in a crisp voice, 'Hopefully that is everything, Dr Blake? Please sign the amended documents.' She indicates the contract before me.

Louis and Frederic enter the room and stand either side of me. I sigh before initialling the changes and signing my life away, knowing that the validity of such a contract under these circumstances is questionable at best. At least Xsade have given me the courtesy of a discussion and the commitment that by the end of the week, I will be out of here. But heaven knows what is ahead of me in the next three days.

'Well done, Dr Blake, I hope you have no regrets. We shall look after you.' I've heard that before, too. She shakes my hand as if we are concluding a momentous deal, which I suppose we are in a way; my hand feels weak in her firm grasp. 'Louis will show you back to your room, and the good doctor shall be with you shortly to make arrangements for your travel.' I stand and follow Louis to the door. 'And one more thing, Dr Blake' — I turn to face her — 'I'm sure you will enjoy yourself rather more than you are expecting, if you just give yourself permission to do so.' She smiles broadly and turns away. Jeez, just how much do they know about me? At that, Louis closes the door to the office and I'm returned to my room.

My bag is packed and the room is made up as if I have never been here. My gut twists in my stomach as I stare aimlessly out the window again, worrying at my bracelet, my one contact with Jeremy who I'm still not sure is my friend or my foe in relation to all this experimentation. I'd give anything to talk to him now and sort all of this mess out once and for all. I just don't know what's ahead of me or whether I'm doing the right thing. I continue to look out the window silently calling out, Jeremy, what have you done to me? Where are you?

Drug companies, who needs them? I suppose we all do in this day and age, but at what cost? I can't help but think that it's all Jeremy's fault that I'm even here, but also can't deny that deep in my heart, I still want to love him and know that he loves me. Even when I'm dealing with this. If only he could make the heartache go away. The back and forth of my thoughts makes me feel confused and numb. Once again, I'm placed in the irrevocable position where I have no choice but to go with the flow.

'Ready when you are, Dr Blake.'

Jeez, will I ever be ready for this? There is no need for me to pick up any bags given the service provided by everyone around me, so I obediently follow Louis and Fred down the spiralled staircase. I absently wonder whether I will ever return to this chateau but I doubt that I will. I enter into a small room off to the side of the enormous arched entrance doorway, where the good doctor (or perhaps the bad doctor, who knows?) is patiently awaiting my arrival. My palms instantly moisten as he greets me and I see an injection and some additional vials waiting on a white linen cloth on the desk.

'Dr Blake, how are you today?'

'I've been better.'

'Are you nervous?' Dr Josef's voice is gentle.

'What do you think?' I glance over my shoulder as the door is closed and we are now alone in the room.

'I will not let anything bad happen to you, I can assure you. Please have a seat.'

'How do I know that? I have no idea who you are or what you will do.' Oh god, I don't think I can do this; I feel like I could faint, this is all too much. I slump into the chair he offers.

'I think I'm going to be sick.' I anxiously look around the room for a bin. He calmly passes me a sick bag from the desk drawer and I hold it close to my mouth. The wave of nausea passes. 'What exactly is going to happen now?

'I am going to give you an injection and then we shall make our way to the hospital. I'm assuming Madame Jurilique has informed you of these details?' He raises his eyebrows and stares intensely into my eyes. He is very distracting. It still feels strange that my captors answer my questions rather than keeping me in the dark. It makes for a pleasant change, I think.

'And what will it do, this injection?'

'It will relax your muscles until you are quite still. The entire process should take less than half an hour. When we arrive at the hospital I will give you another injection and you will then be taken to our clinic. They should be quite painless.' He pauses. 'Are you ready?'

Oh shit. Fuck, fuck and shit. I feel like I could internally combust I'm so nervous. Everything sounds so professional and consensual, yet I'm drowning in fear and he is calmly waiting for me.

'I can assure you that although the sensation is slightly unusual at first, it will be far more comfortable than your arrival at the chateau.' I can't help but stand up and walk over to the door. I turn the handle and open it until I can see Fred and Louis standing guard. I quickly close it and return to the seat. It's hard to sit still and I continue to fidget. I suddenly find some bravado within me.

'Alright, I don't know who you are but it's obvious to me that I have no choice but to trust you and hope that you mean it when you say nothing bad will happen to me. And remember, as you're aware, I have signed a contract with Xsade outlining my terms and conditions.'

'It would be sensible for you to remember that as well, Dr Blake.' Well, touché! 'You appear to be a little restless. Would you prefer to lie down, perhaps?' His voice actually sounds kind and concerned, if you can believe that.

'Yes, I think so.' My jittering body stands up. Oh god, I can't help but think it might be easier if they were nasty and brutal. This eternal politeness is just freaking me out. He indicates the firm bench behind us. I nod and quickly move over to it to lessen the frenetic energy of my nerves. He calmly picks up my left hand and gives it a thorough wipe with an alcoholic swab and carefully inspects my veins. He places a tourniquet just below my elbow and within seconds my veins disclose their whereabouts. My breathing is erratic given the proximity of the injection on standby to pierce into my skin, and the unknown of the next few days. He calmly ignores my rising panic and continues to silently go about his business, fiddling with the vials from the desk before positioning my hand firmly in his.

I can't help one last plea. 'You know I don't want to do this, any of this.'

'I'm aware of that, Dr Blake, but money always has an interesting way of procuring the appropriate outcomes.' The cannula seamlessly slides into my vein and he holds my hand in a tight grip while injecting the contents slowly into my system.

'Money?' I screech. 'You think this about money?'

At least he seems to be good at his job, but I hate injections, and I'm not brave enough to try and snatch back my hand. I have to look away from the proceedings but thankfully it doesn't hurt.

'At the end of the day, most things are, I'm afraid.'

Oh god, how bad does this look? Here I am thinking I could give the money to charity, that I was doing the right thing taking it from a company flush with funds. Now it looks like I've agreed to go through this because of the money I am being paid.

'Well, I'm not, I'd never do this for the money. It makes me feel sick to the core that you think that. I'm doing it for my safety, to be released from here unharmed. Then I can return to my children, so they don't end up without a mother.' He ignores my emotional outburst as he calmly picks up another vial from the tray and injects it again through the cannula. Why am I justifying myself to this man? Once he has finished, he realises the tourniquet.

'Very noble, Dr Blake. It's important you lie still while this moves through your system to avoid any unwanted side effects.' As I lie as still as possible, I can't believe that that is exactly what people will think. By signing that bloody contract it almost endorses the fact that my decision was about the money. And I thought I was being smug about the contract not being able to stand up legally. Now that they have offered me money and I have accepted it, it has all the components of a legally binding contract. Offer, acceptance and consideration. But duress, that has to account for something, doesn't it? Holy shit, what have I done?

I can feel whatever was injected taking over my body. My muscles feel relaxed and there is a comfortable warmth spreading through my limbs. The doctor sits steadily on a chair beside me checking my pulse.

'Can you wiggle your fingers for me?'

I attempt to wiggle them but nothing happens.

'Good, this is working well. Please remain calm.'

Shit, how can my body be anything but calm if I can't move anything?

I can't help but try to wiggle my toes. A weird spasm escapes them and then nothing. My legs are dead weights. I can still feel the doctor's fingers on my inner wrist but I can't move my arm away from him. I'm conscious but completely paralysed. Oh dear, this is not good at all.

'I know this is a strange sensation, Dr Blake, but you will be more comfortable if you relax into it rather than fight it.' I try to remember the last time I wasn't fighting internally over one thing or another, it seems to be an embedded habit recently.

I try to say yes, but my mouth can't form the words. This absolutely freaks me out and although I'm now utterly stressed and panicking internally, I'm lying perfectly still and content externally.

'Use your eyes to communicate. You are doing very well, just remember to stay calm and you will be fine. Just let the drugs do what they need to do.' I desperately try to say no with my eyes but the doctor is now letting two men in white clothes, carrying a stretcher, into the room. I can't move an inch, completely immobile. I can only see what comes into my line of sight or my peripheral vision. This is a really weird, dissociated feeling.

They adjust their stretcher to the height of the bed and on the count of three, easily heave my body from one to the other. A white sheet is placed over me and three straps are secured over my body. The doctor smooths hair away from my face, and I mentally flinch at the softness of his touch before I am wheeled out the door of the room and beyond the great entrance of the chateau. I roll beneath its majestic archway looking straight up before being taken outside and carefully loaded into an ambulance. The doctor follows me in, sits on the bench beside me and once again monitors my pulse. He notices the bracelet on my hand. 'This is an exquisite piece of jewellery, Dr Blake. I hadn't noticed it before. It is a shame you are unable to tell me where it is from. I'm afraid it will not be allowed where we are going, however. I will ensure it is returned to you at the end of your time with us.' I try to scream in desperation, but there is only the silent movement in my eyes. A moment later, I can feel we are moving with flashes of lights reflecting through the windows. This is really too much for me to bear.

* * *

I hear sirens swirling around me as we rush towards the hospital and then heaven knows where after that.

Which reminds me, I still don't even know what country I'm in. I'm not sure which is the stranger feeling, being strapped into a wheelchair hidden beneath a burqa but being able to struggle and tense my muscles, or feeling rather frustratingly yet serenely relaxed, gliding along in a stretcher as if my brain is incapable of sending an effective message to the rest of my body.

As these thoughts float through my mind, I'm being whisked through the corridor of what seems to be a rather small village hospital. I try to scan the entire set-up, keen for any visual information as to what could happen next. Eventually I'm handed over, literally, to some nurses in a small room. The straps are removed as are my clothes and I'm efficiently dressed in a revolting, backless, hospital garment. I know that is the least of my worries but even so …

My limbs are thoroughly washed by the nurses and I'm re-dressed in another hospital robe. Doctor Josef returns to the room and does his usual checks. This time I obviously can't ask any questions. He checks my responses, which are non-existent. He looks pleased with how all of this is progressing. He looks at the clipboard he is holding and flicks through some pages.

'I'm assuming you are still comfortable, Dr Blake?'

I move my eyes up and down. As comfortable as this situation allows I suppose, and very empty.

'I'm going to set up a drip to ensure you have the nutrients you need for the next day or two, so you will not require food after your enema. That should ensure you feel re-energised and promote your overall wellbeing.' God, he makes it sound like I'm in some health spa retreat, instead of lying in a coma with an overactive mind.

He goes about his business. Yet another injection; it's not as if I can stop him. This time a cool sensation filters through my veins. They say you need to face your fears in life … hopefully, after this hospital experience I won't have a problem ever again.

'Once this bag has emptied, I will give you one last injection and that will be it for the rest of your time with us. You will continue to have no muscle control, as is the case now. However, you will feel extremely relaxed, eventually falling into a deep sleep and remain in this state for the next hour or so.' His words alone are making me stressed, which he doesn't seem to notice as he continues to impart information.

'Soon you will be moved to another part of the hospital. During this journey you will not be able see as your face will be covered. Our aim is to complete this transition as quickly as possible. Obviously you will be unable to move, but it is still important that you remain calm during this time as we don't want to put you in any unnecessary danger. Do you understand?'

God, if he tells me I need to remain calm one more time I think I'll scream. If I could, that is.

I move my eyes again. Understand? Sure, stay calm to reduce danger, yeah right, got it!

'You are doing very well, Dr Blake. We should have you back to your normal state in no time.' Bloody hell, there is absolutely nothing normal about my state or

169

my life any more! I feel the urgent need to visually disengage from this process for as long as possible. Maybe I have more to thank Jeremy for than I realised, I think sarcastically. I can't believe I neglected to ask whether the probability of risk or danger in relation to any of these procedures would be high, medium or low. That may have prompted more of a detailed discussion with Madame Jurilique and I didn't even go there ... oh dear.

'Right, we are almost ready.' I start to feel incredibly relaxed, really wonderfully relaxed, and can't help but acknowledge this is a beautiful feeling. Warm, fuzzy and absolutely delightful. Whatever he has given me is a great drug. Although I feel heavy, like a dead weight, I'm also soft and gooey. Happy days. I'm shifted back onto the stretcher.

'Okay, Dr Blake, we shall look forward to seeing you on the other side. Please stay relaxed.'

Hmm, staying relaxed is the only option available to me as I hear something being zipped along my body. It continues until it covers my head and my line of sight vanishes. We begin to move. Just as the good doctor said. I don't care one bit; they can do whatever they want to me when I feel this fantastic ... I can't begin to imagine what the next three days will hold ... then nothingness blankets my brain like a snuffer putting out a candle's flame.

# Part Five

Sorrow is tranquillity remembered in emotion.

— Dorothy Parker

# Jeremy

I lose all sense of which way is up as I continue to fall down the steep hillside. Rocks belt into my sides and legs as I attempt to protect my face and head as best I can. I feel a sharp rock cut deep into my knee but I can't inspect the damage due to my gathering speed. Eventually, I slam thigh-first into a rock and come to a stop. Fuck that hurts, but I have no time for pain. My backpack is crushed between the earth and my back and I have no idea whether its contents have survived the impact. I gather myself up from the ground and limp as fast as I can back down to the village, desperate to tell Sam what I've just witnessed.

I finally make it and push open the door of our small room. There's a woman in the room who looks a few years younger than me. Sam leaps to his feet.

'Jeremy, what the hell happened to you? You're covered in dirt and, god, is that blood?'

'I fell. It's fine, don't worry about it now, Sam, we need to find out which hospital ambulances end up at around here. They have —' I stop myself, both to catch my breath and so I don't say too much in front of this stranger.

Sam realises and introduces us. 'Jeremy, this is Salina. She has been sent as our bodyguard.'

'What? What happened to — oh, it doesn't matter.' I can't really come out and say I had just assumed the bodyguard would be male. I attempt to hide the disbelief in my voice. She looks about five foot seven and is slim with short dark hair cropped around her face. She certainly doesn't look too dangerous but as I'm learning all too well — looks can be deceiving.

'Who sent you?' I feel a desperate need to verify everything first-hand given what I've just witnessed for the second time.

'Martin Smythe. He's responsible for assembling the team in Munich who are on standby for our update.'

'Right, good.' At least she seems to know what's going on. 'I'm Dr Jeremy Quinn. Pleased to meet you.' I wipe my palms against my trousers in an attempt to clean my filthy hand before shaking hers.

'Salina Malek. Likewise.' She sounds all business at least.

'So, tell us, Jeremy, what happened?' Sam urges me to continue.

'Not here, we need to get going. There's an ambulance headed northwest on the road out of this village and Alexa's in it. I'll tell you the rest in the car.'

'It sounds like they're heading towards Bled, there's a small hospital there, otherwise there is a large hospital in Villach across the Austrian border, if the emergency is more serious. Where are the keys? I'll drive.'

I must admit I'm a little surprised by Salina's instant, proactive response, but I'm pleased she seems to knows her way around here. For a moment I am about to insist on driving, but I'm a bit shaky after my fall and subsequent dash to the hotel. I can focus on updating them and cleaning myself up in the back seat. I throw her the keys and she immediately catches them. Good. Fast reflexes at least.

Salina wastes no time finding the open road and I'm impressed with her driving skills; nothing puts me on edge more than being a passenger with a bad driver. I look at my leg and my trousers are ripped, and there is blood still pouring out of my knee. As I fill the others in on what I'd seen, I rip my shirt sleeve and wrap it around the wound to try and stem the flow. At first glance, it looks like it may need a few stitches.

'Bled is about 20 kilometres away from here. Are you sure this is the direction the ambulance was heading?'

'Yes. I'm sure.'

'Were the sirens on?'

'Not when they left the chateau, only the flashing lights, then the sirens started as they turned off past the village.'

'Okay, I think we should do a thorough search of Bled Hospital. It's only small so, between us, it won't take long. We should be able to see whether an ambulance is still there and recently driven. By the looks of your knee, you may need some assistance, regardless.' She glances back toward me and I wish she would keep her eyes on the road.

'I can stitch myself up, but it would be good to use some of their equipment.'

'How was Alexandra when you saw her, J?' Sam asks.

'She actually looked okay. A little forlorn' — I remember the sadness in her eyes as she looked at the Alps and, unknowingly, toward me — 'but otherwise well.' My voice catches on these last words and I swallow hard before continuing. 'Then she disappeared for quite some time. I stayed in my position as soon as I saw the ambulance arrive and the other car being brought to the entrance. The next thing I knew she was strapped to a stretcher, lying perfectly still, before being whisked off down the mountain.'

Fuck, what could have happened to her now, what if she's had a seizure from the stress? As if she wouldn't be scared shitless after all she has been through the last few days. They could have given her a drug and she's reacted badly, drugs have always had a more extreme effect on her than on others. I remember the impact the sedative had on her before we arrived at Avalon. I had thought it would help her, but she took a long time to recover.

'Can you speed things up, Salina, we seem to be taking forever?' I can't take the edge off my voice, more from my own stress than anything else.

'We will be there in less than five minutes, Dr Quinn.' I notice the speedo registers she is going as fast as she can under the circumstances. She continues, her voice brisk. 'Right, this is what we'll do. You two go in together and provide me with a distraction to go and search the rooms and the basement. Hopefully, you can get your knee tended to.' She glances toward me again. Eyes on the road, I plead in silent exasperation. 'Samuel, you can check each person in the emergency wing, in case she is in there. Don't stray too far from Quinn as you are unarmed and obviously these people are dangerous.'

I'm having difficulty assimilating Salina's instructions, when I'm the one who is normally in charge. Unfortunately, there is not too much I can add as everything she has said makes sense. So I keep my mouth closed until we pull up at the tiny hospital.

'Is that the ambulance?'

'Yes, it looks like it.'

'Good, hopefully they are all still here.' She picks up her phone. Obviously, Martin is on speed dial.

'Martin. Malek here. I'm with Quinn and Webster at Bled Hospital. Blake was sighted being loaded into an ambulance outside Kranj and we believe she is inside. We're heading in for surveillance and will send an update ASAP.'

Efficient on the phone as well, obviously.

'Ready?' she asks. 'Remember you are here as a patient, Quinn. Quite convenient that you had your fall under these circumstances.'

I don't like being considered a patient or convenient by someone I barely know. It's not like I'm looking for sympathy, but I doubt I would get it from her anyway. We both nod as she pulls up to the hospital entrance to let us out and then quickly parks the car in visitor parking. I don't need to pretend to limp to the front desk, as the pain is steadily mounting in my knee and hip. The nurse speaks a little English as we attempt to explain my injuries. When she leaves her desk to come around to inspect my leg, Salina quietly slips by into the shadows of the corridor.

I try to explain that I'm a doctor as she escorts me into a small curtained room and indicates for me to sit down in the chair. She insists on finding the locum doctor and wanders off, giving Sam the opportunity to check the rooms on the other side of the hospital.

A friendly young Indian doctor eventually introduces himself and he speaks good English. I tell him I was hiking and that I'm happy to give myself stitches if he can provide the equipment. He looks hesitant until I pull out my medical card from my wallet and then he smiles.

'Okay, doctor, good. Very good.' He shakes my hand before telling the nurse to supply me with what I need. Thankfully, the procedures at this hospital don't seem to be as strict as in the States or Australia. When she returns with the equipment I get to work and as the doctor is still loitering around I decide to find out what I can.

'Do you have many people working on this shift?' It is the least busy hospital I've encountered for many years.

'Only myself and two nurses. We are never too busy here. There is another intern who rosters on occasionally from Ljubljana and one specialist doctor who sometimes brings his own patients, but otherwise it is quiet most of the time.'

'And the ambulance that recently arrived, is everything okay?'

He looks distracted as he fills in the paperwork. 'Ambulance? Oh yes, that is the specialist doctor I was talking about, one of his patients just arrived. Very serious. It's not looking so good.'

I almost pierce the needle straight into my wound at his words. 'What? What do you mean, not looking so good?' I feel myself break into a sweat and I can't keep the angst out of my voice.

He flips over the paper on his board. 'You know how it is, Doctor ...' He looks down again at his paperwork. '... Quinn. You win some, you lose some.'

Fucking hell, what does that mean? He can't possibly be talking about Alexa, can he? Surely he's mistaken. I try to gather myself together and finish these bloody stitches as quickly as I can.

'What do you mean lose some? Was there an accident?'

'I'm afraid I cannot discuss our patients' details with you. I imagine you will be very sore in a few hours. You're bruising now, so it will only get worse by tomorrow. These will help.' He hands me some painkillers for my injuries and effectively dismisses our previous conversation. I know he can't disclose any information but not knowing is killing me.

Sam wanders into the room, shaking his head slightly.

'Thanks.' Bruising and physical pain is the least of my worries. It will be nothing compared to the pain if I were to lose AB. Can't think like that! Where the hell is Salina? She should be back by now.

I'm sorted, so Sam and I thank them for their assistance and head reluctantly back to the car, in the hope that Salina has more concrete news of Alex's whereabouts. I remind myself that she was perfectly physically well at the chateau. At least that's what it looked like through my binoculars. What if I missed something? Nothing could have happened to her between then and now, could it? If it has, they fucking did something to her, and someone will pay. Anger and fear once again surge through my veins and my heart pounds heavily in my chest as I'm forced to wait impatiently in the car.

Salina's brisk efficiency has disappeared as she walks slowly out the hospital doors towards our car. My heart immediately jumps into my throat and I feel sick to the core. Something is very, very wrong. My mind is sheathed in dread as she slumps into the driver's seat and closes the door.

'It's not good.'

'What's not good? What happened?'

She shakes her head. 'Blake was taken to the hospital for a standard procedure. Something went wrong and her body has been taken to the hospital morgue.'

'What?' These words don't make sense through the roaring in my ears. 'That's impossible. What fucking standard procedure? It's a lie, they are lying to you, there is no way she is in the morgue.'

Salina runs her fingers through her hair, looking distraught. Sam is slumped in the backseat, his face ashen.

I can't stand this a moment longer, I can't breathe in the confines of this car, I need to get out. But as I open the door, Salina grabs my arm.

'Quinn, stop. It's true, I saw it with my own eyes.'

'What, what did you see?'

'This!'

She shoves her phone in front of me and I stare in disbelief at the image searing into my retinas.

'What is it, Jeremy?' Sam asks urgently. 'Give me the damn phone.' Salina takes it from my hands and passes it back to Sam.

I can't breathe. I can't speak. I can't move.

My brain and heart are frozen with fear.

Alexandra is dead.

There is no way this can be fucking true. I saw her alive at the chateau. Melancholic, haunted, but alive and breathing. This is impossible, my worst nightmare a reality. After all these years we finally get together, sort ourselves out, recognise the love for each other which has meandered in our subconscious for decades, ever since the first day we laid eyes on each other. No fucking way. It can't be, it won't be. I won't let it. I pound my fists, trying to smash the dashboard, smash anything. My heart feels like it has been cruelly sliced in two, then four, and the cuts are rapidly multiplying as each second passes.

Oh my god, the kids, Elizabeth and Jordan. And Robert. What the fuck have I done? I've ruined a family. A family I was coming to terms with loving as my own. My body feels like a paralysed deadweight as I feel myself going into shock. This is bad … This is as bad as when Michael died, no, it's worse. This time it's absolutely all my fault. I'm vaguely aware of Sam leaving the car. Salina grabs the keys and follows Sam back into the hospital. This is all occurring around me, but is happening as if I'm not part of the scene. My body is anchored to the seat with chains of anguish and guilt.

* * *

I don't know how long I have been sitting alone in the M5. Time doesn't seem to exist in my new reality — a reality without Alex. I can't escape the image of her face in my mind. A face that no longer registers movement or light, only death and darkness. The black body bag encasing her beautiful form that was so vitally alive and breathing just a short time ago.

My hands shake and my body trembles. I'm unaware of the hot tears streaming down my face and pooling in my shirt. My body is physically reacting to my shock and grief without my knowledge, while my heart feels like every bit of love is being squeezed out of it only to be replaced by extreme pain. I thought I knew and understood the pain of loss, but this is an entirely different experience — sheer agony. My emotions are strangling me from the inside out, suffocating the breath in my lungs.

Those bastards have murdered one of the most beautiful women on earth, my best friend and my lover. My god, I swear they will pay for it. Suddenly hate and anger fuel a rush of adrenaline through my veins and I am momentarily overridden from these treacherous emotions. It takes every bit of control to stop myself smashing a fist through the car window and I have no doubt the slashing pain of the glass would be nothing compared to the anguish in my heart.

Instead, I jump out of the car and run straight into the hospital, the stitches in my knee hampering my usual pace and stride. I slam through the doors, turn right past reception and charge down some stairs that I'm hoping will lead to the morgue. I need to see her. To touch her face, her skin, and gently close the lids of her haunted eyes. Every muscle is tense as I swing through some double doors to see Sam and Salina standing before me, both running their hands through their hair in exasperation as they speak to the nurse. The atmosphere is charged.

'What's going on here?' I yell. 'Where is Alexa's body?' I search the empty room and anxiously yank at one of the drawers in search of the body bag I witnessed in the photo. 'Tell me, where is she?' I'm so hysterical I could shake the nurse to make her respond. Thankfully, Samuel's voice distracts me just in time.

'She's not here, Jeremy. This is where Salina saw Alexandra's body, but apparently she's been moved.' I shift my stare toward Salina.

'She was right here, I saw her with my own eyes, I swear to you.' She sounds almost as distraught as Sam, and she doesn't even know Alexa.

'I know, I know, your photo more than proved that.' I can't take the anger and despair out of my voice. I turn to the nurse. 'Where has she been taken?' I scream at her. 'We must know. Now!'

The nurse almost jumps out of her skin before nervously extracting herself from the room.

'What the hell is going on here? This just doesn't make sense.' While we are alone, I attempt to open the drawers again, but they are all locked.

The young, English-speaking doctor comes to talk to us. 'You shouldn't be in here, this is for hospital staff only.'

'I don't give a shit about your rules and procedures, doctor. There was a woman in here, Dr Alexandra Blake ...' My voice catches as I say her name. 'We know she was here, or at least her body was and now it has suddenly vanished into thin air. We need to know what happened.'

'Please, please come out of here, you will get me into a lot of trouble. Please.' His eyes almost beg us to follow his arm, outstretched toward the door. 'Follow me quietly and I'll tell you what I can.'

Reluctantly, the three of us walk out the swinging doors, down the corridor and follow him into a small room.

'You should never have gone in there, it is not allowed.'

'I don't care what's allowed and what's not. Where is her body?'

'Her body has been moved.'

All patience is lost as I grab him by his shirt collar and shove him against the wall.

'Tell us where she has been taken.'

I'm seething with anger when Salina steps in between us and forces me to release him. I slam my fist into the wall in frustration even though I know my tactics are unnecessarily and uncharacteristically brutal.

'Doctor,' she says in a calm and controlled voice and I can't deny I'm a little pleased she still has him firmly pinned against the wall. She's not big, but she's not to be messed with. 'It is imperative you tell us where the body was moved. Dr Blake is an Australian citizen who has recently been abducted and now it seems, murdered, in your country. We have reinforcements on their way and unless you want to spend the next twenty-four hours in custody answering questions, I suggest you tell us immediately where the body was taken.' She cleverly shifts her blazer so he can see her gun holster. This seems to prove a more effective strategy.

'She has been taken to the morgue in Villach Hospital, across the border. That is where Dr Votrubec will conduct a preliminary autopsy to confirm the cause of death. We don't have the facilities in this hospital. That is all I know,' he concludes, eyeing each of us nervously.

'Thank you, doctor, we appreciate your cooperation.' Salina calmly releases him and readjusts her blazer, once again concealing her weapon.

'Right, you two, let's get out of here,' she says with authority, glancing at Sam and me. 'They can't be too far ahead of us.' She takes her phone out to update Martin and agrees we'll meet him and two other agents there.

Although relieved that we have something concrete to do, this knowledge gives me a sinking feeling in the pit of my gut. I really don't want to see Alexa dead but I know that, until I do, this just won't be real. And at least following her body to Villach will defer the phone calls I am dreading having to make.

It takes us less than an hour to cross the border into Austria and locate the hospital in Villach. A significantly larger town and a different country obviously make a lot of difference. Salina insists on waiting for Martin, but I can't stand it. Sam looks mentally and physically exhausted and they wait in a cafe opposite the hospital entrance. Nobody has eaten much all day and it's now late afternoon.

I can't bear the thought of sitting down. 'I'm going for a walk around.'

'Don't do anything stupid, Quinn. Smythe will be here soon.' Just how incapable does Salina think I am, I wonder?

I give her a look of pure frustration and slam out the cafe door. I need to know Alexa's fate. I have a fleeting thought that Salina has never been in love, or that she's so well trained she doesn't show a trace of emotion.

I head straight to the hospital but can't get beyond reception. Eventually, I find myself in the embarrassing situation of being escorted off the hospital premises by security, unable to discover whether Alexa's body ever arrived, let alone whether she is still in there or not. I return to the cafe with my tail between my legs, finally realising the capabilities of Martin and Salina far outweigh my own expertise in this area. They take one look at my face and I'm grateful they decide against a verbal reprimand. I acknowledge Martin's arrival by briefly shaking his hand and quickly grab a chair from another table and slide in beside Sam as they continue their discussion.

'We know they don't want her dead and that the GPS signal stopped at Lake Bled. Agreed, the body bag is convincing, but may equally have been used to throw us off the trail.' Salina and I raise our eyebrows at Martin simultaneously, astonished. He puts his hand up, signalling us to allow him to continue. 'We have been able to establish that Dr Votrubec has nothing to do with the hospital here in Villach and, more significantly, nothing to do with transferring dead bodies across borders. So, Blake's body must still be in Slovenia.' Martin says this as professionally as possible, but I can't help feeling like a complete idiot for being so easily mislead. No wonder they thought I was a psycho in the hospital moments ago! 'We have also been able to establish that he, Votrubec, is financially retained by Xsade and is known to the staff in their Slovenian office.'

'Do you have a list of Xsade executives and their contact details?' I suddenly remember that Moira was hoping to send me the phone records of each forum member. It's a long shot but you never know, they may provide a link …

'Yes, I'll email that through to you now.' Martin picks up his phone and scrolls through. 'Done.' I nod in thanks. We return our focus to his authoritative voice as he continues. 'We will return to Slovenia tonight and split up for surveillance at the chateau and the hospital in Bled.' He motions toward two men sitting at the table behind us. I assume they are meant to be incognito, so don't acknowledge them. 'Salina, you stay with Quinn and Webster, keep your phone on at all times. Accommodation has been organised for you a few blocks from here.' He hands over a document with the details and looks directly at Sam and I. 'It's been a long day and night for both of you. I know it's hard but you need a rest before you can be of any use to anyone.' Well, that certainly tells us where we stand. He looks solemn. 'This situation is dangerous, I don't want you leaving your rooms unless Salina knows. Are we clear?'

I don't think I've been bossed around this much since my internship! It's late and even I have to admit it has been an obscenely long day, so I don't argue with Martin, he's right, we need to rest. We must all look utterly dejected as we say our goodbyes. Martin pulls me aside before we depart. 'Don't lose hope, Quinn. This is not over yet.' I nod my head in desolate thanks. If only I could believe him.

We check into a nearby hotel for some rest. It's clean and tidy and will do for the night. I just don't care. I feel hopeless, in every sense of the word. I know I should eat, so I order room service but find the only thing my stomach can handle is mashed potato. For the first time in my life, I medicate my sleep to numb the pain. I'm out for the count.

\* \* \*

*I'm wandering in a vividly green field, and somehow I sense I'm in Northern Ireland. I can see the fierce waters of the sea smashing against sheer cliff tops. I take deep breaths of the icy air and feel alive and invigorated. I walk for a long time yet my energy never wanes until I notice dark storm clouds rolling in from the horizon. The shades of black and grey tumble over one another until they are almost upon me. Rain splashes down against my skin, making me sodden and weary and I notice there are heavy chains weighing down my arms. My ankles and wrists become bound to an ancient wall. A scream escapes from deep within my lungs only to be snatched away by the ferocious howling winds slamming my naked body against the coarse bricks. A dark fog tumbles forward as though it wants to devour my body; terrified, I struggle against the restraints as it rolls thick and fast toward me. Trapped, I close my eyes and feel its chill ice through my body until at last it passes.*

*As I open my eyes, I sense relative calm and see a blurred vision of red floating in the remains of the mist. I struggle to see more clearly and I discern a figure in a hooded cloak. It moves closer and closer and its warmth infiltrates the deep chill in my bones. The heat intensifies as the ruby figure removes its hood. I stare incredulously into Alexa's beautiful emerald-green eyes. I go to wrap my arms around her, but only manage to rattle my chains. I long for her to reach out to me, but her arms remain unseen, covered beneath the robe, only her face shining through. She kneels before me and without uttering a word takes me in her mouth. She starts slowly at first before her passion escalates and she sucks hard and fast against my rigid cock. I yell in torment at not being able to touch her; there's an intensity in her face I have never seen before, a carnal confidence in her actions — something has changed.*

*My brain can't function under her mouth's ambush as I try to decipher what is going on. She*

*is sucking and pulling as if she is sourcing the
essence of my soul. She doesn't stop until I pump
into her beautiful mouth and she swallows until
I'm drained — something she has never done
before. She looks up toward me from her kneeling
position and I find myself staring into piercing
blood-red eyes the same colour as the robe, and
her lips curl into a salacious smirk. She replaces
her hood and waits on her knees with her head
bowed toward the ground as two other cloaked
figures emerge seamlessly from the mist — both
are in black robes and float either side of her,
lifting her to her feet. Her hood shrouds her face
and I lose all sense of my Alexa. In desperation, I
scream out her name, my body shaking violently
against the chains that keep me bound, my fear
for her, for us, stabbing my soul, but I'm weak
and drained. I watch the three figures turn,
beyond my reach, and float away through the
mist along the moor. I plead and scream for her
return, for her to look back toward me once
more. I feel like my heart has been ripped from
my limp body as I remain tethered and helpless.*

\* \* \*

'Jeremy, Jeremy. Wake up, you're having a nightmare.
Jeremy! You're dreaming.'

Disoriented, I realise I've been woken up by Sam
who is still forcefully shaking my body. I notice the

sheets are soaked in perspiration as I attempt to re-establish exactly where I am.

'Oh, Sam. Right … sorry … obviously a bad dream.' I clear my throat, as my voice is hoarse.

'You were screaming so loudly I could hear you next door, thought I'd better check. Salina had a spare key to your room.'

'Really? Sorry to disturb you, Sam. I'm okay. Might just grab a drink of water.' I notice Salina standing silently in the doorway, checking if everything is alright.

'Here, I'll get it for you, just stay there.'

The potency of the dream still lingers in my subconscious. I've woken up groggy, but as I come to, so does the pain in my heart — my reality is unchanged. Alexa is dead.

'Any update?' There's barely a trace of hope in my voice.

'Not really.' We both sound as dejected as each other. 'We can't access any signal from Alexa's bracelet.'

'That's strange. Do you think it's been destroyed?'

'Well, no … that's the thing. If it were destroyed the program would have reported it, likewise if it were somehow removed. Body temperature enables the signal.'

I look at Sam and wonder if he's just realised what he's said.

'Oh, um … that didn't come out well, did it? Anyhow, there is no signal; the last one was at the hospital in Bled.'

'Exactly where Salina saw her dead body.' The conclusion to be reached suddenly hits me, and I collapse in sobs on the bed, the heartbreak too much of a burden to keep up appearances any longer. Sam tries to comfort me, but I'm not ready for his sympathy and shrug him off as politely as I can. He leaves to give me some space and closes the door behind him.

Eventually, I gather myself together enough to grab a cup of coffee knowing the next call I have to make needs to be to Robert. I pause to think of the strange sequence of events that conspired to bring me into Alexa's life once again, and which led me to contact Robert a few months ago. It was triggered by one of my more casual discussions with Leo at his cottage at Martha's Vineyard. We were philosophising about love and life, and laughing about the fact that we were two bachelors enjoying each other's company without the presence of women. His bachelor lifestyle was by choice — he doesn't believe in committing to one partner for life. Mine was due to pretty much being married to my work and Alexa being taken by some-one else.

\* \* \*

'The way I see it, JAQ' — he always addresses me by my initials, Jeremy Alexander Quinn — 'is that when I cross someone's path it is meant to happen. If our connection is meaningful and I feel like it's meant to be, I become involved until it is obvious that it's no longer working for either one of us. We part as friends who respect each other and the bond we shared together; we keep our fond memories and our paths continue, more fulfilled than if we hadn't met.'

'And that's always worked for you?'

'More or less, although sometimes it doesn't. Take my brother, Adam, for example. We share a similar philosophy but a few years back he met this guy in Australia, at a conference on landscape ecosystems. It was only a brief liaison, but it was intense for both, and Adam really believed their meeting each other was something more than coincidental. The problem is that the guy — Robert — is married with children, and although they have kept in touch ever since, Robert just can't see a way around his existing life and doesn't want to hurt his family.'

Something ignites in my chest. 'Your brother, he's gay, isn't he?' I ask.

'Has been as long as I've known him,' Leo replies with a wink.

'And this Robert? What does he do?'

'I think he's an arborist in Tasmania but he's English. His wife's Australian, I think.' I am suddenly paralysed in disbelief, as he continues. 'Anyway, Adam can't seem to get him out of his mind and hasn't been able to manage a relationship since. I keep telling him to let it go but it's hard for some …' He looks at me knowingly.

'You don't mean Robert Blake?' I interrupt him.

'Yes, I think that's him, do you know him?'

'I don't believe it! This is incredible.'

'What?'

'Alexa Blake! She's his wife.'

'Your AB? The one I've been hearing about forever?'

'Yes.' I think my heart has stopped beating.

Leo looks astonished, but then shrugs and smiles. 'Well, see, just as I was saying. Everything will happen when it is meant to happen and not before. Strange that we've never had this conversation,' he ponders. 'I suppose I don't talk about my brother too much, but look at that — tonight he was on my mind and what a discovery. Who would have thought that your Alexa is married to the Robert my brother loves.'

I remember sitting there, shocked and immobile in front of Leo for quite some time. He sat quietly to let me absorb this information, knowing I was lost in deep thought. Eventually, without a word, he just patted my shoulder and went to bed. He is amazing like that. Because my brain was furiously covering every possible scenario as to how I could get Alexandra back into my life, front and centre.

There were a few things I was desperate to know:

Whether she loved him.

Whether he loved her.

Whether she still loved me.

And I was going to find out. One seemingly innocent conversation with Leo completely changed my life, filling me with hope. I could have kissed him. My existence centred on planning to get her back. Although, even then, in the back of my mind was the consideration that nothing happens by accident with Leo ...

I bury my head in my hands at how such high hopes have turned into utter misery and despair. How could things have gone so desperately wrong? My life is meaningless without her. It is wrong that I am still alive and she is gone. I can't live with the knowledge that my research has taken a mother from their children. Research that need not have occurred. A mother who was so very brave, loving and giving.

A lover who was trusting, divinely sensual, so intellectually and emotionally connected and so remarkably keen to explore the 'psychological unknown'. It's this pioneering streak in her that I was able to tap into during our weekend together, a streak that I'm sure she doesn't understand is such a fundamental part of her psyche. Unlike many other women I know, she had an innate desire to unravel the complexities of the world, to experiment and understand the idealistic and intellectual discrepancies that exist. She honoured me with the privilege of unlocking the core of her sexuality, which she approached with a refreshingly revolutionary zeal. Her desire to overcome and face her fears head-on, enabled us to break right through previously unrecognised medical and scientific conventions … discoveries that I'll never have the opportunity to discuss with her now and ones that, in hindsight, I desperately wish I'd never uncovered.

My level of distress at having to make this phone call is causing my throat to constrict as I prepare for the call. Robert. I dial the numbers, press call, and hold my breath until it goes straight through to his voicemail. I exhale in relief as I realise I'm just not ready to have this conversation and I'm certainly not going to leave such devastating news on a message. It will have to wait.

# Part Six

Nothing in life is to be feared, it is only to be understood. Now is the time to understand more, so that we may fear less.

— Marie Curie

# Alexa

As I come to, my brain attempts to process the emotion of extreme fear but it is simply impossible. I remember Josef telling me to remain calm about fifty times and no doubt this is what he's talking about. As soon as I remind myself of his words, I relax — strange, but true. I feel floppy and fantastic, just as they said I would. Still strapped to the stretcher but my face no longer covered, I am lifted onto something else and suddenly become aware of travelling along some form of conveyor belt. I'm actually going quite fast, essentially making it impossible for my eyes to focus on anything. I close them so I can't see the swirl of motion. I'm grateful my stomach and bowel are effectively empty; at least I'm assuming they are, as this feels like a horizontal rollercoaster, but I have the sense I'm descending, travelling deeper beneath the ground. I slow down and eventually come to a complete stop. How on earth would anyone find this place? I'm immediately covered with a warm, soft duvet that feels crisp, like it has just been near a toasty fireplace and find myself drifting off into a very comfortable sleep.

* * *

'Dr Blake, welcome. My name is Françoise. How are you feeling?'

I open my eyes to find myself staring at a friendly-faced woman who looks about thirty, wearing a white lab coat, with thick-rimmed glasses covering her piercing blue eyes, and her blonde hair pulled sharply back into a tight bun. She stares at me intently, notes something on the clipboard she's holding, and then her face beams with a smile waiting expectantly for my answer.

I sit up and stare in wonder at the clinical environment surrounding me. There are two types of people: those in lab coats without a hair out of place, and those in silver suits that essentially cover every part of their body except for their face. In observing this latter group, I notice that I, too, am similarly attired. I wiggle my gloved fingers and covered toes and feel the top of my head. All covered in the same soft, fine, silver fibre, something like the material of those protectors we put against the windscreen of our cars to shield the dashboard from the heat and sun, but without quite as much shine. Truly bizarre.

'Dr Blake?'

'Oh, yes, I actually feel quite good.' Surprisingly good, I add silently to myself. I feel refreshed and revived, not the least bit dozy. Better than I have in ages, I reluctantly have to admit.

'That's good news and exactly what we were hoping. As we only have you here for a short period of time I hope you don't mind if we start off with our participant questionnaire?' She raises her eyebrows as her smile continues to beam toward me.

'Right. Questionnaire. Okay then.' I glance toward the glass of water on the side table.

'Of course, please, help yourself.' She waits patiently until I have finished. 'Great, let's get started. If you could follow me to the interview room.'

As I move to follow her, I notice the strange suit hugs the contours of my body perfectly, almost like a second skin. We leave the glass-panelled room and walk down the corridor past more silver-suited and white-coated people who smile and nod as we pass, before entering a funky, colourful room that looks perfect for an office-friendly 'coffee chat'. Have they all been to the European school of politeness, I wonder? It's like I have woken up midway through a really weird dream, that's how far from reality I'm feeling at this point. It's utterly surreal. But, I suppose, what else would I expect from the drug company that is so close to releasing a new improved version of female Viagra to the world? I am absolutely fascinated.

For the next few hours Françoise 'confidentially' asks me everything about my sexuality which, at first, is rather disconcerting and quite confronting:

* Describe your first memory of being sexually aroused.
* Do erotic films/romantic movies increase your arousal?
* Does intelligence increase your arousal?
* Does a sense of humour increase your arousal?
* Would you describe yourself as a good lover?
* Do you act on your sexual desires?
* Describe your sexual fantasies.
* Do certain scents cause an increase in arousal?
* Do certain voices cause an increase in arousal?
* When do you most think of sex?
* Do you have anal sex?
* Does the way you dress have any impact on your arousal?
* Is eye contact important to you?
* Does anything in particular interfere with your arousal?
* Do you masturbate — for how long? How often?
* Is sexual variety important to you?
* How important is trust in your sexual relations?
* Does being submissive increase or decrease your arousal?
* Does being dominant increase or decrease your arousal?

And the list goes on, asking about preferences for styles and positions, giving and receiving ... After my initial shyness, I'm surprised how quickly I open up and comfortably answer her many questions. She's obviously trained to make no judgements and I find the entire experience rather enlightening, particularly as I'm used to being the one asking the questions (well, up until recently, of course!). I think she must know more about me now than I ever knew about myself.

Some answers I would classify as astounding for me to hear and they were *my* answers. Who would have thought that watching Penelope Pitstop being helpless and tied up in *Wacky Races* — a Hanna-Barbera cartoon series for goodness' sake — could be a trigger for developing future sexual preferences in the bedroom, or outside the bedroom for that matter. Or all those games of 'catch and kidnap' we use to play as kids, having harmless fun, where I liked to be the captain of the team but always dreamt of someone being smart enough, or strong enough, to catch me. They rarely did, but the thrill of the chase was apparently firmly established as part of my developing psyche. And movies ... a simple question engaged memories from decades ago of watching *Nine and a Half Weeks* that obviously had a profound impact on my fantasies and desires. Instead of feeling repulsed by John's sexual domination over Elizabeth, I was completely turned on by it.

All these tiny experiences and feelings that created excitement and tension in childhood and my teenage years, add up to a sexual profile I've never acknowledged in myself. Jeez, maybe I'm more into the whole submissive–dominant behaviours than I imagined, although I do like to switch every so often. My god, it's truly amazing, and a little embarrassing that I have never fully acknowledged these insights, given my profession. Even my original thesis took a dissociated perspective and concluded that such behaviours are merely part of the experimentation of growing up. But could these insights point to the emergence of a lifestyle preference, or maybe even an embedded part of my overall psyche?

I'd obviously blocked this out when I married Robert, or at least buried these thoughts somewhere. Security and motherhood seemingly superseded all other psychological priorities. There are so many things I have never thought about before such as how and why I might like certain aspects of sex more than other facets. Even more intriguing (and admittedly, gut wrenching) is how many of those aspects Jeremy provides me with to perfection. I must have been like a lamb to the slaughter for him — happily slaughtered, mind you. No, I still can't bring myself to think like that, it's just not true. It was more like the skilful de-layering of an onion achieved through the use of a technical sharp scalpel. Reflecting on my responses to the questionnaire has reinforced to me more than ever that Jeremy has always understood more about my sexuality than I have myself. I allowed him to push my boundaries because, deep down, I wanted him to, I loved him pushing them — and it just so happened he knew exactly which ones to push.

I feel my anger toward him, which built up when I was at the chateau, dissipating and I begin to acknowledge that I need to at least give him the time to explain himself and his actions. I must listen to what he has to say before I judge him too harshly. I was emotionally distraught, needing someone to blame for my abduction and he was my target. Mind you, he certainly has some explaining to do and I'm not letting him off the hook too easily. But why hasn't he come to rescue me ... and, more significantly, do I want him to save me just yet?

Dr Kinsey caused a storm in the US, and many other parts of the world, in the late 1940s and early 50s with his studies on the sexual behaviour of males and females. It's incredible how such a significant part of our day-to-day lives can create such societal divides. Has anything much changed since then? It's as if I have been transported into a high-tech, futuristic Kinsey Institute.

I have to admit, I'm strangely excited that I'm taking part in all of this. It's hard to believe I have landed in this innovative place and have the opportunity (am I really using that word to describe this?) to fully explore my sexuality — on my own terms — in this unique clinical environment. Without the influence of Jeremy and his alluring nature always resulting in me conceding complete power.

Due to the questionnaire, I have discovered that three factors trigger a high state of arousal in me:

intelligence (which he oozes), playfulness (he's the ultimate mastermind) and when I feel overpowered by someone I trust (all the time with Jeremy). And that's without mentioning how incredibly sexy I find him. What hope did I have? He has had decades to perfect his sexual craft with a partner like me. Our recent weekend away together offered me the ultimate combination of each of these factors. Unbelievable! I can't control the excited butterflies in my stomach as I acknowledge this reality, even though my mind reminds me that I still need to remain a little pissed off with him for keeping me in the dark about his results. Maybe Madame Jurilique was more insightful than I gave her credit for. Maybe I just might enjoy myself during my time here if I give myself permission to do so. I can't help but wonder what comes next …

\* \* \*

Now that Xsade knows almost as much, if not more, about my sexual history and behaviour as I do, I'm escorted by the charming and polite Françoise into another rather innocuous-looking room.

'Dr Blake, we would now like to show you a short documentary to provide you with information on how we developed our purple pill for women. It will also help explain the experiments we would like you to undertake. Please make yourself comfortable; it will begin in a moment.'

'Okay then. Thanks.' My manners automatically

kick in within this strangely professional environment as I settle into what looks to be a small, private viewing cinema. Seconds later, the lights dim and an explanation of the corporatisation of female sexual health and arousal begins. The film, interestingly, focuses on many of the preliminary drivers for orgasms and even mentions the issues around scientifically verifying female ejaculation.

Sam's team of elite researchers were discussing this very thing when I met them all for lunch before my lecture in Sydney, which feels like an eternity ago. The film outlines the struggles scientists and doctors have experienced in attempting to both compartmentalise and standardise the female orgasm. It appears that Xsade has achieved greater success than many other organisations, having gathered together a number of female volunteers willing to undergo testing in Xsade-owned clinical environments. I am clearly in one of those testing clinics now. I remember my rather disturbing mental image of women wearing white hospital gowns all lined up with their legs spread open. I shift uncomfortably as I realise that perhaps I wasn't too far from the truth, but who would have imagined the outfits would be like the silver bullet I'm currently wearing?

In essence, the documentary highlights that Xsade prides itself on developing solutions to counteract Female Sexual (arousal) Disorder, with the main prize being Federal Drug Administration approval of the purple pill, because once it is approved in the US, many countries will consider the drug favourably, enabling the cascading effect of ultimate market domination.

Now this is interesting, as I have always been a firm believer that lack of desire in women is more psychologically grounded than physical, at least in the majority of cases. The substantial global success of Viagra — or, to give its proper name, sildenafil citrate — is due to its end result of increasing blood flow to genitals, providing a physical solution to a physical problem.

Xsade's solutions to promote sexual function in females includes a variety of products — topical creams and pills derived from a variety of sources, which include male hormones produced by the adrenal gland, natural extracts from tree bark that stimulate the nervous system, and testosterone supplements. How on earth do they come up with these things? In various combinations and by using sensory therapy, some women reported having orgasms up to seventy percent stronger than placebo. Honestly?

It is finally beginning to dawn on me that I have, in fact, been sent by Madame Jurilique to an orgasm factory. I can't help but smirk at the knowledge that a few of my close female friends — well, quite a few actually — would pay for an experience like this, rather than having to be paid. Are we so different from all those women in the 1900s who visited medical practitioners to cure their supposed 'hysteria'? Technology solved that female disease forever with the invention of the vibrator. And admittedly, we've been buzzing ever since! Now, it seems, we need a purple pill to solve our arousal disorders, a condition that Xsade ensures me is widespread in the female population.

I can't help but be intrigued from both a psychological and professional perspective. The fact that they abducted me demonstrates just how far at least one pharmaceutical company will go to ensure their future profits and market share, but now I feel strangely committed to testing personally what they have come up so I can judge for myself.

Françoise returns to collect me as the documentary finishes and she informs me that I'm now going to meet the physician who will conduct my sensory testing. Given my background and expertise, how could I ever say no to that? We depart the private cinema and I am led into a room that looks like an expensive doctor's office.

'Dr Blake, my name is Dr Edwina Muir. It is indeed a pleasure to meet you. Welcome to our clinical research facility.' She too has her hair pulled back, no make-up, and doesn't appear threatening in any way. I'm not sure what I was expecting.

'Hello.' I shake hands with my gloved fingers, unable to decide whether I feel more excited or nervous as to what could happen next.

'I trust you are comfortable?'

'As comfortable as possible under these circumstances, I suppose.' I'm scientifically in awe of this place, but remind myself that it's not like I'm here of my own volition. Although I do I notice at this point that I'm not hungry, not thirsty, don't need to use the toilet, so my basic physiological needs as listed in Maslow's hierarchy have been met ... and I'm suffused with an odd sense of wellbeing.

'Great. If you'd both like to follow me, we shall get started in the room next door.' She opens a heavy door and I follow her tentatively. The room has a large piece of equipment in the centre. It looks like an exceptionally hi-tech machine, like a cross between something you'd find at the optometrist's for eye testing and a dentist's chair. It is a little daunting. The thought of happy gas seems rather appropriate right now.

'We will conduct the majority of our sensory testing from this equipment. As Françoise will have explained, we aim to establish a baseline for your preferences before progressing to other stimuli. Do you have any questions at this stage, Dr Blake?'

Questions? They all seem frozen in my brain.

'No, not right now.' Very unusual for me.

'Okay then, if you could please make yourself comfortable on the chair.'

I move over and carefully slide myself onto the 'dentist's' chair, which is surprisingly comfortable and supports my legs, head and back.

'Let me explain the suit you are wearing in a little more detail. This fabric has been designed to monitor your temperature, the pulse points throughout your body and record any increase in blood flow, particularly in the region of your genitalia.'

She seems to be getting down to business. If they

have already started recording I'm sure they can see my pulse rate starting to climb — rapidly.

Dr Muir continues. 'It also enables us to monitor the sensory and neural pathways in your brain. This will not cause you any discomfort.'

Well, that's a relief, even though I continue to feel my anxiety levels rising.

'Given the high sensitivity of the equipment we use, your movements will be restricted to ensure the integrity of the results. Having said that, our aim is to maximise your comfort during the entire duration of the experiment.'

It is right about now that I mentally note how my life has taken such a drastic turn so quickly and I'm gearing up for being on the opposite side of an experiment — again. Something to be debated with myself at a later date.

Suddenly I have a question, thankfully.

'Will anyone else be in the room during this process?' Memories and feelings of the experiment Jeremy conducted flood my mind, as I could never visualise who was in the room, and if I'm honest, would prefer not to know.

'Only Françoise to assist and myself. Does that cause you any problems?'

'No, that's fine.' For some reason knowing that there will only be the two women in here with me is reassuring, given the male orientation of last time. It helps put me in a more clinical rather than sexual mindset.

'Are you ready to begin, Dr Blake?' And they always address me using my professional title.

Ready? I have no idea. 'As ready as I'll ever be. I doubt it will get any easier ... Wait, I do have one more question.'

'Yes, of course.'

'Have either of you undergone this testing?'

The two women exchange a quick glance. 'Yes, we both have,' Dr Muir answers, with a smile. 'Anyone in our facilities who conducts testing such as this, is also able to participate in our experimentation process. In this particular instance, we have all happily volunteered.'

'Oh, right.' Well, that makes me feel slightly less concerned.

'Anything else?'

'No, that's it for now, I think.'

'Then we shall proceed. Please, just relax.' Sure, that's what you always say and I can assure you it is easier said than done. I take a deep breath and wriggle and adjust myself in the chair. I'm grateful I'm covered from head to toe, literally. It can't be too bad, can it?

When I'm in position, the chair reclines back halfway, my bottom sinks slightly lower than my legs and my knees are supported slightly higher. It's comfortable and I settle in.

'Please move your arms and legs a little wider, Dr Blake, so they are not touching the rest of your body.'

I spread my legs and arms.

'Thank you.' So polite. I then feel the odd sensation of being pulled deeper into the chair almost magnetically. The force is strong enough that when I attempt to raise my limbs they don't lift at all. My head is trapped in the same way and I'm left primed to experience whatever they have to offer.

'Is everything okay for you, Dr Blake?' Dr Muir asks.

'I suppose so.' I'm apprehensive but not enough to prevent the procedure from continuing.

'We will commence the experiment for the baseline in one minute and will not talk to you until it is complete. It should take approximately thirty minutes and will incorporate stimuli involving vision, smell and sound. All you need to do is remain calm, still, and keep your eyes open.' I hear a door close behind me and assume I'm now alone. Right, calm — difficult but not impossible. Still — can't move so that is sorted. Eyes are open — this is very different from Jeremy's version, interesting. A computer-generated voice in the room counts down from ten. I can't help but try to lift my head and wiggle my fingers and toes but they are all firmly trapped by the suit I'm wearing and whatever is binding it to the chair. *Five — four* — please let me be doing the right thing — *two* — too late now — *one* — here we go!

At take-off, part of the complex machinery moves directly toward my face and I can't shift to avoid the potential collision. It settles softly against my face, the only exposed part of my body. It covers my eyes so I can only assume it will be responsible for establishing my visual sensory baseline.

I focus on trying to control my breathing when suddenly my brain is ambushed with pictures and photos of beautiful and exotic locations of all kinds. Dreamy tropical beaches, majestic valleys and gorges, lush forests and waterfalls, they are beautiful and it calms me a little. It makes me feel excited about what else there is for me to experience and see in the world. It also triggers the realisation that there are absolutely no outside influences in this laboratory, no windows whatsoever.

I don't have time to dwell on that as the pace changes, as do the images. Now I am seeing people in various states of emotion, some laughing, some sad, some exuberant, some pained and grieving. Then it speeds up again and shifts to disturbing images of poverty and war. I'm reminded of the children we sponsor in third world countries, one for each member of our family, which leads me to thoughts of what Elizabeth and Jordan could be doing and how I feel a million miles away from them right now. But the progression of images forces me back to attention. They become more and more horrific, and instinctively I try to turn my head away to protect myself from seeing them, but it is anchored steady.

I close my eyes for a few seconds and open them to return to exactly the same scene of torture, as if the flow and speed of the pictures is sensitive to the position of my pupils. It makes me feel sick to the core that human beings can treat others that way. I feel myself shaking but I'm still firmly positioned in the chair.

Finally, the horror of war ebbs to be replaced by babies and happy couples walking along beaches. I immediately feel the tension ease from my muscles and sigh in relief. Another switch, to household chores — weird — and another to gay couples, and straight couples, then bondage — hundreds of images are flashing before my eyes in rapid succession. Some fascinating and arousing, some utterly repulsive to me.

More images flash of masturbation, cunnilingus, fellatio. As they evolve from sexual to more obscene, it dawns on me that they seem to centre around the seven deadly sins — wrath, greed, sloth, pride, lust, envy and gluttony — depicting both ancient and modern-day reflections of these characteristics. It makes me feel giddy.

Each picture flashes before my eyes for just as long at it takes for me to register what I'm seeing before the next image appears. I'm familiar with this association process from a psychological perspective, but their technology must be at a level of sophistication I never knew existed if it is monitoring my responses this quickly. Amazing.

Then, abruptly, my children are in front of me and I swear my heart stops beating and jumps uncomfortably into the back of my throat. My body immediately tries to wrench itself from the seat, an impossible task. It is the photo they sent me on the phone. Of course, they would have access to that, I haven't seen my phone for days. I feel like my heart is being ripped out of my body and is desperately trying to join them and those angelic faces before me. Tears stream down my face as violent sobs threaten to overwhelm me. Oh god, I need them, I miss them so badly. The photo fills me with such simultaneous love and pain that I feel like I've been beaten. I let out an anguished scream as the image disappears like a mirage.

Just when I think I can't take any more, that the emotions are too much, images of religious significance appear before me: Buddha, Christ, Mohammed, Mother Teresa, sacred symbols, ancient symbols, pyramids, Stonehenge, Easter Island … it's going so fast I find it difficult to believe my brain could assimilate any of it. Just as I begin to close my eyes to give my overstimulated brain some relief, I see a photo of myself in the red dress and blindfold from my weekend with Jeremy — I immediately freeze. All emotion, all breathing, all responses are on hold until I see what will come next.

The photo fades only to be replaced by a close-up of my bound wrists then it morphs into Jeremy straddled over me as I sit helpless beneath him. I can feel my cheeks flush with embarrassment as I wonder how they accessed such personal photos. And more concerning is that if Xsade has them, who else does? This could be my professional undoing.

The temperature seems to have increased and I can hear the type of classical music that makes special times with someone you love even more mesmerising and memorable. More photos from the weekend dance before my eyes, some I have never seen before. And to see Jeremy's face gazing at me so protectively threatens to undo me. That is when I notice a change in smell filter through my nostrils. Oh god, what are they doing to me? It is his smell, the musky, masculine freshness permeating the air around me. My nipples instantly react to this penetration of my senses and I feel myself swell with anticipation. The mere sight of his hands touching my body in the photo was difficult enough to absorb emotionally but all of this combined is sensory overload, it's just too much. Now, it's as if I can feel his fingers stroking my opening in time with the music, eliciting my pent-up juices from deep within me. His smell makes me feel as if he is right here.

I close my eyes and in that second I understand just how much I long for his touch again, and I silently cry out for him in my mind, imagining and hoping for the impossible. My hand automatically tries to respond to my swelling sex and aching breasts and I accidently release an audible whimper at the disappointment of being perfectly immobile.

Then it all stops. Music. Smells. Photos. Including my attachment to the chair. Everything comes to an abrupt end, as I though I've been released from a spell.

'Excellent, Dr Blake. I think we have everything we need for our baseline.'

Whoa, what? It takes me a minute to gather myself together.

'You may feel a little fatigued after this session. We often find that many of our clients do.' Dr Muir's cool voice brings me some way back to myself. 'So please take your time to relax when Françoise shows you to your room.'

I can't remember a time when I've been so categorically dismissed. The images caused such intense emotions, I honestly don't know how to respond. And that thought reminds me: 'Those last photos, how come you have them?'

'Your contract states that the results of our experimentation here will be given to you. That is all we are required to provide.'

Well, finally we have some steely undertone to the superficial politeness I've been experiencing since my arrival.

'Thank you, Dr Blake, I shall look forward to our next session.' I can't even imagine what that may entail, though I suspect this is merely the tip of the iceberg.

\* \* \*

Françoise escorts me back to a plush-looking room for some time to myself. I breathe a deep sigh of relief at being alone and attempt to take my suit off to go to the bathroom. After a few minutes of struggling and flipping around uselessly I decide it's impossible — and I'm grateful I'm alone because I've no doubt I looked ridiculous! It's only when I stop that I notice there is a conveniently covered flap that provides the access for me to urinate.

I lie in the middle of the firm bed and, as if on cue, I suddenly feel exhausted. Before I drift off, I feel the bracelet beneath my silver suit. Thank heavens it's still there. I have no idea whether they have tried to remove it, but I am so happy it is still securely around my wrist. Even though I can't see or touch it, I can feel it against my skin. Unable to keep my eyes open any longer, I fall immediately into a dreamless sleep.

* * *

I wake up however long later and stare at my silver silhouette in the mirror for quite some time. It's weird seeing one's face without any hair, and the curves of one's body without any infringing layers. Hot and cold face cloths have been provided in separate buckets and their alternate use instantly revives the skin on my face. It reminds me of the thermal waters I experienced with Jeremy.

A tap on the door startles me, and my friendly keeper, Françoise, lets herself into the room. 'I hope you enjoyed your rest, Dr Blake.'

I am immediately consumed by conspiracy theories: I've no doubt there are hidden cameras in the room and I wouldn't be surprised if my room was ventilated by some insidious sleeping gas — it's not as if they don't have access to these things, as I've learnt firsthand. But either way, I have woken up considerably calmer and less emotional than I was beforehand.

'If you would please come with me to your next session.' Obviously there is no time to be wasted — she waits by the door for me to exit with her immediately.

Her politeness feels even more odd given I have disclosed so much of my sexual history and desires to her earlier.

Once again we meet up with the now familiar Dr Muir. 'Dr Blake, welcome back, please make yourself comfortable.' She indicates a chair similar to the one I was in before, but without the hefty visual equipment overhead. This looks a little less complicated, at first glance anyhow. I sit down.

'This is another of our sensory laboratories, specifically designed around touch. It is at this time that we shall analyse the liquid exuded from your orgasm.'

Dr Muir seems confident that I will, in fact, orgasm and I'm interested as to whether I can in an environment like this. I could assure them I am nowhere near 'in the mood', but I decide that's my business not theirs. I just want to get this part over and done with as efficiently as possible. She adjusts a few bits and pieces before turning to me directly.

'Do you have any questions?'

'Just one. How many other women have you tested with this procedure.'

'Two thousand, three hundred and fifty-eight. Globally, of course.'

'Oh, right.' Well, that is substantially higher than I was expecting. I feel like an orgasmic lab rat!

'Anything else, doctor?'

'No.' I can't bring myself to reciprocate their polite formality.

'Good. Let's proceed. I'll be next door.' She immediately leaves the room.

Once again I feel the chair magnetically capture me from beneath and I'm stuck in position. That is, until the chair spontaneously separates and my legs are spread wide apart — I'm as far apart as in a traditional birthing suite with stirrups. It's not the most dignified position. Françoise, who is standing nearby, delicately comes into my view to slide a kidney-shaped tray between my chin and my breasts rendering it impossible to see what is happening below. Such privacy. I feel her open the convenient flap between my thighs and the coolness of the air surrounds my sensitive slit. Instinctively, I try to close my legs but obviously to no avail. It's like I'm being prepared for a pap test and I decide that is the mindset I must adopt. People have vaginal examinations all the time, I'm sure this will be fine. She then does a similar thing to each of my breasts; I hadn't noticed seams there in the suit. This essentially leaves me completely covered, except for my genitalia and breasts. I'm not sure whether this specially-designed attire makes me feel any more or less exposed.

The silence in the room is deafening, so the slight vibration of the wand in Françoise's hand sounds like it ricochets around the room. I cast my eyes upward to the lights in the ceiling, which makes the room feel even more clinical, and await my fate. I've never experienced a woman do this to me, but then again I've never been in an environment like this before either, never say never! There is absolutely no other stimulus to put me in the mood, so to speak.

The vibrations begin around my breast slowly and methodically, carefully avoiding my areola. First my right breast, then my left. My breathing stabilises and I feel myself relax a little. It actually feels very pleasant. At the end of the massage the tip barely touches the tip of my nipple, which immediately sends a shiver through me, and she repeats the entire process. I could get used to this ... And then it stops. Damn.

Next thing I know the vibrations are teasing my vulva, slowly and softly. My breathing calms and I adjust to the sensation. Eventually, I feel the wand slip in and out of the entrance to my vagina, not too far, just enough for me to sense the change in pulse and pressure. I tense a little as I adjust to the tempo. It slides lengthways along the edge of my vulva and I'm wide enough for my clitoris to respond to such pleasantries. As I get used to this lovely sensation, I can't help but wonder whether I will actually be able to achieve an orgasm in such an environment. I've no doubt I'm relaxing into it, but these are purely physical factors for me — all science and no psychology.

The pressure then increases substantially along with the vibrations and I groan at the intensity now penetrating and sliding along my sex. She has certainly upped the ante now.

It feels good and my nipples harden as another instrument focuses on my clit more specifically. Okay, this is becoming rather full on — my breaths shorten. As

I'm trying to maintain focus, still staring at the ceiling, my breasts are fully covered with warm silicon cups that suction on to them, massaging them consistently and methodically. However, every so often something tweaks and twists my nipples and the direct stimulus is so intense, I can't resist a yelp escaping in the silence of the room every time it occurs. The only other noises are the discreet vibrations of the instruments Françoise is using on my body, which now feel as though they have significantly multiplied in number. I'm not sure where or how to focus in this strange room of sexual machinery.

Reluctantly, I acknowledge that I'm becoming unavoidably more vocal as the intensity continues to increase, as does the biting sensation sporadically targeting my nipples. My back would be arched off the seat if I could move. My body can't do anything but absorb the sensations bombarding it. And it is intense. So, very, intense. I'm secretly pleased I had the enema and wonder if that has had an impact on my reaction so far.

The heat in my erogenous zones must be going off the scale as Dr Muir continues to monitor my situation from the anteroom. I desperately attempt to isolate in my mind the sensations my body is receiving, to distract and prolong what I now understand will be inevitable. I'd hate to be considered easy! There is a gratifying penetration deep within my vagina, not unlike the purple egg Jeremy bought me all those years ago. Oh jeez, I can't think of him or I'll come undone in seconds. Then my breasts are being continually massaged, slowly and methodically, until the random bite — this is becoming more extreme and shocking as we continue but I must admit, it's working a treat and sending my clit into overdrive. I'm losing focus. My breathing is both rapid and irregular with my G-spot being stimulated so absolutely, so perfectly. It makes my vibrator at home seem like a cheap, dodgy imitation. How will I ever be able to return to something so obviously inferior after experiencing this? Not to mention the simultaneous stimulation of my clitoris and, oh, dear lord … the nothingness is so close, so near … my body is unable to do anything but accept what's being done to it and I can't take it any more …

I hear myself sigh, then groan, as I so desperately try to hold back from moaning into the clinical silence until I finally relent, accept and welcome sensation to come and claim my body and … release! Oh, it feels so good as I exhale and tremble and pump around the instruments that enable my body to achieve such physical pleasure. As I can't move any other part of my body all I can feel is the continual distinctive spasms of my sex muscles. I close my eyes and allow the room to recede until I'm in a more composed state.

All the instruments are removed from my body with such efficiency I can't help but gasp at the cold draft they leave behind, then the silver suit flaps are returned to their more modest positions. In my peripheral vision I can see Françoise carefully labelling things before she carries them to Dr Muir. They both return, the visual barrier is removed and I'm 'magnetically' released from the chair. Dr Muir offers me a glass of water with hydrolytes dissolving in it.

'Well done, Dr Blake,' she says. 'That wasn't too bad for you, was it?' There's a knowing smile at the corner of her lips, experience perhaps suggesting that she has never had too many complaints to date.

'Survivable,' I allow.

I'm a little embarrassed about my noises having echoed around the room, although I reluctantly admit to myself that I doubt I'd say no if, for some reason, they needed me to do it again. What is happening to me? It's really hard to say no to a sensational orgasm, particularly when it releases hormones and tension and puts you in a fabulous mood. That makes it good for everyone, doesn't it? Perhaps they are really on to something with their purple pill, after all. If not, I'm sure they could always successfully diversify into high tech sex toys. I've no doubt that market would be recession-proof.

'If you would be so kind as to provide us with a pinprick of your blood now.' I'd forgotten about the blood.

'Sure.' The glove covering my hand is removed and my index finger subjected to a brief sting before a drop of blood is saved in a Petri dish. Much better than another needle.

'That concludes our baseline testing, Dr Blake.'

'Will the rest of the testing continue in this way?' I ask.

'No, not as such. The next two sessions will measure your sexual arousal based on various configurations of factors derived from the information you provided to Françoise during your questionnaire, on the visual baseline experiment we conducted earlier and, of course, on the results from your recent orgasm.'

'And this suit enables you to continue to monitor these variables?'

'That's right, doctor. The development of these suits has been instrumental in ensuring the accuracy and consistency of our results.'

'Do you mind if I ask you a few more questions?' My usual curiosity seems to be asserting itself.

'Not at all.'

'How many people are you testing in this facility at any given time?'

'Females?'

'There are others?'

'Yes, men and children are used for testing other drugs we are developing. This department can accommodate up to fifty women at any given time. We currently have twenty with us and anticipate the arrival of another thirty by the end of the week.'

'Really? Where do they come from?' I had no idea this place was so extensive. I imagined people being recruited from the streets for orgasm testing, lining up as if at a lemonade stand.

'They are paid volunteers, Dr Blake. We pay them well for their time and commitment to our laboratory.

Unemployment is high in Eastern Europe, as is the number of refugees looking to live further west.'

'Oh, I see.' It sounds like she honestly believes she works for a benevolent society.

'And this is all focussed on your purple pill?'

'No. We are in the business of developing drugs, Dr Blake, that's what we do. Our purple pill is but one product line. If you'll please excuse me, I do need to continue testing in another room now and you should get some rest in preparation for your next session. Françoise will show you back to your room.'

Clearly, I'm being dismissed again and I try to quell an unsettling feeling about this whole set-up. It looks perfectly above board, even sounds perfectly above board in the context of Dr Muir's discussions, but I can't shake off the sense there are sinister secrets lurking beneath the polite, professional and clinical interior.

My thoughts are distracted by Françoise's ever-friendly presence waiting by the door to escort me back to my room. Heaven knows what could happen next. Dr Muir's convoluted, yet vague answer told me nothing. I'm not actually scared but the slightly discordant nature of this facility is putting me increasingly on alert. And here I am, venturing into the unknown … at least with sight and knowledge this time around. I would have thought I'd be used to it by now!

* * *

Once again, I'm returned safely to my room, I notice the post-orgasm glow of my sliver-framed face in the mirror. I wonder if people who don't know me could tell? I've no doubt Jeremy would notice the second he glanced at my still-flushed cheeks. I wonder what he would think about everything here? Strangely enough, I don't feel embarrassed about it. I'm sure he would be very eager to hear what I've been up to and I'd be eager to tell him …

I feel the strain in my heart at this thought and at his absence. Why hasn't he come for me yet? He promised. Are we so far hidden below the Earth's surface that my bracelet has become redundant, I wonder idly, feeling its presence beneath my shiny sleeve.

Francoise stands in the doorway and smiles toward me. 'Do you have any questions or requirements before I leave you in peace for a while, Dr Blake?'

Of course I do. 'Will I be alone in the next session, like before?'

'No, this will be a group session, with other paid volunteers.' I can't help but ponder whether the other paid volunteers were abducted from Heathrow and visions of the movie *Taken* start floating around in my head. That film is about two girls who are abducted into the European sex slave trade. Jeez, where did that come from? I think of Elizabeth and can't imagine the horror I'd feel if that happened to her … It would be a living hell for a mother, or father for that matter. I wonder if Robert and the kids even know what's happened to me. God, I hope not. Hopefully, it will be over soon enough — they'll be none the wiser and we'll be back to a normal life, that's my ideal ending anyhow ...

'Anything else, doctor?' Her question disrupts my disturbing thoughts.

'Oh, no, Françoise, that should be fine, thanks.'

'She closes the door behind her.

I turn my attention to the brochures that have been left on a bench outlining other products Xsade is currently testing. As I flick through the information sheets, I am a little astounded to discover that some of these products already exist in the marketplace. Creams for dryness, increasing blood flow, improving the strength of the female orgasm. Depending on the volume or potency, you may require a prescription but I've no doubt they are readily available over the counter in most less regulated countries. I think of my friend who regularly travels to Thailand to acquire 'household pharmaceuticals' for a fraction of the cost in Australia.

Honestly, are we that desperate for additional stimulation that we are willing to put manufactured hormones and chemicals on our skin and our private parts? But is it really any different to what has happened for centuries with the Chinese desiring shark fin soup or deer penis for their sexual potency and aphrodisiac qualities? Should we be embracing the artificially manufactured products so that animals no longer need to suffer? I shake my head. I'm obviously not going to resolve any of these global issues now and I feel a little fatigued. Given there is not much else to distract me in the room, I lay down on the bed for a nap until the next experience begins.

* * *

Some time later, Françoise arrives to collect me and we head in the opposite direction this time, once again passing friendly, polite people who are seemingly happy to be in this bizarre facility. I no longer feel the least bit conspicuous in my slinky silver outfit and have become accustomed to my surroundings remarkably quickly considering the length of time I've been here.

This time we enter a large circular room and Françoise escorts me to a position against the wall. There are already another five silver-suited females in the room, like me being strategically positioned by their keepers, and another has entered just after me.

My body is pressed firmly against the wall, my legs and arms spread apart so no part of my body is touching another. Our keepers ensure everyone is positioned the same way — close to each other but never quite making a connection. They give each other a silent nod and depart the room at the same time as the magnetic connection between our suits and the rubbery wall fastens its grip on our bodies. It seems is if this is the position we'll be in for a while.

Our eyes automatically scan the other faces around the room to ascertain where we are at with this, how we are feeling. As we don't know each other at all, it's difficult to decipher. A few look anxious, one looks excited, very excited by the looks of it. Her nipples are protruding through her suit — jeez, and nothing has even happened yet. One looks bored and another one tired. But interestingly, no one speaks.

I'm not sure how my face looks to them but I feel rather bright-eyed and bushy-tailed, intrigued as to exactly what will unfold. I don't have to wait long before two naked people enter the room, one male and one female. There's an audible collective gasp between us, then silence as our eyes remain fixed on the centre of the room.

Soothing opera music that I can't place wafts through the speakers as the couple stands directly facing one another, completely ignoring our presence in the room. As soon as a delicate soprano voice joins the music they begin to kiss each other, slowly and cautiously at first. They touch each other's cheeks tenderly as they embrace, gently stroking and caressing. They look like they're in love.

Their seeming passion deepens when a tenor takes over and they explore each other's nakedness with a greater sense of desire and more deliberate use of their hands and tongues. It takes no time before his erection is pressed against her belly and her nipples harden against his taut chest.

We are close enough to sense the changes in their physiology as the level of sexual intensity increases along with the drama of the voices and music. I feel as though I'm privy to an illicit viewing of an intimate erotic opera. I can't help but glance around the room.

The silver woman opposite is mirroring the breathing of the lovers she's witnessing and it's almost as if she'd love to morph into the scene with them. Fascinating. The one next to her is rolling her eyes and yet another seems totally distracted, her face reddened as if she's struggling to move her hand, which she can't, desperately straining to wriggle her body away from the wall. Another has her eyes closed and looks rather lost in the music.

My attention returns to the lovers before me as two more naked bodies enter the room. Good grief. The music stills as if something major is going to happen and the lovers look as though they have been caught a little off guard — until they welcome the new arrivals into their embrace. The tempo quickens and suddenly the limbs of two male and two female bodies intertwine — caressing and stroking and kissing each other as though they are fused as one.

I've seen women naked before, but not like this, not charged with sexuality like the women in front of me. And I've certainly never looked directly at naked women, noticing every twitch, every rise and fall of their breasts, every quiver of their nipples.

The music is loud and I'm sure the oxygen in the room is being replaced with pheromones. The scene unravelling before our eyes is impossible to ignore. The four bodies glisten with sweat and lust as the exploration of each other's bodies deepens and intensifies and I can hear their cries over the music.

The air becomes heavy. I've never been this close to other people having sex before — it's as if I'm watching something private, forbidden, and yet for some reason, it doesn't seem wrong. I have never been into pornography but I imagine the presence of technology or a screen might perhaps provide some kind of filter. This is raw, real and we are witnessing it with absolutely no barriers. I can literally feel the lust vibrating within the confines of the circular room, there's nowhere for it to escape.

One woman is moaning and sighing as if it is becoming too much for her to bear. She seems desperate for touch but she is trapped, immobile as we all are, left with no choice but to absorb the sexually-charged atmosphere. I feel the knowing fire in my lower belly and my own body's arousal in the face of such abundant desire. Every set of nipples around the room is on high alert; even the woman with her eyes closed isn't spared, confirming there's more than visual stimulation causing our reaction.

The music changes again. It becomes darker, edgier, and the slippery bodies disentangle from their self-created sexual nest.

Soft black ropes are released from the ceiling. The newcomers seductively separate the original lovers and deftly weave the fabric around their arms, binding their wrists together. Arms now pinioned high above their heads, their bodies are unable to touch but their eyes remain locked. The room electrifies. The music meanders as the newcomers take a moment to acknowledge and appreciate their captives, lightly stroking their skin as if contemplating what pleasures will next take their fancy. I'm a little embarrassed that my loins and breasts are throbbing with anticipation as to what might happen, but I'm mesmerised by the scene, barely aware of the other silver-suited women wrapped around the walls. The intensity of my feelings is inexplicably linked to the bound beings at the centre of the room.

They blindfold the man and his erection immediately becomes even more rigid, leaving the bound female to watch. There is no denying she is turned on by this and I can't deny that my arousal ramps up a notch as I feel my heart pounding faster. The male and female suck and tease him to the point of orgasm, which doesn't take long given the previous foreplay and his body trembles and shakes.

At the last second the blindfold is removed and we are left to watch the tormented face of the bound man just before he comes and he releases a euphoric groan as the woman on her knees swallows his seed in her mouth without spilling a drop, something I've never been able to do. She licks her lips as if she's received a potent elixir. One day, I concede, maybe I could try it, I've never seen it from this perspective and it's a powerful image …

The bound woman simultaneously throws herself back against her restraints as if she is feeling every sensation with him. They allow his limp body to recover turning their attention to the highly aroused female. She too is blinded and left to feel everything their touch incites.

I can't help but release my own whimpering moan as the memories come crashing back through my mind. Now, I'm watching as others once watched me. If I weren't pinned to the wall my legs would have given way at this sight. My body floods with warmth and emotion that's so intense, it's overwhelming.

I watch as they suckle her nipples and fingers, and tongues entice her opening, lightly biting her inner thighs on the way. I am throbbing below, my own sex pulsing to the music, perfectly attuned to the bound woman's body, to what's before me. I was fearful of what others may have seen of me during my experience but now I'm absolutely overawed by the apparent beauty of sexual acts between consenting adults. I had no idea watching could have such an undeniable impact. I've never seen another woman orgasm before. Not even myself in a mirror. I'm both captivated yet quietly appalled that I can't bring myself to turn away. I always considered it such a personal, private affair. Now, I want to see what Jeremy sees in my face, in my eyes when he takes my body to such extremes. I'm silently begging for them to remove her blindfold as they did with the man.

Her moans are becoming increasingly excitable as the woman stands behind her, opening her thighs for the man; his fingers continue their play, as do his teeth on her breasts and her groans crash and bounce around the circular room. His penis is hard and fully erect and I picture him penetrating her hard and deep right now. The vision of it in my mind is so real, it takes my breath away. I can no longer distinguish between what I'm seeing and what my body wants me to feel. His fingers disappear deep into her sex, the blindfold is removed and his thumb finally ignites her orgasm. I don't think I've focused on a face more in my life, as if I'm studying the mesmerising artwork of Da Vinci's *Mona Lisa*.

It is as though her life is suspended, breathless, still, as if some angelic force has frozen her body and mind with pleasure. The music softens, my own breathing pauses along with everyone else's in the room, and I feel as though I'm flying with her, somehow connecting to her, until finally her breath is expelled with an intense cry, as her gratified body jolts and spasms back to life, to this reality. The music resumes with a bursting crescendo at her climax and dies off as the juice of her orgasm literally flows down her leg. Her eyes remain unfocused on the room, her body hanging limply around her.

It's only then I hear another pleasured moan and turn to see another orgasmed face the other side of the room. Absolutely extraordinary. Can that really occur? I only need to recognise my own dampness below and shortness of breath to confirm the answer to my question. I scan the room and see most sets of eyes are clouded with a lusty haze, no doubt mine included if my aching clitoris is any measure.

What an experience. I feel exhausted and have done nothing except stand against a wall. None of us touched or pleasured, just watching others — the results pumped out from these suits should be truly mind blowing for Xsade.

\* \* \*

Back in my room, I find my suitcase filled with my clothes but unfortunately still no handbag. Françoise informs me that I can relax in here for a while until my final session and that I'll no longer be required to wear the silver suit. Happy days. She helps me out of it via some tricky fastening that was out of my reach and, although it was comfortable, I'm relieved to be free. It's quite surreal being unable to touch the skin on your own body.

She hands me a robe to cover my naked body and carefully folds the suit into a special container. I'd love to see their testing laboratory, but what I want now is a bath and sleep. I feel shattered. I can only imagine how the four performers in the room feel … or maybe they're used to it?

I've been relaxing and dozing for a while when a disembodied voice interrupts and tells me to be ready with my bag packed for my final session in ten minutes. Almost there … I'm assuming my 72 hours must almost be up. I wouldn't know, I've lost all concept of time since arriving here. I close my bag and attempt to wait patiently on the edge of the bed for Françoise's last knock on the door. I have to admit I'm a little anxious about this last session and what may occur. I harden my resolve. I've come this far and survived unscathed. How bad could it be?

I am led to a new room, which is favourably lit with the sort of lighting that makes skin look soft and sensual, as if you're shrouded in romantic candlelight —

no doubt it is only clever artificial illusion but needless to say I'm grateful.

It is sparsely furnished except for a huge black beanbag. It looks strangely inviting. I bend down to run my fingers along its length to feel the soft velvety material.

The room is decorated with elaborately draped pale purple, almost lavender, silk scarves that flow like a meandering stream around the blackened walls of the room. The effect is simple, stylish and clever. The fabric is silky soft and superfine; I can barely feel it as I slide it smoothly between my finger and thumb.

In the corner of the room I spy a small table with a glass of water and the infamous purple pill nestled at its side. In the other corner, much to my surprise, is a bottle of vintage Dom Pérignon chilling in a silver ice bucket surrounded by three crystal champagne flutes. It appears I'll be having company.

I'm not sure whether I should open it or wait. I've been told that nothing will occur in this room until I have taken the purple pill. If I decide not to take it, I shall be escorted back to my room before a final 'exit interview' and then my contractual commitments are complete, except for the final pinprick of my blood. Then I'm free. I can't believe how elated that makes me feel. Ecstatic, even.

I reflect on the fact that after my initial concerns, I've been treated really well. My time here has been nothing short of fascinating and — if I'm being really honest — even tantalising. I've learnt so much about myself, sexuality, female libido, and the desire of drug companies to cure female sexual disorders — and, of course, make stacks of money. It's impossible to ignore the capitalist reality of such products.

However, the idea of being so close to speaking to my children and seeing Jeremy again — wherever he is — suddenly puts me in a pre-emptive celebratory mood. So without further ado, I walk over to the 'almost approved' purple pill and promptly swallow it so I don't change my mind with my usual vacillating self-talk. Done.

Making that decision has given me added confidence and ease, or perhaps I'm more comfortable wearing my own black and white dress and sensible black slip-on shoes instead of being covered from head to toe in that strange silver suit. Whatever the reason, I decide to pop open the Dom.

Immediately, some slinky, sexy eastern music begins to echo around the room as I pour myself a glass and 'cheers' myself for making it this far through the 'ordeal' — which is what I'd presumed it was going to be. They have confirmed that I don't have female sexual arousal disorder, which is no surprise to me after the recent changes in my sex life. But I do wonder, if I had undergone similar analysis before Jeremy flamboyantly re-entered my life, would my results have been different? Would I have been the perfect recipient for this drug of theirs?

Apparently, this final session has been designed around a potentially unfulfilled fantasy of mine —

integrating elements of pleasure, desire and the unknown. I honestly can't even imagine what it could be — so, if I don't have the slightest inkling, how would they know what I want? I thought I'd pretty much done everything with Jeremy but then again, if I let my mind wander, I can think of a few things I wouldn't mind exploring when I see him again ...

I flush at my raunchy thoughts and take another sip of champagne to bring my mind back into the room. My last mission in the clinic of sexual experimentation. It should be enlightening, if nothing else. The good thing is, if I want it to stop, I only need to walk out of the room and that's it — all over. I still have a choice so I can't complain.

I take a few more delicious sips — it's been a while since I've had an alcoholic drink — and take a mental note that as yet, I don't feel any effect from the pill. At least, I think I don't.

The door opens and a stunning woman enters slowly. Her skin is dark and she is wearing sheer white harem-style pants that sit low on her wide hips with slits either side of her legs. A matching silky scarf is folded over her ample breasts and wrapped halter-neck style, leaving her shoulders bare — her obviously erect nipples not disguised in the least by the material that covers them. Her belly and back are flat and bare and their darkness is a stark contrast to the white flimsy material. Her hair is jet-black and wild, defying gravity in a rigid afro.

Ignoring me, she saunters seductively in time with the music over to the bottle of Dom and pours herself a glass, as I stand staring at her, mesmerised and barely breathing. Her arms are toned and muscular and move like liquid silk. Finally, she raises her eyes and her glass towards me in silent cheers, and takes a long sip with the most sensuous, plump lips I have ever seen in my life. I almost let out a sigh, I'm so overawed by her beauty.

Without uttering a word, she places her glass down to fill the third champagne flute. I feel like my body has been frozen in place even though I can't deny the warm glow of anticipation beginning in my belly and loins. Much to my shock I feel myself moisten with anticipation. Obviously it must be the pill having this effect on me, surely?

She stands confidently with a glass of Dom in each hand, her presence filling the silence of the room.

The door opens again and a Japanese woman with pale skin, unusually large doe-like eyes and a perfect, neat nose, bounces delicately across to join us. She is dressed in a black version of the same outfit, has a pierced belly button and a chain hanging over her hips linking through it. Her hair is also jet-black but impossibly shiny and plaited into a braid that slithers down her back and past her pert arse. Black on white and white on black, they look amazing together. She smiles at me and looks excited as she accepts the champagne.

They both take long silent sips, simultaneously licking their lips after they've tasted the delicious bubbles. My body releases me from its frozen spell and I subconsciously raise my glass to my lips as they do.

They both meet my eyes, mine the only ones infused with any anxiety as to what comes next. This continues until we complete our drinks.

Ms Africa (as I have mentally dubbed her) takes the glass from my hand and guides me into the centre of the room; the music's seductive tempo shifts audibly up a notch, as does my pulse.

This is my potential fantasy? Hell no, other women? Surely this can't be it. Although, I must admit they do look so soft and seductively beautiful in their outfits ... Oh dear lord ... Jeremy would give anything to witness this! I notice the security bulb unobtrusively positioned in the centre of the ceiling, most likely recording everything, and absently consider that if he had access, he probably could. Somewhat emboldened by this thought, I can't deny a thrill of anticipation as to what will happen next. I blame the pill!

The Japanese woman's fingernails slide slowly over my shoulder, along the edge of my dress. I inhale sharply as she slides over the material covering my breast and exhale as she continues her journey to the other side. Ms Africa stands behind me and unzips my dress, so it can be pushed off my shoulders. It falls to the floor in one fluid move. My shoes are removed one at time, deliberately, slowly, the music and touch our only forms of communication. I feel myself flush with excitement and nerves but there is no part of me that wants to stop this from progressing.

The sexual tension in the room steadily escalates and it's making me hot — everywhere. As my bra is removed my nipples are standing to attention, my blood is pounding to ensure their immediate pertness. As my bra drops away, my panties are sliding down my legs and I stand centred in the room, completely still yet mysteriously engaged, awaiting their next move, their next touch.

Simultaneously their breasts slide around my body as they circle me. I inhale sharply, for the first time in my life I experience the sensation of breast caressing breast, nipple against nipple through the silky fabric. It's intoxicating.

They move away, as if releasing me from a spell, and my clothes and shoes are bundled neatly under the table. With grandly elaborate movements they whisk the lavender scarves from the walls and swirl them around the room with such skill they could be ribbon dancers in gymnastics. Eventually the flimsy material lands lightly draped over my body. Their bodies twist, turn and spiral rhythmically to the music as exotic silk floats around my naked flesh, taunting and teasing until I feel desire thoroughly spread through all my erogenous zones. The scarves oscillate between barely caressing my nipples to sliding between my thighs with enough intensity to prompt my clitoris to swell and throb.

The music changes slightly, the bass lightens and the strains of a guitar flit through the air as I come to realise they are wrapping my entire body in the sheer silk. They begin at my feet and ankles, delicately wrapping one at a time, before continuing along each leg and towards my thighs, wrapping me around and around.

As they reach my apex, I gasp and they gracefully swap sides continuing their circular motion, maintaining all fluidity in perfect unison with the music around my body, covering my buttocks, my belly, my breasts, my chest. My arms become their focus as I'm wrapped from fingertip to underarm and up over my shoulders.

My body is pulsing with lust and desire, as I fantasise about being part of their secret harem. I've never been intimate with another woman and have never allowed my mind to wonder what it would be like, to touch and explore the female form … would I be brave enough now?

My breathing shallows again as they wrap the silkiness gently around my neck, cover my lips, my nose and my forehead before sealing me up with a knot around my high ponytail, the only requirement Françoise gave me for this session. Now I understand why. I feel my hot, short breaths move in and out against the silky layer covering my mouth, my arousal impossible to ignore.

My vision is now through a haze of purplish pink as my entire body is mummified in the fine, sensuous, fabric. Every sense is heightened and feels extreme as my arousal ratchets up the scale. My breasts and groin ache as both women take a step back to inspect their artistry. Experiencing such an exotic sexual ritual has left moisture pooling between my thighs. I feel so lightheaded I could faint with lust.

They each take one of my wrapped arms and guide me backwards towards the velvet beanbag. I am lowered softly on to my back, looking up towards their beautiful faces. Am I dreaming? Will I wake up in a sweat suddenly wondering if I have bisexual tendencies I never knew existed? Will I have changed my position on the Kinsey heterosexual–homosexual rating scale after this experience? Maybe I don't know myself at all ...

My meandering mind screeches back at the sensation of two mouths suckling on my breasts. Oh. My. God.

I gasp in shock, only to breathe in the fabric and exhale a groaning sound as their lips and tongues flicker and fondle, their hands massage and pinch and play with thigh, belly and arms — all through the silky sheath. Fingers softly edge around my lips and as I sigh in delight with the sensations, a tongue pushes through to my mouth but can't penetrate past the material, distracting me from the continually adjusting position of my body on the beanbag.

I'm rolled over and the sucking and biting continues on my back, my butt, under my arms, the soles of my feet ... It is as if they are bringing every nerve ending in my body to the surface. I could cry at their soft stroking of that especially sensitive spot near my tailbone and that's before they continue along my crack as my inner thighs are being simultaneously nibbled.

All of this sensation is made strangely more arousing by the additional layer shrouding my skin. There is no rushing, no force, just the perfect sensual tempo of their touch. After everything I have experienced today, I feel like I could come any second, should the friction increase ever so slightly.

I lose focus as my sensate body takes over, something I only ever believed Jeremy was capable of eliciting from deep within me ... The feelings are so exotic, so rhythmic and intense, it's as if the room itself is charged with our innate femininity. Our three bodies are entwined, forming an indescribable mix of black, purple and white.

I'm captured by the moment and can no longer stand my passive role in this scene. I need to play and fondle and feel them just as they are playing with me. My bound silken hand reaches out to touch a breast and I'm delighted as I feel the responsive nipple. My hand is considerately kissed and gently guided away before being I'm rolled over again on my back, this time my legs are raised higher than my upper body due to moulding of the bean bag.

Ms Japan positions herself between my legs and anchors my hands my hands firmly by my side. I see her cheeky, perfect smile and her eyes meet mine just before her face disappears between my thighs. Oh god, is this really happening? I throw my head back and my body jolts at the gentleness of her breath blowing past the silk in through my vulva. Is it meant to feel this incredible? The pill, it must be the pill, I counter, but my goodness they are very good at this. With such skill between them maybe any woman would have a hard time resisting their sensual ambush, regardless of their sexual preference?

Ms Africa is above me, upside down, holding my shoulders in position as her beautiful lips dedicate themselves to my breasts and I think I'm dying a blissful death as her bountiful bosoms brush against my face.

The women's rhythm is in perfect unison as they control my sensate ride in perfect synchronicity. Their tongues, their breath, their suckling, their biting has me on the cusp so many times over I can't even remember my own name. They use the sublime material to pull and tug and tighten so I am forced to feel even more pleasure than I ever believed possible.

The room starts spinning and my breath is short and fast. I feel like my speeding pulse is about to implode every sexual part of my body. I cry out in need of release, but they are experts — just as I'm on the edge, they disrupt the flow, change the tempo, create a pain of intense pleasure, a sensation that distracts me from my desperate destination. My body is so overwhelmed, I can do nothing but give myself over to them, conceding I have no control and they have it all. Their dominance over my body firmly established, bringing me so close to the orgasm my body is literally aching for, only for them to deny it, over and over again. The pleasure they're creating within me is delightfully tortuous. I can barely breathe it is so intoxicating and I'm losing all sense of self. And their skin has never touched mine — not once during this entire experience.

A fleeting notion interrupts to make me wonder if maybe that's the problem — perhaps that what's missing. Oh no, I'm forced to acknowledge this random thought has let my conscious mind back in which will now mean the torment will continue. Oh dear god. I can't take any more.

The twirling of tongues and suction through the silk continues on my nipples and clitoris, the tremendous pleasure turns to sexual pain as they bite and nip, ensuring I'm swollen, raw and desperately wanton.

I pant and scream yet again with the all-absorbing intensity until it suddenly stops ... I have no resistance left as my legs are bent at the knees, spread wide open, as far as they can stretch without causing damage and held firmly in position. The layer of silk covering my opening is carefully separated. And I feel a soft, gentle breath blow around my aching vulva and then it directly targets my swollen, hot clitoris and my god I come, and throb and explode and shake and come and shudder until my body bounces back from the ceiling. My mind finally left the room, once and for all.

I lose all sense of time and self as I lie sated next to these exotic women, my entire body still wrapped and covered bar one opening that is still hot, wet and pounding. Eventually, the silken fabric is carefully unravelled from head, limbs and torso, heightening my self-awareness until I'm given a robe to cover my naked form. The soft cotton rubs achingly against my raw nipples. I'm unable to deny the impact the women have left on my sensitive skin.

I can't quite fathom that I experienced an orgasm that acute without any penetration whatsoever — incredible. Although with the way I'm feeling in this delirious state, I'd give anything for Jeremy's thick hard cock driving hard and fast into me. Just the thought of it excites my loins and elicits an agonised groan from my throat.

I can't help but acknowledge that Xsade are definitely on to a winner with their purple pill.

I hear a rap on the door and Dr Josef lets himself into the room holding his little black bag and characteristic stethoscope around his neck. He quickly dismisses the women and it feels strange, after everything I have just experienced with them, not to say goodbye. We didn't speak one word the entire time, although *my* sounds — gasps, groans and screams — were certainly more than amplified. We give each other a small wave as they silently leave the room. I'm still lying on the black beanbag, flabbergasted at what I've just experienced and I tighten the tie around my robe, conscious that I'm naked underneath.

Josef comes up to me and opens his bag. Back to this again, I think vaguely, as he suddenly whispers very close to my ear: 'Don't say anything. I need to get you out of here, tonight.'

Just as I'm about respond with a 'What ...?' he grabs my finger and firmly pricks the skin of my middle finger to distract me. Ouch! Well, that has certainly disrupted my recent euphoria. Angrily, I look into his eyes and notice a sense of urgency in them.

'We can't be here for too long, they will think something is amiss.' He wipes my blood on to a slide, covers it up and assists me to my feet.

'Are these your clothes?'

'Yes.'

'Good. Quickly, get dressed, you need to come with me.'

'I can get dressed back in my room. I need a shower —'

'Dr Blake, you are in imminent danger. You have one chance to get out of here as per the terms of your contract and one chance only — that is with me.'

He grabs my elbow and moves me to the corner of the room where my clothes are bundled and, much to my mortification, attempts to dress me.

'Okay, okay, here, give them to me.' I snatch my bra and undies from his hand and quickly put them on. 'What is going on?'

'Please, keep your voice down and keep your actions normal. Everything is monitored in here.' I thought as much.

'Alright, but tell me what's going on.' I pull my dress over my head.

'Your blood results have presented certain interesting outliers and they are preparing to take up to a litre of your blood as you sleep tonight, before they release you.'

'What? But they can't, we agreed, the contract stipulated —'

'I know, and that is why I'm here to help you escape. If nothing else, Dr Blake, I am a man of my word. The research doctors plan to ignore what was agreed between you and Madame Jurilique. I have no idea whether she organised it or not, but I cannot take the risk. I need you to follow my every instruction to ensure our safe departure from this facility.'

'But how do I know I can trust you?' I grab the lapels of his white lab coat and pull him near. He looks good up close and I inhale his scent deeply. Jeez, this pill must still be playing havoc with my hormones. I instantly release him and flush with embarrassment.

'I'm sorry, I ...'

Thankfully, he ignores my previous action.

'Only you can decide that, Dr Blake, but whatever decision you make must be made in the next five seconds.'

I'm shocked by his words, but also distracted as the door begins to open and he punches me in the stomach, causing me to double over in pain just as Dr Muir and Françoise enter the room. What the hell was that for? I think, but can't say as I'm still gasping from his surprise attack.

'Dr Votrubec, I'm surprised to see you still in here,' says Dr Muir. 'Do you have your sample?' I quickly glance between Josef and the women from my bent position, my arms still wrapped around my stomach, and I notice an almost undetectable nod of his head toward me.

'Dr Blake is experiencing hot flushes, causing abnormally high peaks in her temperature and heart rate since the end of this session. That is why I was called here as she is ultimately my responsibility. She also just mentioned feeling waves of nausea, as if she could vomit. I will be taking her to the clinic where she will remain under my observation until these after-effects subside.'

'I'm sorry to hear this, Dr Blake. Are you feeling these symptoms now?' I sense a hint of scepticism in her voice as she turns from Josef to myself.

I quickly glance at each of them before deciding on Josef. I attempt to respond to her question, but instead start heaving and dry retching, further folding my body over as if in pain.

'Oh my goodness, I see. Of course, she will definitely need to be given something for that. How unfortunate.'

Dr Josef gathers me in and puts his arm around me, bundling me effectively out of the room.

'I'll return Dr Blake to her room when the symptoms ease, Edwina.'

'Oh yes, good.' She shakes her head, looking perplexed, as we pass by. She turns to Françoise near the doorway. 'This nausea still seems to be occurring sporadically in our clinical tests. We really need to get to the bottom of it before—'

I don't hear any more as Josef steers me down the corridor, turns the corner, then down another long corridor. I have no idea what the time is, but there is no sign of the usual bustle of white lab coats and silver-clothed 'experimentees' wandering around. Josef moves at a silent, deliberate pace with his arm still firmly gripping my shoulder, steering me through the labyrinth of the laboratory. Suddenly, quick as a flash, he whisks me through a door and we disappear into the fire escape. 'Follow me,' he whispers, 'we need to be quiet and quick.'

Not really understanding why, but responding to his tension, I do as he says and we descend two flights of stairs before exiting the fire escape. I scuttle behind him as we walk at a rapid pace along yet another corridor. To my left is a solid concrete wall and to my right is a long glass window. It is heavily tinted and as I take a closer look I can see what appears to be hundreds of faces, being herded along in lines. Some look fatigued, some bored — there are both men and woman — and then I notice there are children with haunted eyes.

I instantly come to a stop, staring in disbelief at what I'm seeing. Dr Josef is ahead of me, but senses my absence behind him. He retraces his steps and grabs my elbow.

'Please, Dr Blake, we have no time to waste.' He tries to pull me along while I continue to stare.

'What is this?' I push my face closer to the thick, tinted glass to see more clearly. 'Who *are* these people?'

'I have no time to explain, please hurry, we cannot be seen here.'

'Can they see us?'

'No, I will explain everything when we are safe. Please come quickly. We are both in grave danger.' He implores me to action, and I move, but not before I take one last lingering look at the people on the other side of the glass, who look like they have been shuffled from one existence to another, some with suitcases, some with only the clothes on their backs. I shudder as I suddenly think of the Jewish people being rounded up in World War II and vehemently shake my head to dislodge the disturbing image. It wouldn't be anything like that, surely? His grip drags me forcefully away and we reach a crossroads. He fumbles with some keys, eventually finding the right one, swipes it across a security pad which opens and he enters a code. The door opens and we are confronted with a stairwell spiralling upwards. He guides me through, re-enters a code on the other side, waits for the door to close securely behind us, and we begin our ascent. We climb and climb, round and round. My legs haven't had this sort of workout since a horrifying step class at the gym maybe three years ago.

'Josef, how much further?' I pant as quietly as possible. For the first time my stomach painfully realises that it hasn't been fed much for a while. I feel rather dizzy and fatigued.

'We have a little way to go,' he says kindly. 'Here.' He extends his hand toward mine and I grasp it to help me move forward. Up and up and round and round we go. How long can this continue? I feel like we could be at the top of a skyscraper. Finally, we reach the end and I collapse on the edge of the last step, puffing and out of breath. Again, he finds the right key and the door opens.

A rush of fresh air reminds me how long it's been since I've breathed in the outdoors. My lungs rejoice but the temperature sends a chill over my sparsely-covered body. I step outside. Oh not again, I can't help but think — where am I this time?

# Part Seven

Life is a series of natural and spontaneous
    changes.
Don't resist them; that only creates sorrow.
Let reality be reality.
Let things flow naturally forward in whatever
    way they like.

— Lao Tzu

# Alexa

It's almost dark but I can see that we are surrounded by water and I can thankfully just make out some land not too far away.

'Do we have to swim?' I really don't think I have the energy for that. What a bizarre couple of hours, well, days really ... actually, could be close to a week, for all I know. Oh, just shut up and stop thinking, I admonish myself.

Josef is busy at some sort of pylon, untying a small boat. Thank goodness.

'Here, jump in and put this on.' He hands me his white coat and I can't help but think he might hand over his stethoscope to complete my look. I'm obviously delirious.

Quietly grateful there isn't a second pair of oars as he conscientiously rows the boat, I take a moment to look around and see a picturesque lighthouse behind us, where we apparently just appeared from the depths of the laboratory. Recognition suddenly dawns on me.

'Oh, my god! We are at Lake Bled?' I ask, completely astounded.

'Yes, have you been here before?'

'I cycled around here years ago,' I say. Along with every other tourist who comes to Slovenia. 'Xsade's laboratory is beneath all this?'

'Yes, but it is not a laboratory that is publicly acknowledged. It provides a useful gateway between Eastern and Western Europe. Not many people know about its existence, very few are aware of this emergency access through the boathouse.'

Unbelievable! One of the most beautiful fairytale locations in Slovenia, if not all of Europe. I absently wonder how my own fairytale might end and whether I'll ever truly escape from Madame Jurilique's wide net of influence. At least it feels like I'm making progress thanks to Josef. I can just make out the shadowy outline of the Julian Alps in the background. If my memory serves me correctly, before the church was built on it, legend has it that Bled Island was home to the temple for Ziva, the Slavic goddess of love and fertility. I'm in shock, could my life get any weirder? I shake my head and vow to never ask that question again, and decide to wait until we get wherever we're going until I ask any more. This is really just too much. I think Josef appreciates my silence as he continues rowing.

* * *

After tying up the boat, we eventually end up at his uncle's house, a short walk through the village. We are greeted with such enthusiasm it is clear that Josef's uncle is very proud of him. He raises his eyebrows at Josef as his head inclines towards me and Josef shakes his head.

His uncle, who is a small solid man with a thick, salt and pepper moustache and well-worn clothes, seems to know not to ask any questions and welcomes us into his small, neat home. The fire is lit to take the chill off the crisp night air and the room is infused with the aroma of a hearty stew. It warms me from the inside out. Josef guides me through the living room and into a small bedroom.

'I haven't been able to organise too much at such short notice, but please help yourself to what is available.' He indicates clothes laid out on the bed and some towels, soap and toothpaste. I remove his white lab coat and gratefully replace it with a soft cashmere cardigan.

'Thank you, Josef, I don't know what to say. I think I'm still in shock about this sudden change in events.' Although I would have thought I'd be used to it by now! 'Could I ask you a favour?'

'Yes, of course.'

'Would you mind if I used your phone briefly to call my children. It has been days … and … well …' My voice catches in my throat and I'm suddenly overcome with emotion. 'I'm sorry …' I stutter.

He regards me with a compassionate look, then strides across the room and wraps gentle arms around me. I immediately tense, not used to an unfamiliar man showing me such affection. He feels my anxiety and releases me, instead reaching out for a tissue and handing it to me. Josef seems like a kind and sensitive man who will do me no harm.

'Thank you. I just really need to know they are safe and let them know I'm okay as well. It's been a while since they've heard from their mum.'

With a knowing sadness in his eyes, he replies, 'I understand, but please be brief in case they are already tracing my calls. Actually, it will be safer to use Uncle Serg's phone, just to make sure.'

As he turns to leave the room, there is a loud knock on the front door. He frantically motions for to me move behind the door next to him and quickly raises his fingers to his lips to ensure I do so as quietly as possible. What now?

I hear voices in a language I don't understand, which I assume now to be Slovenian, as Josef stares out through a tiny crack in the door. His uncle raises his voice in response to the questions he is being asked and Josef closes the door silently behind us, resting his back against the wooden slats. He closes his eyes briefly as if he is trying to protect me from registering his fear and anxiety, but I can sense it in his body. He is on high alert. I swear my pounding heart is the loudest noise in the room.

I suddenly think of Anne Frank and consider the emotions she would have dealt with on a daily basis, obviously facing far more dire consequences of being found. I feel nauseated at the thought of being discovered. Are they here to take me back to the facility? To take my blood — do they really want it that desperately? Oh, dear lord, now that I'm out, I don't want to go back. I need to speak to my children. I honestly don't believe my heart can take much more of this.

The voices die down and we hear the front door of the small cottage close. I let out a sigh of relief, as does Josef. He places his hands on my shoulders and looks directly into my eyes.

'They are asking the residents in each household in the village whether they have seen a woman who is seeking help.' He frowns. 'They are describing you: slender frame, brown, wavy hair just below shoulder length, green eyes and English speaking. They obviously know you are missing. We will be okay, but we can't stay here long. You must eat first because you are already in a weakened state, then we need to move. I will get the phone for you.'

I move to the edge of the bed to sit down, unsure of the stability of my legs. Josef hands me the phone, anxiety etched in his eyes. 'Don't talk too long. We don't have a lot of time and I don't want them to trace your call from here.' Then adds with sympathy: 'I'll give you some privacy.' He turns and closes the door.

My fingers tremble with the realisation that I finally have access to technology again. I quickly dial my home number before anything else happens to disrupt me and take a deep breath in an attempt to compose myself for the conversation.

'Hello?' A groggy voice answers.

'Hi, Robert, it's me. Did I wake you?'

'Alex, hi … well, it's pretty early in the morning.'

'Oh, so the kids are asleep.' Disappointment washes over me.

'Yeah, of course. School doesn't start till the sun comes up.' I can hear his sleepy smile. 'How are you?'

'Oh, ah, I'm good. I just really wanted to talk to them, say hi, you know …'

'You don't want me to wake them, do you? They've been getting your text messages. Sounds like you've been really busy.'

'Oh, well, yes, I have I suppose.' I've been sending messages? How convenient. 'Sorry I haven't called.'

'Are you okay? You sound funny.'

I can't help the tears sliding down my face. 'I'm okay, just busy and tired. Are you all okay?'

'Yeah, we're fine. Jordan's started a new group project at school so we had a few of his mates over, and Elizabeth has been practising for her school concert. She's taking it very seriously, of course.'

My heart swells with the normality of his words; I feel I could stay listening to him talk about their activities forever.

A knock on the door indicates that my time must be over.

'Oh, Robert, sorry to interrupt, I need to go. I have, er, another meeting now. Sorry I can't talk longer. Please tell them I love them so much and give them a huge hug and kiss for me as soon as they wake up.'

'Of course. Are you sure you're fine, you don't sound it?'

I straighten my shoulders to affirm to myself that I am, particularly as I know they are safe and sound, sleeping in their beds. Josef stands by my side.

'Yes, just a little tired. Love to you all. I'll call again soon. 'Bye.' I press end and reluctantly put the phone in Josef's waiting palm, attempting to quickly wipe the tears streaming down my face. I want to speak to Jeremy but suddenly realise that I don't know his mobile number by heart. I'm only used to dialling it from my phone's address book. In any case, I suspect that now is not the time to make another call. Josef still appears worried about his uncle's visitors.

'Thank you, Josef,' I say softly, acknowledging the risk he has taken in ensuring my safety and peace of mind. He takes my hand and leads me out of the room to the kitchen table to eat. The goulash is hearty and delicious as I realise it's the heaviest meal I've had in my stomach for days. I feel full and suddenly weary with the weight of everything that has occurred since I stepped off the plane in London.

After the food, Josef gives me a moment to freshen up before ushering me outside and towards a car.

His uncle has given him some water, bread and fruit for our journey, which I'm assuming may be long, and I thank him for his hospitality. I can only hope he doesn't suffer any repercussions from harbouring us in his home.

He hugs me as if he is my uncle and hands me a blanket to keep me warm. He can barely speak any English, but his body language is kind and engaging. I rub my stomach to indicate how much I enjoyed his home-style cooking which triggers a giant grin on his face. I think it is the first time I've had such a heartfelt smile for at least a week.

Josef bundles me into the passenger seat while he takes the driver's seat. I fasten my seat belt and lay the blanket over my body. I could ask questions, but exhaustion is settling into my bones and along with a full belly, I feel like I could easily drift off to sleep. He is focussed and silent as we drive off into the unknown darkness of the night.

# Jeremy

It has been days since we received any signal from Alexa's bracelet, but I can't bring myself to leave this part of Europe. My rational brain understands that she must be ... dead — the word is still difficult even in my thoughts — but my instinct tells me I'm missing something, something obvious as if it is right under my nose, and that's probably because her body has simply vanished. How the hell do you destroy a family and tell children their mother has died and they'll never lay eyes on her again? This has been ripping me apart for the last two days.

Since Martin's arrival, I finally convinced Sam to check in with the other members of the forum and glean any further information. Apparently Dr Lauren Bertrand made other commitments the second the forum was postponed. Professor Schindler from Germany was still keen to catch up with Sam on some of his recent work so they've decided to meet up in London with the other two members from the United Kingdom on an informal basis. I have the feeling he was almost relieved to be leaving me to go back to the world he knows and, of course, to take his mind off the predicament we face here.

Salina has been very patient in accompanying me to retrace our steps since our arrival in Ljubljana. Or should I say Martin has assigned Salina to me to ensure I don't cause undue trouble. I just know something is fundamentally askew.

Martin has had one of his men stationed at the chateau since just after his arrival here, and he has reported that it seems to have been abandoned. I insisted on returning there myself and we searched the surrounding gardens and looked through the windows. I even climbed a trellis against the wall to peer into the next floor's windows, and almost came crashing down, much to Salina and Martin's horror. I doubt they'll let me be too involved in any further action now — but there was no sign of life anywhere. It felt wrong, as if everyone had to pack up and leave quickly, unexpectedly.

I had the same hunch when we returned to the hospital in Bled. It was still operating, of course, but none of the staff who were on duty the night Alexa's body was discovered were on duty when we returned, and no one could say when those others would be rostered on next.

It's as if everyone who was involved in Alexa's disappearance has undertaken a code of silence or, literally, vanished into thin air. Each path we tried to venture down was blocked, or simply petered out. Martin was becoming as frustrated as me.

The only positive link we've made is between our forum member Lauren Bertrand and Madeleine Jurilique, the European Managing Director of Xsade. They made a number of phone calls to each other over the past few months and attended a Swiss finishing school together in their youth. Unable to discover whether their relationship is significant or not, Martin sent one of each of his men to track the two women down and source more information. Apparently this has proved a more difficult task than we first thought. We are still awaiting updates.

It has been hard to work out exactly what we should do, but there is no way I am going to give up, and I won't until my heart stops beating.

* * *

It's now just Martin, Salina and myself who are left, drinking short blacks in a cafe in Ljubljana, not wanting to leave any stone unturned just in case we find a trace or hint of anything, but with each passing hour I become more despondent. As they sit absorbed in some documents that have just come through I excuse myself and walk outdoors to call Lionel McKinnon — our Chair — and advise him that Alexandra will no longer be involved in the forum in any capacity, but I can't bring myself to tell him what happened. It still feels too raw and somehow premature. Perhaps I'm living in complete denial.

I continue walking around the cobbled streets in a semi-daze, not really noticing the last of the sun shining through the clouds as my thoughts rush through my brain, unabated.

Even if she were alive, under no circumstances would I condone Alexa being involved in any further experimentation. I always thought she was exceptional, but even I was shocked by the results of the experiment I persuaded her to undertake.

Our weekend together somehow triggered an unusual sequence of events that overly stimulated her nervous system, resulting in her neuroendocrine cells releasing spontaneous surges of adrenaline. This, combined with the secretion of pituitary hormones into her bloodstream, seemed to enable Alexa's levels of serotonin and oxytocin to unexpectedly peak at the same time that her neural pathways were showing heightened activity.

These irregular and unusual findings boded well for our work on depression but most significant of all were the results of her blood tests at Avalon. Alexa's red blood cell antigens stemming from an allele — essentially an alternative form of gene with distinct DNA coding that can be passed on from parent to child — showed particularly unique characteristics.

Never in a million years would I have thought that her blood would uncover a previously undiscovered self-healing agent. I always guessed as much but now I have absolutely proven she is truly an enigma.

This instantly became so much bigger than a cure for depression. The worst-case scenario would simply mean that she had an almost unique blood type; the best-case scenario is that her blood could potentially be used to fight cancerous cells.

Unfortunately, the best-case scenario for humanity is the one that places her in the highest category of personal danger. When our computers were hacked into, I needed to come up with a plan to let people believe that all type AB blood had the same characteristics that we discovered in Alexa's, without providing the specific details. If the truth were discovered ... well, maybe it was, which is why they have her and I don't.

I wanted to explain it to her in person, after Ed Applegate, my research partner, and I had spent more time analysing the details of these peculiar results. The more I discovered, the greater the risk in talking to her over the phone or via email, particularly after the continued hackings. I just couldn't take the chance. I decided to present some of the results in Zurich to distract other scientists and researchers from her direct involvement, ensuring publicity and casting the net wide to include volunteers with an AB blood grouping.

This had been a successful strategy, or so I thought at the time. Obviously, there was at least one company who had illegal access to our results and decided to go straight to the source, Alexa.

If only I'd followed my gut instinct in the first place we would never be in this horrendous mess, but I couldn't get that blackmail letter out of my mind. My self-loathing is absolute. If I had never re-entered her life, she would be a mother happily looking after her children, untouched by these recent horrors. I've been attempting to keep myself preoccupied, distracted, hoping that I'll wake up and find that this is a nightmare.

I know I must try calling Robert again, something I've been putting off for too long because it is just too hard to form the words in my head, much less say them out loud. I dial and try to temper the emotion welling up inside me. Knowing I can no longer avoid the inevitable, I take a deep breath as the phone rings.

'Robert, hi, it's Jeremy.' My tone is flat, neutral.

'Jeremy. Well, what a surprise. It seems to be the day for everyone to call.'

'Everyone? What do you mean?'

'I just spoke to Alex a while ago and now here you are, too.' It takes a moment for his words to register.

'What, are you serious? You just spoke to AB? How, when — she —'

'Slow down, Jeremy, is everything all right over there? Alex sounded a little weird and I've never heard you like this, what's going on?'

'You are one hundred per cent sure you spoke to Alex?'

'Sure, I —'

I interrupt him, my pulse racing. 'Can you tell me exactly when?'

There is a pause, and there are little voices in the

background. It sounds like one of the kids is talking to him. I struggle to contain my impatience. 'Please, Robert, I can't tell you how important this is.'

'You're not with her?'

'It's a long story that I can't go into right now, but no, I'm not with her. How long ago?'

'About an hour or so.'

'And she was okay? You're sure it was her?'

'Who else would it be? Of course it was her.' He sounds a little indignant, understandably so, I suppose. 'She sounded tired but she was really just asking after the kids.' Hope and relief and love flood through my body simultaneously.

'Oh, my god, Robert. I can't thank you enough. I need to go, I'm sorry, I'll call you when I can.' I hang up and race back to the cafe, interrupting Martin and Salina's conversation.

'Martin, what's the latest on Alexa's bracelet, any signal?'

'Why, what's happened?' Sensing my urgency, he immediately flicks through the screens open on his laptop. 'You know we haven't had a signal for days.'

'We might have a signal now. Robert just spoke to her an hour ago.' I can't keep the excitement out of my voice, it's flooded with hope. 'I don't know if she's still wearing it, but it sounds like she's very much alive.' I restlessly pace the room waiting for what feels like an eternity until the system finally kicks into gear.

'You're right, Jeremy. There, she is back on the grid, there she is …'

I can't believe what I'm seeing and neither can Martin. We stare transfixed at the screen. Salina lets out a loud sigh. The release of our pent-up stress and tension is as instantaneous as it is spontaneous and the three of us embrace with firm hugs and claps on the back. My lungs feel like they can breathe again, like my heart has been resuscitated.

Martin returns his focus to the screen as the signal zones in on a more accurate location. She is in Croatia, heading towards Split. I'm so absorbed in staring at the map, I jump when my phone rings.

'Quinn here.'

'Dr Quinn? Dr Jeremy Quinn?' A lightly-accented male voice.

'Yes, speaking, who is this?'

'My name is Dr Josef Votrubec.' I become instantly suspicious. It only takes me a spilt second to recognise his name from the hospital in Bled.

'Do you have Alexa?'

'That is what I'm calling about. I do, I helped her escape —'

'Is she okay, when can I see her?' I'm so overwhelmed by sudden news, I'm shaking. Relief penetrates every pore in my skin.

Martin insists I hand over the phone to him so he can make arrangements. I've lost the plot. I can only hope that Dr Votrubec is true to his word and that my Alexa is unharmed. The last thing we need now is another wild goose chase and by the serious tone of Martin's voice on the phone, he'll be taking no chances.

# Alexa

When I wake, it's still dark, but I sense the sun is not too far from creeping over the horizon. I glance toward Josef, who looks weary but content.

'Where are we going, Josef? It looks like you've been driving for a while.' I try to stretch out as much as possible in my seat.

'I have, but I wanted to make sure we weren't followed so I took the coast road. We're heading towards Dubrovnik and we'll stop there.'

'Have you heard from anyone?'

'I've heard that they have been searching for you all night. They can't raise too many alarm bells, given your unusual arrival at the chateau and the facility.' He glances toward me and hands me a bottle of water. 'It wouldn't have taken them too long to work out it was me who helped you escape.'

'What will happen to you now?'

'Well, I guess I'll be looking for another job,' he says with a nervous chuckle.

I take a sip of water and regard him thoughtfully. 'Why did you do it? Why did you risk everything for me?'

'There are a few bad people in Xsade. Plenty of good ones also, but the bad ones seem to have more power in the company at the moment and they are willing to do and risk anything to have their way. I cannot work for an organisation I no longer trust or for people who are willing to endanger the lives of others. I know you signed an agreement and that is what I think we should work with. But when they didn't achieve the results they were hoping for the scientists wanted to do more tests, tests you hadn't agreed to. This is totally against my personal values and was the end for me. I knew I had to resign, but my conscience wouldn't allow me to leave you there. I could only hope that you would trust me enough to escape with me.'

I sit quietly for a while, trying to absorb his words and understand the risks he has taken on my behalf as I stare out toward the dramatic coastline becoming visible in the growing light. 'Thank you, Josef. I'm not sure how I can repay you.'

'After all you have been through, Alexandra, please don't think you ever have to repay me. I only wish you never had to be involved in the first place.'

'Josef, who were those people we saw on the way

out of the facility?' I ask gently, unsure as to how he'll respond even though we are alone.

'They are people from Eastern Europe who are willing to be paid to try the drugs Xsade is testing.'

'Is it safe?'

'Some are safer than others. They are willing to risk their bodies to try to improve their quality of life and the lives of their children. Xsade pays them and provides them with accommodation. Some testing is worse than others, but drugs do have to be tested on humans at some stage. How else would they get to market?'

I think about how we stumbled upon drugs for HIV, chemotherapy ... Then more specifically for women, the contraceptive pill, the IUD and now hormone-infused implants, among other things; how readily we accept chemical solutions to manipulate our natural hormonal cycles. Someone has to test them; indeed, many people trial new drugs. Now I've become one of those people. I can't help but wonder whether the success of Xsade's purple pill will depend on women's willingness to alter their personal chemistry for the sake of a few sexually aroused hours or days? I suppose I just did exactly that. I physically shudder the thought away.

'The people you saw were being sorted by their blood group. Hungarians have the highest proportion of AB blood in the world so they were called in as a back-up plan when you refused to give Xsade your blood.'

'Oh, I see.' Jeez, that has to be a little concerning doesn't it? My brain can't accommodate the different tangents that this conversation is triggering right at this moment. So I deliberately change topics.

'What do you think you will do, Josef?'

'First of all, I want to ensure your safety then I think I will return to my wife. I haven't seen her for days.'

'You're married? I'm sorry, I had no idea, I should have asked.' I feel awful; I've been so caught up in my own circumstances, I hadn't even spared a thought for the person behind the title.

'Do you have children?'

'No, unfortunately we haven't been blessed with children. My wife had an ectopic pregnancy and the prognosis isn't good. But you never know what scientists will be developing next, so we don't give up hope.' He attempts to hide his emotion behind an empty smile.

'I'm sorry, Josef, but as you say, you never know what will happen. The world is advancing so fast in so many ways.' I feel sad for him and can't help but remember my own intense desire to procreate all those years ago. We continue our journey in silence, lost in our own thoughts.

I'm a little surprised when he pulls the car smoothly to a stop. The scenery is breathtaking. We are parked by the sea at a small marina tucked in behind a rather secluded coastal headland. There's probably fewer than thirty yachts and motor boats moored here.

Josef rushes around to open my door and assist me out of the car and I stretch my legs. It feels great to be outside and I inhale the fresh saltiness of the air deeply into my lungs. I squint my eyes at the sun rising over the horizon.

Josef escorts me down a long jetty towards a sleek-looking speedboat. There are two figures sitting in the boat and for a brief second I pray that Josef really is on my side and not leading me into a trap. I attempt to calm my nerves and tell myself firmly that I am not that bad a judge of character.

As my eyes adjust to the sunlight and shadows, one of the figures climbs out of the boat and starts walking in our direction, wearing a navy shirt and cream cargos. It takes me a second to realise it is Jeremy walking steadily towards me, arms open, as if appearing out of a mirage.

I tentatively take a step forward before rushing full force into his arms and he envelops me securely against his chest, as tight as he can. Tears pour down our faces as I hug him harder than I have anyone in my life. My heart feels like it could explode with love and relief as I continue to sob and bury my head into the warmth of his body.

Eventually, I look up into his gorgeous smoky green eyes and his soft lips find mine, kissing me lightly, carefully, as if assessing my fragility, but it isn't long before his mouth is hungry for my own. His palms cup my face and we kiss deeply and passionately, our tears blending together. There is a franticness between us as though it could be the last time we have the opportunity to connect in this way. It feels as though

Jeremy is making sure I'm real and tangible and not a figment of his imagination. I have never wanted or needed another human being so much in my life, and judging by his reciprocating urgency, neither has he. I can only hope like hell I'm not dreaming because I've never wanted a reality more than I have this one, right now.

We finally draw breath from our very public display of affection and I'm giddy from the intensity of it. Jeremy has his arm firmly anchored around my shoulders and it doesn't feel like he will ever let go. My smile is wide as we step back to acknowledge Josef, who is patiently waiting.

'You look happy, Alexandra.'

'You didn't tell me, Josef!' He just shrugs innocently. 'Jeremy, this is Josef. Obviously I don't need to introduce you.' The two men shake hands.

'I can't thank you enough. You don't know what she means to me.' Jeremy places the palm of his free hand over his heart as he says these words and tears well up in my eyes again.

'I believe I just had a sneak preview,' Josef says with a smile and I blush at his words. 'I'm so sorry you had to endure any of this.' Josef's voice is apologetic as he takes both my hands in his and kisses them gently. 'I wish you every happiness for your future.' Jeremy reluctantly releases me so I can give him a proper hug goodbye.

'Thank you again, Josef, for everything. I will be forever indebted to you.' Jeremy and Josef do a quick man hug; full of meaning, but not sure exactly how to let each other know physically, type of thing.

'Don't keep her out here for too long, Dr Quinn. There is no need to take unnecessary risks.'

'I won't be letting her out of my sight, Dr Votrubec. We'll be in touch.'

Just as we say our final goodbyes we hear a screech of tyres rounding the sharp hairpin bends on the road, speeding towards the marina.

'Jeremy, get Alexa in here now,' calls the man in the boat.

The next thing I hear is the engine roaring into action and Jeremy pulls me to the edge of the jetty and hauls me into the speedboat. He then jumps in and lands beside me. I'm a little speechless as the boat shifts to full throttle, pulling away from the marina and forcing me back into the cushioned seat.

I'm left with the receding image of Josef's aghast face and two men running up the jetty with guns pointed in his direction. He raises his hands to his head as they approach him. The boat I'm in is moving so fast out to sea and around a jagged rock face, I don't have the opportunity to see what happens next.

Jeremy draws me into his embrace and we remain silent in each other's arms until we are certain no one is chasing us. As we are the only visible boat in the safety of the otherwise empty ocean, the speed and noise finally slacken a little.

'Oh my god, Alexa, I can't believe what you've been through. Votrubec is right, we need to get you out of sight.' Jeremy yells to the driver, 'Let's get out of here, Martin,' and receives a nod in agreement.

The speedboat changes course and we make our way along a dramatic headland. I am still in shock about everything that has happened in the last ten minutes and we can't talk over the sound of the massive motor, so I remain silent and snuggled into Jeremy's warm body as we continue to travel at rapid speed.

Eventually, we slow down and I see an enormous luxury yacht tucked around a hidden outcrop. We are skilfully positioned alongside the magnificent vessel.

'Oh my goodness, you mean out of sight on this boat?' I'm in shock. 'You certainly never do things by halves, Jeremy, do you?' He holds my hand steady as I take a careful step onto the ramp.

'Never when it comes to you, sweetheart.' His words seem to cause him some anguish as his face looks strained. I know that I'll feel safer when we are inside and out to sea and have some much-needed time to catch up on everything that life has thrown us recently.

# Part Eight

We do not quit playing because we grow old,
we grow old because we quit playing.

— Oliver Wendell Holmes

# Alexa

My world instantly transforms as I board this luxury cruiser. It is the most incredible boat I have ever laid eyes on, let alone set foot upon. Beautiful timber decks; both outdoor and indoor dining and lounge areas. A spa on the starboard deck. Our speedboat has miraculously disappeared into a purpose-made garage; it's as if the large cruiser we are now on has swallowed it up entirely.

Jeremy introduces me to Martin, who was apparently protecting us at Avalon, and from what I understand will be accompanying us for the foreseeable future if Jeremy and Leo have anything to do with it. And to Salina, who looks small, strong, smart and savvy. I shake her hand warmly because it looks as though she could give Jeremy a run for his money. I like her instantly. And then I meet the rest of the crew, including a chef, the captain, and a few boathands to help out with all the things that generally need doing around a boat.

All the while, Jeremy's arm is anchored around my shoulders. To be honest, it's too much to absorb just now, but then again, I have felt like that for a while. The wild ride continues.

'Do I even ask how you managed to arrange this?' His arm is still protectively around me, as if he'll never let me go. I don't want him to.

'A good friend of Leo's … it isn't being used until next month so he was more than happy to lend us both boat and crew for the next week if we needed it — which we did.'

'Aha. Okay then.' I slide my fingers along the lounge suite as we make our way deeper into the boat. There really are some obscenely wealthy people in the world. I'm a little overcome by my situation, compared to the looks on the faces of those people lining up to allow the use of their bodies for drug experimentation.

'Are you okay, Alexa, do you need to lie down?'

'Yeah, I think I do, actually. There is just so much we need to discuss, Jeremy, I honestly don't know where to begin.' The events of the past week have drained me both physically and emotionally. And now I'm on a dream cruiser with Jeremy — I feel like I've been dropped out of Dorothy's tornado and landed in Oz.

'I know, sweetheart, I feel exactly the same way. I thought you were … well, for days … I didn't know …' Tears well up in his eyes and he can't continue. I hug him tight so he knows I'm here, so he can feel I'm here, finally, with him. I can only imagine how I would be feeling if the situation had been reversed, not knowing whether he was dead or alive. You wouldn't wish it upon anyone.

'Can I use your phone, Jeremy? I really need to speak to Elizabeth and Jordan. It feels like it has been forever and they should be home and awake now.'

'Of course, I'll go and let the crew know we're ready to sail. I'll be right back.' He stares lovingly into my eyes, gives me another lingering kiss and reluctantly lets go of my hand.

The relief when I hear their chirpy little voices is as overwhelming as it is calming; finally the knots in my stomach begin to unravel. They are happy, talkative and completely unaware of anything I have been through. It sounds like the messages Xsade sent on my behalf were fairly generic and inconsequential. Thank god! I send a prayer of thanks to the universe.

They miss me as much as I miss them and they really try hard not to talk about a big surprise they have for me. It works, sort of ... My heart swells with love for them. Robert confirms everything is going fine, that yes, they are eating well and that my mother has been sending over additional meals just in case he has been too busy to cook.

I laugh at the joyful, mundane, everyday life of parenthood and wouldn't give it up for quids. I can't help but think that so much has been going on over here and they have been none the wiser, their lives chugging along normally. This knowledge is enormously reassuring and I'm eternally grateful they haven't been dragged into any of this mess.

Jeremy returns and I hand him his phone back with a smile on my face and love in my heart. My relief is monumental. 'Thank you.'

'Everything okay with the kids?'

'Everything is great. They have no idea what has been going on here and are very excited about some surprise for me, which is so cute.'

'I can't wait to meet them properly. They certainly sound like real little people these days.'

'They are gorgeous, Jeremy. You get to realise how much children mean to you when you are taken away from them.' My voice quivers and his arms are around me in seconds as I bury my head into his chest in tearful happiness. 'You know, the one thing I missed and thought about more than anything, was not being able to kiss them goodnight. There is no greater privilege for a parent than to be able to tuck their child in and give them a kiss goodnight while they fall sleep. So peaceful and angelic, their little cherub faces dreaming their sweet dreams.' His finger gently catches the last tear cascading down my cheek.

'I'm so sorry, Alexa. I never meant for any of this to happen, or to put you in danger. Can you ever forgive me?'

'I love you, Jeremy, I always have. Don't doubt for a second that I've been through a lot, but it has worked out. We are here and we are together. All that is missing is my children, but speaking to them was the next best thing. We will get through this.'

The pain etched on his face is almost crushing. I stand on my tiptoes to kiss his lips, his chin, his cheeks in an attempt to smooth away his anguish. It takes a moment for him to soften, but I'm happy to persist until he kisses me back and we become lost in the moment. God, I've missed him.

'Would you like me to run a bath for you?' His lips caress the nape of my neck so perfectly as he utters these words, his hands gently resting on my hips. I immediately consider where else I would love his lips and hands.

'Absolutely. I haven't had one for ages and I'm looking forward to getting out of these clothes. I must stink.'

'You actually smell surprisingly good. Let me help you with your clothes.' He drops the cardigan from my shoulders, sliding it down my arms and unzips the back of my dress, letting it fall to the floor. I'm left standing in my new black underwear that I bought especially for this trip. Finally, he gets to see it. 'New?'

'For your eyes only ...' I say cheekily as I look into his eyes in the mirror above the basin. Then I remember that isn't exactly true — other eyes have seen it before him. He smiles while absorbing the sight of my body until a frown shadows his face.

'What's wrong?' I ask, sensing a change in his demeanour.

He slips a strap of my bra over my shoulder, lowering the cup covering my breast. He stares in shock at what he sees, running his finger down from my breast to my stomach. I catch a glimpse of what is causing his reaction just before he turns me around to face him directly. Oh dear. Nothing like this has ever happened between us before.

I remain silent and still as he continues a close inspection of my entire body. His fingers linger along the tops of my legs and stop at my inner thighs before he finally speaks.

'What did they do to you?'

I'm not sure whether to be embarrassed, angry, upset, thrilled or proud. Combinations of these emotions flow through me as though I've just taken a spin on the jackpot on a lottery machine. Jeremy's eyes look as though he is going through a similar process albeit with vastly different emotions. I wonder which one he'll settle on? I decide to cut to the chase before his mind comes to a complete stop.

'They did many things, Jeremy. None of them harmed me; some of them scared me a little.' I remember my inauspicious journey to the chateau. 'But when I was in the facility, it was mutually agreed, and to be honest, I learned quite a lot about myself.'

'But you have small bruises all over your body. If I didn't know better I'd say they were love bites.' I can't help but smile at his use of such a teenage word. 'You think it is funny?' He looks unamused.

'A little, I have to admit.' I am unable to keep the smile from my face. 'Don't you?'

'Alexa, you were abducted right in front of my eyes, shuffled from country to country, vanished for over three days and I thought you were dead and you now have bruises and marks on your body. How can you stand there smiling and tell me they didn't hurt you?' He sounds distraught as he turns me back around and raises my arm so I can see the marks on the inside of my upper arm as clearly as he can.

'I promise you, Jeremy, they didn't hurt one bit.' I raise my eyebrow and wonder where this will take his analytical thought process.

'You, you … enjoyed it?' He looks utterly astonished.

'Surprisingly, much more than I would ever have believed.'

'With other men?'

I hesitate.

'Please, I just need to know, tell me the truth. How did you get these?'

'From two women.'

'And they didn't cause you pain?'

'Quite the opposite, actually.' My eyes are wide open, awaiting his response. He has always wanted me to explore the 'other side' — that is, with women — and I'd never been brave enough. On a few occasions, he'd gone so far as to provide me with the opportunity, but I never went there. And now I have, well, sort of … at least, they did with me.

'Oh, well … I suppose that is different, then.' I can sense his entire body and mind absorbing this new information. His previous fear and anger is making way to curiosity and fascination.

'I can assure you, Jeremy, you've put me through worse … and better, admittedly.' This time I can't help but laugh. I've never seen him so unsure of himself and his emotions. It's strangely empowering.

'Jeremy,' I say clearly, 'a bath would be great, thanks.'

'Hmm, yes, a bath, of course.' Still not entirely at ease with our conversation he goes about his business of making a bath, which gives me an opportunity to inspect my body and the bruising more thoroughly. It's not too bad, although there are a lot of them I must admit, more than I would have thought. 'Your earlier comment was quite accurate, Alexa.'

'What was that?' I yell out so he can hear me over the running water.

'We do have a lot to discuss.'

This should be interesting.

* * *

I can't describe how incredible the bath feels for my body. I melt into the steaming water, and once again the aroma of lavender and jasmine fill the air and my body finally feels as if it has the opportunity to release the tension it has been harbouring for days. I'm not surprised when Jeremy undresses and joins me. I get the sense that he isn't game to leave me for more than a few seconds, in case I should vanish again from his grasp.

I know this is where I belong but I also know we have much to resolve between us before we can move forward. He cradles my body between his legs and wraps his arms possessively around my shoulders. I let my head rest against his chest and feel more secure than I have in days, but I'm not sure that it is the truth. I have to ask: 'Am I safe now, Jeremy? Is there any risk they will find me?'

'That's a good question, sweetheart. Let me explain to you everything that happened after we left Avalon.'

\* \* \*

Over the next twenty-four hours, Jeremy explains everything that he was planning to tell me personally during our scheduled meeting in London — before our plans were more than rudely interrupted.

He tells me about the blackmail letter and for a moment my head swirls. I flash back and remember my difficulty in interpreting his sense of urgency and underlying fear during our weekend away, and now fully understand why it was so difficult for him to resolve. Sometimes the decisions we make in life are to protect the ones we love, to distance them from potential pain. Not knowing whether the blackmail threat was real or not, and not knowing our true intentions and feelings for each other confused us both and clouded the decisions we were willing to make.

If only we had trusted each other enough to have a 'real' conversation. If only I had known that he had known about Robert's sexual tendencies while I remained completely naive, I may have not been so hesitant or nervous. I barely had time to think about anything that weekend, so much was coming at me, so blindly, so fast. It had been so long since Jeremy and I had connected emotionally, let alone sexually … neither of us were as sure of ourselves as perhaps we should have been.

Hindsight is a great thing, but it doesn't alter the past or the decisions we made. Would I change anything? I'm not sure. I'd never put my children in danger, so maybe he made the right decision on my behalf, regardless, and I'd be lying if I said I didn't have a lot of fun playing that weekend. More fun, in some ways, than I had ever had as an adult. Is that irresponsible?

I have to acknowledge that I willingly agreed to partake in the experiment and can't deny gaining many personal insights and learning a lot as a result. After all, I'm always trying to live a life without regrets.

What I haven't come to terms with is the 'uniqueness' of my red blood cells. This is a complete shock. The potential healing ability that Jeremy describes is almost unreal to me.

I ask him whether it has been genetically passed to my children, but he's unsure and, at this stage, unwilling to conduct any tests on them to find out. He has become even more protective since he is now aware of the heightened risks and dangers. It's almost as if he is taking the approach of 'the less we know the safer we'll be', which goes against the grain of his career. But I suppose he has never loved anyone like he does me, and the fact that I know that now, beyond any shadow of a doubt, makes me the happiest woman on earth. I smile and hug myself indulgently. Even if I have enigmatic blood that people want to steal ... a deep shudder travels down my spine at that thought.

Once again, I find myself unconsciously stroking my ever-present bracelet. Jeremy assures me they are investigating a way to modify it to ensure it can be traced underground or underwater, since the Xsade facility, located *under* Lake Bled, blocked the signal. I hope they do, I never want him to lose me again!

* * *

After a few days sailing at sea, I feel refreshed and alive. The ocean air has been good for my lungs and the sun has added a little colour to my otherwise pale skin. I feel hesitant about returning to London so soon after everything that has happened so we decide to sail to Barcelona while we still have use of the boat.

My bruises have pretty much cleared up, thank goodness. Jeremy was not happy with seeing them on my body — understandable, I suppose. He said whenever he sees them he can't help but blame himself for everything I've been through. So instead, we have been making very gentle, exceptionally romantic love in the shadows, completely absorbed in the mystery of our togetherness and deliberately avoiding the future that awaits us when we disembark.

Over dinner last night on the outside deck, he asked me to describe exactly what I went through at the Xsade facility, in excruciating detail, as only Jeremy can. He wanted to know my answers to the questionnaire, how I was feeling at every step of the process, what surprised me, what made me scared — everything. At first I wasn't sure if I wanted to talk about it, or wanted him to know, but he sat there, encouraging me to speak and to open up to him. He listened patiently for hours, absorbed in every word, every facial expression. Once I began, and lost any sense of inhibition, I couldn't stop talking. I realised I needed to talk about the fear and anxiety I experienced, how I felt about him when Madeleine Jurilique made me doubt his love for me, and my anger towards him at his supposed betrayal.

He showed more concern for my emotions than my accusatory words as I continued my story. It was just the therapy I needed. His body language changed almost imperceptibly when he asked thoughtful questions about my experience in the 'orgasm factory', as he liked to call it. I think it helped him come to terms with the fact that they didn't keep me in some hideous dungeon, and made the whole situation more bearable and light-hearted for both of us. His eyes were blazing with concentration as I explained the actual experiences I observed and was intimately involved in. He didn't judge me, my actions or responses, just listened attentively as though he needed to intimately understand my perspective.

I somehow felt cleansed during this process. Knowing everything he had been through as well and his desperation to ensure I was part of his life, along with his need to protect both me and my children, reinforced the unbreakable bond between us — that our lives should be lived together, never apart, from this point forward.

# Jeremy

It is our last night together on the boat, as we near Barcelona before flying to the United States. Alexa is wearing a sexy black negligee and I'm in my boxer shorts. We're just chatting and I have the great privilege of admiring and stroking the luscious silky curves of her body. Her reactions to my touch are even more pronounced since we last met, it's incredible.

She believes we are going to Boston to meet up briefly with Professor Applegate and for me to pick up some things before escorting her back home. I can't stand the thought of her travelling without me, her abduction is still far too raw in my heart; I don't imagine that will change for quite some time.

Leo, via Moira, has insisted that Martin and Salina escort us at all times until we find Madame Jurilque and understand exactly what her intentions for Alexa might be. Once again, I'll be forever thankful that Leo is part of my life. I'm completely indebted to him.

I'm thrilled that I've been able to arrange, on the sly, with Robert for him to fly over with the kids and meet us in Orlando, Florida. He's actually a great guy. I can reluctantly understand why Alex would have chosen him to be a father to her children. Since Avalon and the momentous conversation between Alex and Robert regarding their true feelings about their marriage, he has been in regular touch with Adam, Leo's brother. So the kids will stay with us and he'll fly on to London and finally meet with Adam, after all these years; it will be interesting to see whether it all works out. I hope so.

I figured Disney World would be the perfect place for me to get to know Elizabeth and Jordan and would distract Alexa's mind from everything that's happened recently. Although I have to admit her resilience has been astounding and her libido has been on fire. I was anticipating having to be very patient with her, give her time to recover after everything she has been through, but she seems almost insatiable. I'm certainly not complaining, but I know that being reunited with her children needs to be our priority ... and sooner rather than later, so we can work out how to best reorganise our lives, together rather than on separate sides of the world.

Everyone is so excited about arranging this as a surprise for her and I'm grateful Elizabeth and Jordan have managed to keep it that way, even though we've had a few close calls, which makes me laugh. Alexa is completely puzzled as to what they could be planning, but seems happily distracted and I love to see her this way. For the first time in weeks, I feel like everything could actually work out for us.

I'm gently stroking her inner wrist and playing with her hair. 'So you honestly want this, Alexa?'

'Yes, I do.'

'You certainly seem more assured of your desires and arousal since your experience at the orgasm factory.'

'I'm very sure of my desire for you, Jeremy, and your innate ability to arouse me.'

'Thank you, I'm very pleased to hear it.' And relieved, I have to admit quietly. 'So you really want to play …'

'More than you can imagine. I want to play now. It will be different when we are with Jordan and Elizabeth. We'll be parents first and foremost, not lovers. It won't only be our time. My focus will be on them. This moment is just about us and I don't want to waste it.'

She breathes a deep sigh before straddling her legs over my body and pinning my hands either side of my head, a position I have her in regularly. I can't help but smile up at her glowing face, her dark hair cascading past her shoulders, but not quite touching her breasts. I know she isn't strong enough to keep me in this position, she knows it too.

'So lovers it is then.'

As if guessing my thoughts she says, 'For now, absolutely. It feels good to be on top.'

'I'm starting to wonder if I should be a little concerned about how much you're beginning to like this position.'

She laughs. 'Not as much as I like others, though ...'

She is certainly more playful and even more — dare I say it — abandoned than she ever was during our weekend away. Doubt shades my mind, but she seems happy, more confident, in her body and in our relationship. Perhaps the purple pill factory really did provide her with an opportunity to appreciate her sexual self. She certainly looks and feels sensational! My whole body agrees with that thought. Well, if the love of my life wants to play, who am I to deny her?

'And you trust me?' I ask her.

'Yes, I trust you, Jeremy. What do I need to do to prove it to you? I understand now why our weekend together was so extreme, so many different forces at play. But, more than anything else, I know you did everything because you loved me, you wanted me back in your life and you were protecting me and my children.' She strokes my cheek softly. 'You keep forgetting that even though I didn't understand how and why everything was going on at the time, like I do now, I made a choice. I chose you — every step of the way that weekend. You pushed me further than I've ever gone and I loved it. I might have questioned it, but I loved it. You tapped into the essence of me, opened me up like no other — as you said, like the roses blossoming. And here I am, a little tarnished, but certainly still blooming. Because I love you and I know you love me, always have and always will. Believe me, that instils more trust than I ever believed possible.'

The faith in her eyes is almost enough to undo me. What a speech. I wasn't expecting such eloquence, but it is also exactly what I needed to hear. 'You honestly never cease to amaze me.'

She peppers my face with light kisses, her delicate lips barely touching my skin as she continues to straddle my body. She rubs her cheek against my three-day growth. I still can't believe she likes the feel of it.

'You and I, we're destined to be together, we know that now and I can't wait for our new life to begin. We still have issues we need to work through and we will. But for now ...'

'Yes, Dr Blake?'

She slides her tongue teasingly along my lips. 'Well, right this minute, Dr Quinn, it's playtime.'

'It certainly is.'

I flip her over so our positions are exactly reversed, the only difference being that I know she can't extract herself from beneath me unless I let her. I return her feathery kisses before upping the intensity and devouring her delicious mouth and she squirms with delight beneath me. I remain straddled over her body as I reach to the bedside drawer and pull out two black leather wristbands, each with a connector, just like the ones from our weekend. I watch her face carefully as she registers exactly what they are.

'Do you want to play this much, Alexa?' I will never force her to do anything she doesn't want to do, ever again, even if I believe she wants it. I've learnt my lesson.

She nods her head. Her nipples become instantly erect at the sight of the bondage restraints. She readily offers me her free wrist so I can wrap it in the black leather. The look in her eyes tells me she is already moist below. I feel myself spring to life as I do the same to the other wrist. She is watching me intently, always more quiet in these circumstances than at any other time. I know it is because she is so in the moment with me, fully absorbed in what will happen next.

I slip the strap of her negligee over her shoulders. As soon as she explained to me how she felt about seeing the two couples together in the circular room, I noticed the timber beam in the corner of the room and have been waiting for an opportunity to use it. But only when she was ready, and it seems she is more than ready now.

The first time she had seen another woman come, and the way she described it and described her response to it, made me stiff while I listened to her, watching her sexy mouth form the words. I didn't dare interrupt; I needed to know everything, every detail about how she felt and what she experienced, so I could learn more about what drives her arousal, to prove to her and to myself that I can fulfil her sexual needs.

I lift her carefully off the bed and over to the beam and her eyes widen in surprise. I can't decipher whether she had noticed it previously, but there is a cheekiness about the way reacts that makes me think this is what she may have been hoping for. My intentions are clear now at least and she smiles knowingly, raising her arms above her head. Wow, she has become so much more proactive in her own submissive way. I attach the two connectors above the round wooden beam, connecting her wrists together, and move back a step to take in the sight of her bound, beautiful naked body.

'Are you comfortable enough in this position?' Her silence continues as she nods her assent.

She is stretched out, on the balls of her feet as if she is wearing high heels. Her body is to die for, her round breasts teasing me to take them in my mouth but it's not time for that. I absorb the visual feast of her waist, her hips, her stomach. My attraction to her is absolute.

I walk deliberately around her, admiring her backside as much as her front, gently kissing the blade of her shoulder as I pass. I return to her face and cup her cheeks in the palms of my hands staring intently into her eyes, boring into her soul. I kiss her deeply until she is breathless, sighing audibly against her bounds. God, I've missed her so much. She is my world. She has been denied me for so long, in so many ways, and now she is mine and I am hers. I'm ecstatic that this has finally become my reality.

I lean down to kiss her belly and am enticed to poke my tongue firmly into her bellybutton, the core of her being, keeping it hard, and swirling my tongue around before sucking her skin back toward me. She gasps and I look up at her face to monitor her response. My hand slips between her thighs to physically confirm the look in her eyes.

There are barely any remnants left of her small bruises, but I remember exactly where they were on her body and now I have free access to replicate each and every one of them, with my own mouth. For once in my life, I don't follow a methodical process or have a definite plan. I listen and watch her body and how it feels beneath my touch to determine where to suck and nibble and bite. Something carnal within me ignites and seems to be driving my desire to mark her, to override where I know the others have been with their mouths on my woman. I can't stop as my tongue, lips and teeth intensify their ambush on her most sensitive areas.

'Oh, god, Jeremy.'

'Do you like this?'

'Yes ... but ...' I suck her nipple slowly, and widen my mouth to absorb more of her breast, using the pressure of my tongue to great effect before biting the bud of her nipple and simultaneously stroking the inner layers of her labia.

'Oh god ...'

'Yes, but ... what is it, sweetheart?'

I repeat my actions on the other breast while continuing to tease her vulva with the strokes of my fingers. 'I'm listening.' Her moans intensify and I'm pleased I locked the door to our room. 'Would you like me to stop?'

I spread her legs open so my mouth has access to her inner thighs and continue my nibbling and sucking of her soft white and pink flesh, knowing some will leave marks and others won't.

'No ... no, don't stop.'

There is a gorgeous sheen heating her skin and her eyes are beginning to glaze over with the intensity of sensation. I ease off, not wanting her too close this soon. We're certainly not done playing yet.

I step away from her body, my eyes intensely admiring its beautiful form.

'You look stunning, Alexandra. You are oozing lust and love, I'm in awe of you. I swear I could play with you all night like this. How have we never entertained this position before?'

'Please, don't just look, touch me. I need to feel you.'

'I need a minute, sweetheart. You are getting hot and bothered too fast.' She sighs in frustrated response, left dangling in the corner, eyes glazed over with desire.

I walk to the bedside drawer and return with two items.

Her eyes widen even more as I place both of them on the edge of the bed and sit beside them. Fascinating ... her eyes are telling me a thousand words, she is licking her bottom lip, but remains defiantly silent.

I cross my legs and rest my palm against my chin, taking a moment to contemplate my next move. I decide we could probably both do with a drink so I walk over to her, bound and silent in the corner of the room and give her a gentle kiss on the lips.

'I'll be back in a minute.'

'Jeremy, you can't leave me like this!'

'Oh, good, you're talking again. I need more words, sweetheart. I need to know how you're feeling at all times. Have a think about that while I'm gone.' I can't resist giving her a quick slap on the butt to ensure I have her attention. The look on her face confirms I do now.

I return to the room with a chilled bottle of Sancerre in an ice bucket with two glasses.

'Thirsty?'

She nods.

I slide the chilled bottle along her raised arm and slide it along the contour of her body. She shivers against the cold sensation on her hot body. 'I'm sorry, sweetheart, I didn't hear you. Would you like a drink?'

'Yes. Please.'

I open the bottle, pour some into a glass and take a quick sip before gently raising it to her lips to taste. 'Do you like it?'

'Perfect.'

'As are you.' I can't resist a quick suck on her nipple and she gasps. 'When you go all quiet on me I worry you're not enjoying yourself.'

'You know I am.'

'More?'

'Yes, please.'

'Here, have a bigger mouthful. It's too good not to. Ready?' She swallows quickly, which is just as well because she lets out a laugh.

'Jeremy! You can't leave me hanging like this.'

'Hmm, I can actually, both literally and figuratively.'

'But I know you won't.'

'True.' I take a mouthful of the wine and place it back in the bucket.

'So many things to play with in this room, don't you think?'

'Yes.' A single word from a voice full of lust.

I pick up a piece of ice from the bucket. 'You were getting a little hot and flustered before so I thought the ice might cool you down.' I slide it under her arms, across her breasts, taking time to circle her nipples, then her bellybutton before inserting it into her sex and closing her legs between the strength of my own.

'But we've done this before, haven't we?' Our faces are close to each other, her breathing is becoming erratic.

'Yes.'

'And you liked it?'

'Yes, I did.'

'Tell me how much.'

'I liked it a lot.'

'With another man, is that what you liked, Alexa? Having two of us at the same time?' Her cheeks instantly blush at the memory or my question, perhaps both.

'I liked it, but I love being with you more.'

'More than this? More than what we are doing now?'

'No. I like this more.'

'Well, that's good to know, I appreciate your honesty.' I release her legs and walk towards the bed.

'And what about this, my love? Did you like this, too?' I pick up the blindfold from our weekend and run its fabric beneath my fingers.

Her body goes limp as her sex glistens between her thighs. Her arms keep her in place, high above her head.

'Tell me.'

'Yes, I loved it.'

I move over to her and gently slide the silk across her face, across her mouth and finally over her eyes.

'Oh, Jeremy.'

'Tell me what it means to you.'

'It symbolises everything. Us being together ... discovery.'

'Go on, Alexa, please. I need to know,' I encourage as I continue floating it over her body, seeing what sensations it will elicit, what emotions.

'You awakening my body again, sexually, just as you are now. You opened me up, Jeremy, finally allowed me to feel like I'd never felt before.'

I slide it between her thighs and she gasps. My cock instantly reacts to her movement. 'You're the last person I need to convince about the impact of visual stimulation.'

I rest it over her shoulder so it dangles down her back and on to her nipple. I will never take her sight away again unless she explicitly asks me to, of that I am sure. Right at this moment, I want her to be able to see everything.

'But what about this?' I hold up a black leather crop with a red paddle on the end.

'I've never seen it before.' Her breath is short and light, her breasts rising and falling rapidly with the intensity of her arousal. It's fascinating to watch.

'No, you haven't seen it before, but you have certainly felt it.' I slide it across her belly, under her breasts, over her nipples, in between the cheeks of her buttocks and finally between her thighs as though I'm delicately playing with the bow of a violin, tuning her body.

She closes her eyes and releases low, rumbling moans as I complete these strokes and the sexual energy in the room heightens and intensifies. The response is sudden and shocking. Her paroxysm occurs the second it slides between her legs and I hold her body firmly against mine in case she does herself damage. I feel the rhythm pumping through her as she gasps and groans, struggling against the sensations ambushing her body.

Christ! I've never witnessed anything like this. It takes me a moment to think to release her wrists from the beam, it happens so quickly. I hold her body off the floor with one hand and struggle with the connector for a moment before it releases and she collapses into my arms.

'My god, Alexa, what's happening? Are you all right?' I hastily move her convulsing body to the bed, wondering whether she has had some form of seizure and I lie with her firmly in my arms until the shudders subside enough for her to regain focus. In the meantime, I carefully wipe her hair away from her face, desperate to look into her eyes. 'Sweetheart, are you hurt? What just happened?'

She smiles up at me beneath her thick lashes and kisses my chest.

I thank god she seems to be all right.

'Alexa, please, tell me. What happened? What was all that about?'

'Wow, that was intense. The most intense ever.'

'What are you talking about? Here, let me get you some water. Are you hurt?'

'Hurt, goodness no, but it's a bit embarrassing, isn't it?'

'This has happened before?'

'It's been happening since our weekend together, but never anything like that. I suppose it is because it's the first time we've played since our weekend, the blindfold, the crop ... it's the symbolism of what they represent to me ... the memories, the feelings, my god.' She pants out her words trying to catch her breath before taking a sip of water and collapsing back on the bed. 'Just give me a minute. That was really full on.'

My brain is working on overdrive and competing with my rising-back-to-the-occasion cock — now that I know she is unharmed. My cock is thrilled when Alexa's hands hastily remove my briefs and she wraps her naked body around mine, but my brain still registers concern. 'Sweetheart, you need to —'

'Enough with the talking, Jeremy. I need you inside me and I won't be taking no for an answer.'

All coherent thoughts instantly vanish from my mind and my body takes over all control, as does hers ...

# Alexa

What a surprise! How they managed it without me knowing, I'll never know. I think I spent the first hour or two crying when I finally had Elizabeth and Jordan back in my arms, which confused them no end. I had to keep telling them they were tears of joy, because they wondered what on earth was wrong with their mummy after the first fifteen minutes.

We have had the most fantastic four days; it just couldn't have been more perfect. We've been to Magic Kingdom, Animal Kingdom and to the Epcot Centre today. We have played and laughed and eaten so much food.

I've been trying to put off Typhoon Lagoon until my body is respectable and love bite-free enough to be seen in a swimsuit after my last night on the boat with Jeremy. My body delights in the sexy memory;

hopefully, we should be clear to go tomorrow. Everyone of us is happily exhausted and I don't think I've stopped smiling since we all got together.

I keep checking on the kids while they sleep, ensuring they are tucked in and kissing them gently on the forehead. I am constantly thankful I have been blessed to have them in my life. They fill my heart with peace and love. I close the door as quietly as possible behind me, so I don't disturb their slumber. The smile on my face is a direct reflection of how immensely happy and alive I feel, on holiday with my new family unit. I almost need to pinch myself to believe that things have gone so well.

Jeremy has been fantastic with Jordan and Elizabeth. He's managed to achieve that almost impossible balance of both friendship and respected authority figure. So far they have accepted him into their lives far more favourably than I could ever have hoped for; fingers crossed it continues. It seems as if the family discussion that Robert and I had with the kids, way back before I left for London, prepared them more than I'd anticipated for the change in their parents' lives. Funny how children can be far more accepting of such change than adults. They know they are dearly loved by both of us and that's what counts the most.

Jeremy is on the lounge, looking gorgeous, casual and relaxed as he checks his messages on his phone. My heart could burst with the enormity of the love I feel for the people in this apartment. He diverts his attention from his phone to me, his face broadening in a smile. I don't remember ever feeling this way: as if I could literally overflow with happiness. It's oozing out of me.

'How are they?' His outstretched arm snuggles me into the warmth of his body.

'Perfect, just perfect. They are absolutely exhausted from the trip over and the sheer excitement of having a week at Disney World. I think they'll be sound asleep for a while.'

'You look happy.'

'I couldn't be happier. I can't quite believe this is my reality, after everything that we've been through. I could pinch myself.'

'No need for you to do that, Alexa. I'm always happy to help.' I raise my eyebrows at him, give him a light pinch instead and snuggle in closer.

'They're great kids, Alexa. You and Robert have done a great job. You should both be very proud.'

'We are, J,' I beam, 'but I'm even happier that they seem to be accepting you in my life.'

'I hope so. I honestly don't know what I would do if I lost you again, sweetheart. I can't bear to think about it.' A twinge of a frown creases his brow, his hand absently playing with the loose hair at the back of my neck, twisting and turning it between his fingers.

'What's wrong, Jeremy? Did you receive a message?' I glance towards his phone.

'Not yet, still no sign of Josef and it seems as though Madeleine de Jurilique has vanished into thin air. As Jeremy continues, I send a silent prayer to the universe that Josef is safely back with his wife, particularly after everything he risked for me. I'll feel much better about this whole situation when they know where she is and ensure she is no longer a threat. Salina's still on the trail with another agent, but hasn't been able to uncover anything further about her whereabouts. I also just received an email from Sam, who sends his love. He's on his way back to Australia after catching up with some of the others.'

This attracts my immediate attention. 'What's happened with the forum? I can't believe I haven't asked.'

'It's the last thing you needed to think or worry about, Alexa. It's been indefinitely postponed. I don't want you being involved in it at all now, sweetheart. It's too risky.'

I don't argue with him. Just nod in agreement as he holds me tight. I know I'm not ready for anything like the global forum just yet. I want everything to return to normal, for a while at least, if that's possible. I need to draw breath and be a mum and get used to my new duties as the love of Jeremy's life. Gosh, my heart could just explode. I look up at Jeremy's face and see that it has become anxious, almost angry.

'I can't believe Lauren Bertrand betrayed me, betrayed us, like that. The thought that she put you in such danger ... It's outrageous. Passing on information of your whereabouts, leaking our results to Madame Jurilique and Xsade, all for an expense account here or a free holiday there ... It just infuriates me how people can live their lives so selfishly, never considering the consequences of their actions on other people. If you hadn't bumped into her in Singapore, maybe things would never have gone this far.'

'From what I know of Madame Goldy, she would have found a way to get to me with or without the assistance of Lauren, Jeremy. She's really not the sort of person you want to mess with. I promise you.'

'After what she put you through, that bi—'

'Jeremy, please, I don't want to talk about her. It's disrupting my blissful state.'

'Sorry, sweetheart, I know, it's just that it still makes me so angry.'

'It's okay, we're good. We're here together, just as we should be. My children are safe and well. Robert's meeting with Adam. All we need to do is work out the simpler details of our lives, like which country we should live in —'

'Plenty of time to work that out, my love. We still have another few fun-filled days at the never-ending supply of theme parks and I want you to finally meet with Leo in person before we head back Tasmania.'

'You mean, the mysterious Charlie? You are honestly going to introduce me to Leo after all these years?'

'Not just you my love, the kids too. He wants us to spend some time with him when he returns from the Amazon. He managed to get in touch with Moira.'

'Wow, I can't believe it. I've always wanted to meet the most important man in your life. We must be special.' I'm feeling an overwhelming sense of serenity, as if all barriers are finally dissolving between us so we can become a true partnership.

'You, and your children, are the most important people in my life, Alexandra. I'll love you and protect you until my dying breath.'

Could more perfect words ever be spoken? I'm in love more than I ever, ever imagined or believed possible. What a wonder!

# Epilogue

There's a knock at the door and Jeremy extricates himself from our interlude on the lounge. Probably Martin doing his usual check that everything is fine with our little foursome. I hug the pillow to replace Jeremy's absence. We really need to discuss where we will live and how our lives and our careers, can be managed. I suppose we need to wait to find out about Robert and Adam before we can make any firm decisions, as neither one of us will want to be separated from Elizabeth and Jordan. I try to put this out of my mind as it can't be resolved yet. We'll work it out eventually.

Jeremy's taking a while, so I walk into the kitchen to open a bottle of wine. Maybe Martin will come in for a drink; he must be getting bored hanging out in Orlando, following us around theme parks.

I head towards the front door to see Jeremy engaged

in what looks to be a very agitated conversation with Martin.

'Is everything okay out here? Do you want to come in for a drink?' I indicate the bottle I have in my hand. They glance nervously at each other before looking directly at me. Jeremy ushers Martin in and locks the door behind him.

I busy myself getting some glasses out of the cupboard and pouring our wines. I pass one to each of them. 'What's going on? You are both looking very strange.'

Martin places a thick A4 envelope on the kitchen table.

'What's this?' I ask, as I reach across to slide the envelope towards me.

Jeremy finally finds his voice. 'Alexa, don't, please!' He looks instantly pained.

'What's wrong, Jeremy? Are you going to tell me or will I just open it and find out for myself?' His face looks agonised, so much so I think he's immobilised.

I look towards Martin before I open it. He slowly nods.

I slide out the contents and read the covering letter.

*Dear Doctor Blake,*

*I do hope you have had a wonderful time recuperating in the Mediterranean with your lover and have enjoyed the delights of Disney World with your sweet children, Elizabeth and Jordan.*

*It is so unfortunate that you were not able to properly conclude the entire 72 hours at our facility. After having provided us with such useful information, there is but one element we now require.*

*Should you not be forthcoming in relation to our requirements we shall once again be forced to take circumstances into our own hands. The enclosed news headlines are but a small sample of the strategies we will employ to ensure that we acquire what we need from you, so please let me be clear.*

We need your blood.

*If, for some reason, you decide not to cooperate with our request within the next ten days, we shall be forced to proceed with our global 'Do you really know Dr Alexandra Blake?' campaign. Needless to say, I shouldn't have to remind you that we have some wonderfully explicit photographs and video clips to authenticate our headlines.*

*While I have your attention, I should also mention that should this not procure your participation, we would look to acquire the next best thing — the blood of your children.*

*I shall look forward to working with you again in the very near future.*

*Sincere regards,*
*Madame Madeleine de Jurilique*

I then spread the attached pages out on the table. Printed on them are mock-ups of the front pages of international newspapers.

### SLUT MOTHER SHUNS KIDS FOR KINKY SEX EXPERIMENT

### DR BLAKE BARES ALL — CHECK OUT HER BEST ANGLES HERE

### PSYCHOLOGIST TURNS PSYCHO —
Would you leave your kids with this mother?

### ADULTERY — SADOMASOCHISM —
is this what you teach your kids?

I take one look at the headlines and immediately throw up into the kitchen sink.

Jeremy stands behind me, rubbing my shoulders as I vomit and tears pour down my face, as if every ounce of happiness is physically extracting itself from my body. He passes me the hand towel and I wipe my face. He hugs me tight as I sob into his chest.

'When is this going to end?' I look desperately at the men standing before me. 'I don't think I can take any more.'

Jeremy and Martin immediately move into action mode and start poring over the vile papers covering the kitchen table. They talk about this strategy and that scenario, what we should do next. They make phone calls to Salina and Moira and leave messages for Leo and Ed and whomever else they can think of.

So frenetic is their activity, they don't even notice that I leave them to go and lie on the bed with a cold washer covering my eyes.

How has this become my life?

So plain and boring one minute, so exhilarating and exciting the next. So wrong and scary, then so beautiful and happy and perfect.

Now this! How dare she! Everything I've worked hard for, down the drain in one malicious heartbeat if this becomes a public scandal.

Those photos will haunt me until my dying days.

Make the most of your happiness ... you never know when it will be taken from you. I had it ten minutes ago and now it has vanished.

Past ... present ... future.

I walk into the children's room to check on them yet again, ensuring they are still sleeping soundly, now ensuring their safety, and take a moment to absorb their innocence — an innocence I can never return to — I try to breathe it deeply in to my body.

I slowly walk back to the kitchen where Jeremy and Martin are seated, still in deep, frenetic discussion.

'Please, stop. Stop all of this.'

Jeremy gets up, his strong arms immediately opening to hold me in a firm embrace. I push him gently aside. 'Please Jeremy, sit down.'

'What is it, sweetheart? Don't worry, we'll get through this. I won't let her touch you or the kids, I promise you.'

'I've made my decision.'

*The heart-stopping conclusion ...*

## *Destined to Fly*

The compelling and thrilling climax to Alexandra Blake's sensual journey.

Alexandra has returned to the world after her captivity and is left with a heady mix of emotions. Strangely empowered, her feelings of pleasure and exhilaration are tinged with fear, but now she must reconcile the decisions of her past and how they may determine her future.

Alexandra knows it is she alone who holds the key to the answers so desperately sought by both her lover, Jeremy Quinn, and her captors. In order to unlock the secrets within her, she must embark upon a quest to explore long-forgotten sexual rituals and despite believing that she has experienced everything possible in her erotic adventures, she discovers that there is still so much more to learn ...

At last she will learn what freedom truly means and understand the real purpose of the role she was always destined to play.

## How it all began ...
# Destined to Play

It's simple. No sight. No questions. 48 hours.

Dr. Alexandra Blake is about to give a series of prestigious lectures, but the butterflies in her stomach are for a far more exciting reason ...

After the lecture she is meeting up with Jeremy Quinn, esteemed doctor and dangerous ex-lover - the only person with whom she has ever let her guard down completely. After a few glasses of champagne in his luxurious penthouse suite, Jeremy presents her with an intriguing offer: stay with him for the next forty-eight hours and accept two extraordinary conditions, the first of which leaves her utterly at his mercy, and he will give her an experience more sensual and extreme than any game they have ever played before.

This scorching novel is an erotic exploration of trust and betrayal, experimentation and control, lust and love. Forget *Fifty Shades of Grey*, this daring debut will leave you breathless for more ...